The FINAL REVEILLE

★★★ *The* **FINAL** ★★★
REVEILLE

A *Living History Museum* Mystery

AMANDA FLOWER

MIDNIGHT INK
WOODBURY, MINNESOTA

FIRST EDITION
First Printing, 2015

Cover design by Kevin R. Brown
Cover illustration © 2015 Tom Jester/Jennifer Vaughn Artist Agency
Map by Llewelyn Art Department

Midnight Ink, an imprint of Llewellyn Worldwide Ltd.

Library of Congress Cataloging-in-Publication Data
Flower, Amanda.
    The final reveille / by Amanda Flower. — First edition.
      pages cm. — (A living history museum mystery ; #1)
    Summary: Kelsey Cambridge becomes a prime suspect when the tight-fisted nephew of her living history museum's main benefactor is murdered on the grounds amid a Civil War reenactment.
    ISBN 978-0-7387-4473-5 (softcover)
    I. Title.
    PS3606.L683F56 2015
    813'.6—dc23
                      2014033919

Midnight Ink
Llewellyn Worldwide Ltd.
2143 Wooddale Drive
Woodbury, MN 55125-2989
www.midnightinkbooks.com

Printed in the United States of America

DEDICATION

For Suzy

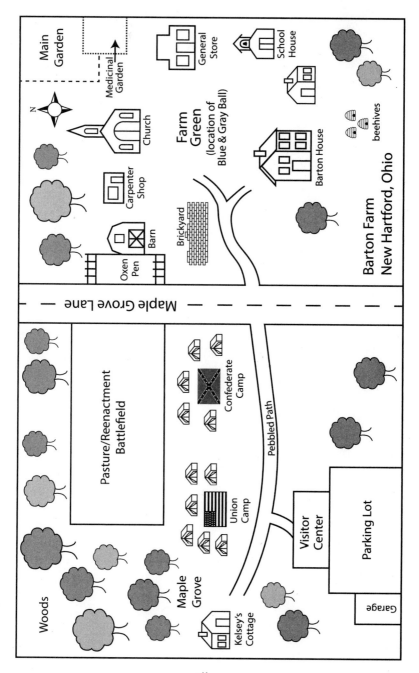

Barton Farm
New Hartford, Ohio

Main Garden

Medicinal Garden

General Store

School House

Church

N

Farm Green
(location of Blue & Gray Ball)

Barton House

beehives

Carpenter Shop

Barn

Brickyard

Oxen Pen

Maple Grove Lane

Pasture/Reenactment Battlefield

Confederate Camp

Union Camp

Pebbled Path

Woods

Maple Grove

Kelsey's Cottage

Visitor Center

Parking Lot

Garage

Beat! beat! drums!—Blow! bugles! blow!
–Walt Whitman

ONE

THE UNION SOLIDER GLARED at his Confederate counterpart. "You're lucky I'm all out of gunpowder, or I'd blow you all the way back to the Mason-Dixon Line."

"Oh you would, would you? I'd like to see you try." The Confederate soldier was red-faced as he tugged on the collar of his heavy denim jacket. The Confederate encampment behind him, a cluster of several dozen white cotton tents held upright with wooden poles, bustled with activity. Children in their breeches and cotton shirts ran barefoot from tent to tent in an elaborate game of hide-and-seek while their mothers started the long process of cooking lunch over their tiny fire pits. The Confederate flag hung proudly from every flag post. On the Union side, the encampment was almost identical with the exception of the thirty-five-starred American flag displayed at every campsite and Abraham Lincoln strolling in and around the Union tents, repeating the Gettysburg Address to anyone who would listen.

Crack! Crack! To my right, a battle raged in the grassy field. As the sound of musket fire broke the silence of the usually tranquil river valley, the regiment from the Ohio Volunteer Infantry charged toward their adversaries with a triumphant yell. The Confederate Division of the King's Brigade also charged forward brandishing their bayonets and stout knives retrieved from their boots.

As the two opposing armies met, the clatter of metal on metal reverberated across the field. Soldiers from both sides fell to the ground with cries of pain and disbelief. The Union and Confederate soldiers in front of me ignored the demise of their comrades just a few feet away.

While the two soldiers argued, a third man lay fallen less than a yard from my feet on the other side of the wooden rail fence that surrounded the pasture.

"Water, please, Miss?" he murmured.

I looked down at him. He was another Union solider. His right arm was flung out dramatically above his head, and his left arm lay across his chest as if covering a wound. His blond hair was encrusted with mud as it had rained the night before the battle. His forage cap had a tear in the brim and one of the brass buttons was missing from his dark blue wool shirt. Despite his condition, a smile teased at the corners of his mouth.

I peered down at him. "I'm sure your medic will be along shortly."

The soldier shook his head with a twinkle in his eye. "I am the medic. There's no help for me. Can't you tell I'm dead?"

I raised an eyebrow. "You don't look dead to me."

He winked, closed his eyes, and resumed playing dead.

The Confederate soldier, who was a large man with a handle-bar mustache, grumbled. "I see your men aren't trained well enough to stay dead when they're hit straight on by a musket ball." He appeared to be at a serious risk of heat stroke.

The Union solider who stood across from him was at least twenty years younger and looked like the poster child for enlistment. He held his kepi, his regiment-issued hat, in his hands, and his dark hair was brushed back from his forehead. He touched his cleft chin as he thought of a comeback.

"Please calm down," I cried over the din, clutching my ever-present notebook.

The two arguing men stared at me in surprise. I may be a tiny woman, but I know how to project my voice when needed, a trick I learned from my father who was an amateur stage actor. It's a skill that came in handy in my job as the director of Barton Farm, a living history museum situated an hour south of Cleveland, Ohio.

Now that I had their attention, I asked, "What's the problem?"

The Confederate soldier wiped his brow. "He stole a canteen from my encampment."

"Why would I steal anything from you? I'm surprised everyone in your company has shoes!"

The Confederate soldier's face turned even redder as he struggled for a rebuttal.

This was the first Civil War reenactment I had hosted, and I didn't want any casualties. I stepped in between the pair, who were now attracting more attention than the battle raging on the Barton Farm pasture. "What are your names?"

"I'm Sergeant Wesley Mayes," the Union solider replied.

"And I'm Corporal Henry Adams," the Confederate soldier said. His flushed cheeks began to lighten.

"Adams?" Wesley snorted. "A fine federal name for a Rebel."

Henry's nostrils flared, reminding me of the Farm's oxen when they were in a foul mood.

"Is this true about the canteen?" I asked Wesley, using the voice I usually reserved for unruly grade schoolers visiting the Farm on a field trip.

Wesley placed his kepi on his head. "No."

"Liar!" Henry accused. "I saw you in my camp."

"You must have mistaken me for someone else," Wesley said coolly.

"We aren't going to settle this now," I said. "Henry, if you would like to file a complaint, there are forms in the visitor center. At the same time, report the missing canteen to the front desk. We'll keep an eye out for it in the lost-and-found."

"That's it?" Henry cried. "That's all you're going to do?"

"Listen." I put my hands on my narrow hips and straightened to my full five-foot-two height. "I have one hundred and forty-two reenactors, thirty Farm staffers—most of whom are seasonal and believe Abraham Lincoln fought in the Revolutionary War—and nearly four hundred visitors here. I don't have time to hunt down your canteen."

Wesley grinned and polished the third brass button on his coat with a handkerchief.

Henry sniffed. "Well, I will certainly report this to my commanding officer." He stomped away.

Wesley called after him, "Just remember who won the war!" before strutting back to his own encampment.

The flirty dead solider opened his eyes again. "You handled that well."

"Can't you stay dead?" I asked.

He snorted a laugh.

"Kelsey," the soft voice of my assistant, Ashland George, whispered into my ear. She teetered back and forth on her ostrich-like legs. A stiff wind could topple my gawky assistant and send her sprawling into the middle of the battlefield.

"What is it?" I felt sweat trickle down my back. June wasn't usually this muggy in the Cuyahoga Valley, but we'd had an early spring that led into a long hot summer.

Ashland's eyes, fringed by blond lashes, blinked at me from behind her glasses. "Umm, well." Her voice was as powerful as a baby chick's. She certainly didn't know how to project. *Maybe I should ask Dad to give her some tips.* I scanned the crowd. He was around the Farm somewhere, along with my five-year-old son, Hayden. Undoubtedly, the pair was in loads of trouble already. I wondered if they had anything to do with the missing canteen.

"Well," she said again. Ashland was a doctoral candidate in American History at a nearby university. I tried to imagine her teaching a theater-sized classroom of two hundred undergraduate students. I knew that was part of her job as a teaching assistant, but the image didn't fit.

I became concerned. "Is anything wrong?"

"Cynthia is here and would like you to give her a tour of the reenactment," she said.

"Of course. Where is she?" I couldn't imagine why Cynthia's appearance would tongue-tie my assistant. Ms. Cynthia Cherry was Barton Farm's benefactress and, for lack of a better word, my boss as she was also the chairwoman on the Farm's board of trustees. "Is that all?"

"Her nephew is with her," she added in a rush. "They're waiting inside the visitor center."

I made a face. "Why is he here?" I asked. I could count on one hand the number of times Maxwell Cherry had visited the Farm. He was Cynthia's only heir and did not approve of the money Cynthia donated to the Farm through the Cherry Foundation, which Cynthia's tire tycoon father had created over a century ago to promote the arts and culture in Summit County. Barton Farm certainly wasn't the only museum the foundation supported, but we were the most expensive.

Ashland clenched her hands together in front of her, not answering.

I tapped a rhythm on the back of my notebook. "Well, this should be fun."

TWO

WITH ASHLAND SHUFFLING CLOSE to my heels, I wove through the crowd of reenactors and Farm visitors back to the visitor center. Two little girls ran along the path knocking a wooden hoop with a stick, one dressed in Civil War–era clothing, the other in shorts and a fluorescent tank top. Their yelps of glee made me smile. The visitor center was fifty yards beyond the trail. It was the only "new" building on the property; all the others were over a century old. However, under Cynthia's guidance the architect had made the building fit with the Farm. It resembled an overgrown ranch house, with white wooden siding and forest green shutters.

It wasn't all built for the nineteenth century, I thought as I stepped through the automatic glass doors. I entered the great room with high ceilings, exposed maple beams, and polished pine floors. There were glass doors on either side of the room. The first set led to the Farm, and the doors on the far side of the room opened onto the parking lot. Just before them was our ticket counter and gift shop. Children hopped in place as they anxiously waited for their parents to pay for their tickets so they could enter the Farm and tour the encampments.

On the opposite side of the room from the ticket counter, a hallway framed with wooden beams led to the restrooms, a small cafeteria, and my small office.

I spotted Cynthia and her nephew along with a dark-haired woman I didn't know. She was busy admiring the large black-and-white photographs of the Farm that surrounded the great room. Each picture was from a different season of the year. Even in the dead of winter, Barton Farm was picturesque. Our official open season ran from the middle of April through the end of October, but I had hoped to speak with the board of trustees about opening for special occasions throughout the late fall and winter. Perhaps for a snowshoeing hike through our woods or sleigh rides around Christmas or maple sugaring in March? The Farm held so much potential, and I'd only touched the tip of iceberg in my two years as director.

Cynthia held onto the mother-of-pearl knob of her black walnut cane with strength and assurance. "Kelsey, dear, this is spectacular!" she said with her usual enthusiasm. She wore a lavender pantsuit paired with a ruffled blouse and reading glasses hanging from her neck from a beaded chain. Her improbable red curls bounced on the top of her head. "You've outdone yourself again! Maxwell circled the parking lot three times before he found a spot. The place is packed. What an achievement for our little museum." She air kissed me on both cheeks.

I blushed at the praise but did not disagree. Despite a few scuffles between the North and South, the reenactment was a success. The Farm visitors were eating up the history and atmosphere, just as I knew they would when I approached the board of trustees with the idea seven months ago.

The reenactment was a four-day event, running Thursday through Sunday, with battles every day. The grand finale would be a Blue and Gray Ball, a Civil War–inspired dance in the middle of the village. Tickets for the ball had sold out even before the reenactment began.

Cynthia smiled over my shoulder. "Ashland, it is always nice to see you, my dear. I enjoy our little visits."

Maxwell rolled his class ring back and forth over his knuckle. "Are you sure you're following code to allow this many people on the grounds?" He was a small man, only a few inches taller than me. His narrow face and pointed nose gave him a ratlike appearance.

"Yes, the fire chief was here last week to assess the grounds, and some members of his firehouse are here today as reenactors." I held my hand out to the dark-haired woman at Maxwell's side. "Hello. I'm Kelsey Cambridge, director of Barton Farm."

She shyly shook my hand. "Portia Bitner," she murmured. I barely heard her over the cannon shots outside. She was an attractive, tall woman, at least half a foot taller than I was, and had long straight black hair tied at her neck with a yellow ribbon. Her ponytail hung over her shoulder, and she held it as if it was a personal security blanket.

"Where are my manners?" Cynthia asked. "Kelsey, this is Maxwell's fiancée."

Behind me, Ashland gave a sharp intake of breath.

I turned, but she was flipping through her notebook, which was identical to my own. Perhaps I'd imagined the sound.

Maxwell gave me a triumphant glare. "Yes, Portia is truly the one for me." He reached for the woman twenty years his junior who towered several inches above him. After the slightest hesitation, she folded her thin hand into his.

Not long after I started working at Barton Farm, Maxwell Cherry had asked me out on a date. I turned him down, claiming I wasn't ready because of my recent divorce. It was an excuse on my part. Even if I found him remotely attractive, I would have never dated Maxwell. He had no respect for history. I smiled sweetly. "Congratulations!"

"I'm just tickled by the whole thing." Cynthia's curls bounced. "Can you believe I'll finally have a niece-in-law after all these years? I never thought Maxwell would settle down. It's been one girl after another for a decade. I can't even remember all their names. Maxwell is nearly fifty."

Maxwell scowled. "Aunt Cynthia, I don't think Ms. Cambridge needs to know all the details."

"Oh, pish. Kelsey is practically family," the older woman replied and grinned at me. "Since Portia is with us and this is her first visit to the Farm, I want the grand tour, Kelsey." She shook her cane at me. "Don't leave anything out. With your help I'm hoping to convince them this is the perfect location for their wedding."

Maxwell bristled. "I already told you we have no intention of getting married here." His gaze followed a boisterous family of five leaving the visitor center for the Farm. "We prefer a more formal setting."

"It's the bride's decision," Cynthia said as she winked at Portia. In return, Portia nervously tugged on her ponytail.

"I'm happy to show you the Farm." I put on my best tour guide smile.

The trio and Ashland followed me out of the visitor center, and I turned toward the reenactors' camps. I thought showing Cynthia and her party how authentic the reenactors were would impress them, though in truth, it probably wouldn't impress Maxwell.

Portia touched my arm. "Can we go this way?" She pointed in the opposite direction of the camps.

I spun on my heels, and Cynthia's drawn-on eyebrows disappeared into her hairline. "Is something wrong, Portia?" she asked.

The tall woman blushed and continued playing with her hair. "No, only you've told me so much about the Barton Farm that I would much rather see the actual farm than the Civil War reenactment."

Cynthia waved her comment away with a bejeweled hand. "You can see Barton Farm any old day of the week. The War Between the States will only be here a few days."

On that note, I began walking toward the battlefield again.

"What if," Portia spoke up again, causing me to turn around a second time. She cleared her throat. "What if we tour the village first? Would that be all right? I'm so eager to see it. You said there was a church there," Portia added.

Maxwell watched his bride-to-be closely. For a half of a second, I thought his nose twitched liked a rodent's, but that could have been my imagination.

Cynthia's eyes sparkled. "Yes, and it's the perfect location for your wedding. Do you mind visiting the village first, Kelsey?"

"Of course not," I said hesitantly. My Mama Spidey sense was piqued. Whenever Hayden insisted he wanted to do something so adamantly, I knew he was hiding something from me. Usually it was a frog in the bathtub. I smiled, hoping to put Portia at ease. "Actually, this is a great time to visit the Farm since most of our guests are watching the reenactment. It won't be nearly as crowded as it will be after the battle."

Portia gave me a half smile in thanks.

I guided the trio down the pebbled path that led to Barton's mock village. The path stopped at Maple Grove Lane, which divided the Farm's property in half. On the west side of the road was the visitor center, my cottage, and a handful of out-buildings. It also held the grazing pasture for our five cows and two oxen, which was currently the location of the battle. During the reenactment, the animals were staying in the south pasture, as far away from the reenactment's noise and uproar as possible without leaving Barton property.

The east side of the road held the Barton family home (a three-story brick colonial), the main barn, and the village. The village was a quarter-mile circle of six buildings. Only Barton House was original to the property. The rest were relocated to the farm piece by piece from other parts of Ohio with the intention to preserve them. After transport, they were reassembled on the property as enormous three-dimensional jigsaw puzzles. Cynthia's Cherry Foundation fronted the money for the moves and reassembly of all of those buildings, which included the church, schoolhouse, two homes, a carpenter's workshop, and a general store.

The largest of those building was the whitewashed, single-steepled church. It was Cynthia's pride and joy. As we approached, the church looked like it was ready for its beauty shot. Its pointed steeple stood in a backdrop of the bright blue summer sky. Beyond the church were the homes of our villagers, seasonal workers who played roles of men and women living in northeastern Ohio in the mid-nineteenth century. In honor of the reenactment, they were spending the entirety of June living in the specific year of 1863.

Laura Fellow, a high school history teacher and my partner in crime since we met in first grade, sat outside of the church under a massive chestnut tree, carding wool. She wore a blue shirtwaist and skirt that went all the way to the ground. A pale cameo closed the collar at her throat, and she'd parted her strawberry-blond hair down the middle and pinned it into a bun on the back of her head. Despite the near-ninety-degree heat and stifling humidity, she looked a cool as can be as she spoke with a young teenager in droopy cargo shorts and a band T-shirt two sizes too big for his thin frame. The only indication that she might be warm was the rosy color on her plump cheeks.

As we approached, I heard a snippet of Laura's conversation with the young visitor. "A cell phone you say. I've never heard of such a thing. What does this cell phone contraption do?"

The teen held a smartphone in his hand and waved it back and forth in front of her face. "It makes calls? You make calls, don't you?" the boy said with a malicious twinkle in his eye.

I suppressed a smile. He didn't know who he was messing with. In addition to being my best friend, Laura was one of my best first-person interpreters. She knew her nineteenth-century American history backwards and forwards and never broke character in front of a guest.

Laura smiled sweetly and her green eyes sparkled. "Oh my yes, I make calls. Every time I call on a friend I bring them a pie. I'm well known for my pie crust. I know I should be more modest, but it's the best crust in the village."

The boy yanked at his shorts, which were threatening to fall off. "How can you take a pie on a call?"

Laura cocked her head, and as the sunlight broke thought the chestnut's thick foliage it fell on her red-gold hair, giving her a deceptively angelic appearance. "By calls you do mean going to visit a friend or neighbor at his or her home, do you not? Because that is what I mean when I say calls."

The boy scowled. "This is lame." He stalked away.

Laura rose when we approached. "Good afternoon. Welcome to Barton Farm."

Cynthia tapped the end of her cane into the grass. "Laura, I enjoyed seeing you put that whippersnapper in his place."

Laura simply smiled. "It's kind of you to say. It is nice to see you, Cynthia." Laura nodded at Maxwell, but didn't pay him the same compliment.

"Portia, this is Laura Fellow, one of our twelve first-person interpreters in the village."

"Interpreters?" Portia looked just as confused as the teen had been.

"We're kind of like the reenactors, except we don't have guns," Laura said.

"The first-person interpreters dress up in period clothing and act out the part of someone living in this part of Ohio in the mid-nineteenth century. That boy who was just here was trying to make her drop character." I felt the sunrays beat down on my dark hair, and I lifted my heavy braid off of my neck and stepped into the shade. "We also have third-person interpreters. Those are people who work here and wear Barton Farm polo shirts like mine. Many of them are crafters who make the crafts and goods we sell in the gift shop using only nineteenth-century technology."

"That means no power tools," Cynthia said. "Isn't it fabulous? Everything is made by hand."

Portia had a strange expression on her heart-shaped face, but before she could reply, Maxwell screamed.

THREE

"WHAT? WHAT IS IT?" I demanded.

He hopped from foot to foot. "Bee!" Maxwell screeched.

"Where? Where?" Portia shrieked.

Ashland covered her face like she couldn't watch the scene unfolding before her.

"Are you stung?" Cynthia asked. Her voice was high-pitched.

Maxwell flapped his hands back and forth.

"Maxwell!" Cynthia cried. "Calm down! All of your excitement will only attract the bee."

Maxwell froze in place, arms held straight out in front of him in a universal gesture to stop. I doubted the bee could read hand gestures.

"Are you stung?" Cynthia asked again.

He shook his head and dropped his arms.

Laura choked back a laugh. I shot her a look.

Cynthia started coughing uncontrollably and tapped her cane into the grass. Portia patted her back.

Laura pulled an unopened water bottle from her basket. "Here."

Cynthia took a long swallow. She cleared her throat. "Thank you. Maxwell's allergic to bees. We just learned this a few months ago when he was stung on my estate. He gave us quite a scare, and we rushed him to the hospital."

"You were never stung as a child?" I asked in disbelief. Hayden was only five and had been stung on at least three occasions.

Maxwell scowled at me. "No."

Cynthia seemed to have recovered from her coughing fit. "Maxwell wasn't one for playing outdoors as a boy."

"It's a serious allergy, and I'm glad to know about it," I said. "We'll skip the garden path to be sure. The gardens are teeming with bees and other insects this time of year. Maybe we should avoid the Barton House too. Our gardener, Shepley, keeps his beehives back there."

"Why would you keep beehives? Don't you care about the visitors that you are putting in danger?"

I smoothed a stray hair back into my French braid. "Yes, we care about the visitors, and the hives are twenty yards behind the main house. There is signage to warn any guest who might have an allergy. At the same time, we want to be historically accurate. The Barton family kept bees the entire time they lived on the property. The honey they made was sought after, and they even shipped it back to Connecticut, where they were from originally, to sell in the markets there."

Maxwell glowered. "History won't matter if someone dies."

"Let's go inside the church," Cynthia said. "Kelsey, do you mind if I guide them through the church? It's my favorite building." Some of the twinkle was back in her eyes. "I'm going to do my best to convince them this is the perfect place for the wedding."

"No, of course I don't mind," I said. "I'll wait outside."

"When's the wedding?" Laura asked.

"As soon as possible," Maxwell said. Portia nodded in agreement.

After they went inside the building, I notice Ashland hovering a few feet away. "Ashland, why don't you go check on the reenactment?"

She blinked. "Yes. Right away. I'm sorry." She hurried down the path back to Maple Grove Lane.

Laura watched her go. "What's she sorry for? I swear, Kelsey, that girl is not cut out for this job, or any job really."

"She's still learning," I said defensively.

Laura rolled her eyes and hid the water bottle back inside her basket. It would not do if any of the Farm visitors saw her drinking from a plastic bottle. "Maxwell and Portia are certainly an odd couple. You know a pretty young woman like that would only marry him for Cynthia's money."

I sighed. "Laura, that's not nice."

She shrugged. "It's true though. When Cynthia goes, Maxwell's going to be the richest man in the county, maybe in the northeast corner of the state. He's probably disappointed she's held on this long."

"Laura!"

She changed the subject. "That bee probably came from the brick pit, though, not Shepley's hives. They're burrowing in there again to escape the heat. Benji was stung in the foot earlier this morning."

Benji, one of our third-person interpreters, specialized in making bricks by hand. I shielded my eyes from the sun and looked down the pebbled path to the brickmaking area. I spotted Benji holding a hand-formed loaf of mud over her head. She threw the loaf into the nine-by-thirteen wooden brick mold. The family watching clapped.

"Is she okay?"

"She's fine. I had some antihistamine in my first-aid kit and gave it to her. Benji's a trooper. You should see her toe, though. It swelled up to the size of a lemon."

"Did someone file an incident report?" I asked.

In the early summer, a New Hartford city employee had reprimanded the Farm for not reporting injuries and incidents and slapped us with a hefty fine, which Cynthia ended up paying. I never wanted to be in that position again and had drilled into the staff that even the smallest accident needed to be filed in an incident report. Now the township complained I reported too much.

"I radioed Ashland and she came over and filed one. I knew you would be too busy with the North and South duking it out."

I relaxed. "You're right. Before Cynthia arrived I was in the middle of breaking up a fight over a canteen."

Laura grinned. "Wars have started over less."

The teenaged boy who had been trying to make Laura crack jumped out of a rhododendron bush. "Ah-ha! I heard you say first-aid kit and radio."

"My dear," Laura said with all the confidence in the world. "The first-aid kit is nothing new, and the radio was invented in 1860." The lie slipped off Laura's tongue as if she was simply pointing out the grass was green.

I inwardly groaned and prayed the teen wouldn't Google *radio* only to find that it wasn't invented in 1860 as Laura claimed but several decades later.

"Oh," he said, deflated. Confusion crossed his face.

After the boy left, Laura turned to me. "Don't give me that look."

"What look?" I asked.

"That holy anachronism look. So what if I told him the wrong date? If he goes home to look it up to prove me wrong then he'll never forget when the radio was invented. In that case, we taught him a history lesson, right?"

I cocked an eyebrow. "Is this how you teach?"

"Absolutely," she said with a grin. "Remember, my friend, people will believe anything if you say it in just the right tone."

I grimaced. "Regardless, I hope that misinformation doesn't come back to haunt us."

Laura laughed. "Kelsey, you worry too much."

I pulled my shirt away from my body, hoping a nonexistent breeze would cool me. I didn't know how Laura could stand the dress she wore, not to mention the corset and petticoats underneath. "Someone in every operation needs to be the worrier. It might as well be me." I noticed that the family in front of Benji's station had moved on. "Can you wait here in case Cynthia and Maxwell come out? I want to check on Benji."

She nodded. "No problem."

"Hi, Kelsey," the young brickmaker greeted me. Benji had her black braids pulled away from her face with a wide headband. Sweat glistened on her forehead as she scraped the excess mud off her worktable. She'd worked for Barton Farm as a crafter every summer since she was a junior in high school. As a Farm veteran, she had her choice of the crafts, which included candle dipping, basketweaving, and pottery, but every year she returned to the brick pit even though it was the hottest, filthiest, and most labor-intensive demonstration of them all.

I picked up her display brick, which was already fired in the Farm's kiln. The bricks Benji made that day would also be fired if they passed her inspection. The weight and consistency of the homemade brick felt so different than manufactured ones. Unlike the mass-produced materials, no two homemade bricks were identical. Benji also had a machine-made brick on her table to allow guests to see and feel the difference between them.

"Hi, Benji. Laura said you were stung in the toe this morning. Are you okay?"

"Yeah, I'm fine." She walked around her waist-high table and showed me her toe. On her right foot she wore a sock and tennis shoe. On her left foot, she wore a purple flip-flop. The second toe on her left foot was the size of a large strawberry. At least it wasn't as big as a lemon as Laura had described it. "The bees are back in the pit," Benji said. "It's my fault. I should have checked before jumping in. I just wanted to get in early and get the mud ready since I knew so many guests would be here for the reenactment."

As she spoke, a bee dive bombed the pit behind her, a five-by-five hole in the earth framed on all four sides by wooden boards. The bee burrowed into one of the tiny holes he or one of his friends had made there.

Another bee leaving its mud homestead buzzed my ear. I waved it away. "We'll take care of this, Benji."

She wiped her brow with a pink bandana. "I guess being stung is part of the job, and I can take it. I'm a little worried about the visitors, though. What if one of them is stung? We don't know who might be allergic."

Her comment made me think of Maxwell. "No, we don't." I stepped out of the way as another batch of tourists strolled up to her station.

FOUR

I RETURNED TO THE church yard just as Cynthia, Portia, and Maxwell reemerged from the building. Cynthia leaned heavily on her nephew, who helped her down the cement steps.

To my surprise, Sgt. Wesley Mayes, alleged canteen-stealer, stomped up the pebbled path. I sighed. I had hoped the battle of the canteen had ended. But instead of walking up to me to complain, he headed straight for Portia with a scowl on his face.

"What are you doing here?"

Portia looked stricken. "Wesley, it's nice to see you. I didn't know you'd be here."

"Like hell you didn't. You know my regiment's schedule just as well as I do."

Portia gripped her ponytail for dear life.

Laura whispered into my ear. "Uh-oh."

I shot her a look. Laura winked as she placed a straw sunhat on her head and tied the blue ribbon underneath her chin. She was a dead ringer for Little Bo Peep—if Little Bo traded in her sheep for a heavy dose of sarcasm.

Maxwell scrunched up his face. "Portia, who is this man?" Maxwell looked him up and down. "Besides someone playing dress up."

Portia's eyes darted this way and that. "Maxwell, this is my…umm…"

"Can't you even say it?" Wesley wanted to know.

Portia shot Wesley a pleading look to no avail. Even angry, Wesley was handsome. It struck me seeing Wesley and Portia so close together what a more attractive couple they made than Portia and Maxwell did. I wondered what the story was behind their relationship but quickly decided I didn't want to know.

Cynthia stepped forward. I noted that she leaned heavily on her cane for support. It was the first time I'd ever seen her do that, and I felt a twinge of worry. "I don't believe we've met. I'm Cynthia Cherry," she said. "This is my nephew, Maxwell Cherry. Kelsey's the Farm director, and this is one of our interpreters, Laura Fellow."

Laura curtsied, and I made a "cut it out" gesture.

"Who might you be?" Cynthia asked.

Wesley glared at Portia. "Why don't you tell them who I am?"

"Wesley's a friend." She blushed and looked the sergeant straight in the eye. "And Maxwell is my fiancé."

"Your fiancé?" Wesley looked like Portia hit him in the stomach with one of Benji's bricks. "Did he wave money from the Cherry Foundation at you?"

Portia opened and closed her mouth, but no words came out.

He scowled. "Now I know why I wasn't good enough for you, Portia. You had a millionaire waiting in the wings." Tears welled in the corners of his eyes as he did a precise military turn and headed back to the battle.

"Do you feel like you just witnessed a bad remake of *Gone with the Wind*?" Laura whispered.

Maxwell glared at Portia.

"Maxwell, I'm so sorry, I can explain," Portia said.

He was tight-lipped. "We will discuss this later."

Cynthia looked confused. "Portia, who was that young man?"

Portia licked her lips, and she looked at Maxwell, all the while tugging at her hair.

I suggested we return to the visitor center for some refreshments and to watch the battle. By the time I finished guiding Cynthia, Portia, and Maxwell back across the street, the battle was over and both the living and dead soldiers were walking off the field with smiles on their muddy faces. I glanced at the weekend's schedule that I'd taped to the back of my notebook. Their next scuffle in the cow field would be tomorrow.

"I'm so sorry you missed the battle, Cynthia, but you can still tour the camps. Or if you'd like to catch your breath in the visitor center where it's cooler, you're welcome to."

She patted her forehead with a tissue and shook her head. "No, I think I'm ready to go home."

The usually upbeat Cynthia Cherry looked pale, and I felt a twinge of alarm. I placed a hand on her shoulder. "Are you feeling okay?"

She smiled. "Yes, of course. I'm sure it's just the heat." She patted my hand, and the diamonds and sapphires on her dinner ring sparkled in the sunlight.

"*Woof!*"

I saw Hayden walking Tiffin, our brindled corgi. Both of them looked tiny weaving around and among the soldiers. When the little dog saw me, he broke into a run, pulling Hayden behind him.

"Look who's here," Cynthia cried. Her weariness seemed to be forgotten. She tousled Hayden's sandy blond hair and bent down to scratch Tiffin under the chin. The little dog rubbed his cheek into her palm like a cat.

My father was a few steps behind my son and dog. He wore a Union Army flak jacket with jeans and running shoes. My father had the same color hair as my son, although his was more gray than sand-colored now. He was a short man with a potbelly laugh and a twinkle in his eyes that made some wonder if he was an overgrown leprechaun. He wasn't. As much as my father reveled in the comparison, he was closer to a jovial Napoleon, as his family was of French descent not Irish.

Cynthia shook hands with my father. "It's so nice to see you again, Roy."

My father kissed her hand. "It's wonderful to see you too. You get younger by the day."

Cynthia's crepe paper–like skin blushed. "I've been using a new face cream."

"It's working wonders," he praised.

Hayden reached into his shorts pocket and pulled out a musket ball. "Look what I found, Miss Cynthia."

She leaned over to ooh and aah at Hayden's discovery.

"Ms. Cambridge," Maxwell said from behind me into my ear.

I jumped. I hadn't realized he was that close.

"I'm sorry to startle you. I wonder if you have a moment to speak to me," he said.

I felt uneasy. I couldn't remember a single time Maxwell had asked to speak to me privately since I'd turned him down for a date two years ago. "Sure." I led him a few feet away.

"I'm glad we have a chance to speak while my aunt is occupied." Maxwell touched his silver hair.

I glanced back at Cynthia and my father. He was turning on the old French charm and flirting shamelessly. I knew it was harmless. My mother had been the love of my father's life, and he hadn't looked at another woman since the day she died twelve years ago. Besides, he was at least twenty years Cynthia's junior, possibly more if I was ever able to pinpoint Cynthia's age other than somewhere upwards of eighty.

"You are?" My brow shot up.

"Yes, you see I'd like to talk to you about my aunt's health."

"Her health? Is something wrong?" I asked.

"Aunt Cynthia is a proud woman and would not be happy that I told you this, but she's ill."

My chest constricted. "Ill?" I glanced back at Cynthia, who was grinning down at my son. Hayden waved his arms in the air as he told her a story at his usual hundred miles a minute rate.

"She's suffering from congestive heart failure."

I gasped. "I had no idea." I chewed on my lower lip. That explained Cynthia's unusual tiredness during the tour. "Why didn't she tell me?" Cynthia was like an elderly and doting aunt to me. She had gone way above the call to make the transition to life on the Farm as comfortable as possible for Hayden and me. She never turned down one of my requests. Not that I ever asked for anything the Farm didn't absolutely need, but I knew other museum directors who had a much harder time getting their benefactors to loosen their purse strings.

"She didn't want to worry you."

For good reason, I was worried. "Is there anything I can do?"

He shook his head. "Little by little, I have been taking over Aunt Cynthia's affairs to prepare for the transition."

I didn't like the sound of this, not the least little bit. "Transition?"

"It's time for Aunt Cynthia to rest and enjoy the time she has left. Soon I will be handling the charitable contributions from the Cherry Foundation. As part of the transition, I'm reviewing all of our contributions and will decide which of those contributions we should continue"—the corners of his mouth tipped up in a little smirk—"and which we shouldn't continue. I think you will agree that my aunt has been more than generous to your little farm here."

My muscles tensed. I willed my body to relax. I didn't want Maxwell to see that this conversation upset me, although it did.

A lot. "I hope you will ask Cynthia for input to find out which organizations she would like to continue to support."

He sniffed. "She's run the foundation for nearly forty years. It's time for someone with fresh eyes to take over. Of course, I wish it were under better circumstances. I hate the thought of my aunt being ill."

I bit my tongue to hold back a smart remark.

"However, I believe that we need to focus our contributions on organizations that help society as a whole."

"Barton Farm does that. We are dedicated to educating the community."

He wrinkled his nose as a Confederate soldier walking by spat tobacco juice into a juniper bush. "I suppose that's something you will have to prove."

My mouth felt dry. "That sounds like a threat."

The corners of his mouth tipped up in a half smirk once again. "It's not a threat, just a statement of fact. In this economy, we can't throw away the foundation's money on organizations without lasting power."

I felt my hackles rise and my volume jump to just short of yelling. "Lasting power? That's one thing Barton Farm certainly has. We share Ohio and American history with our visitors. Look around you. We have nearly four hundred guests here today, and this is only the first day of the reenactment."

"That may be, but I know in general your ticket sales are down."

I clenched my jaw because it was true. Would Cynthia share this information with Maxwell? If he was taking over the foundation, I suppose she had to. "What are you saying?" I asked.

Maxwell checked the time on the designer watch on his wrist. "Let me put it this way: I'm not going to put more money into a sinking ship, or in this case, a sinking museum."

Portia called over to us, "Maxwell, we're ready to go. Your aunt is tired." She supported Cynthia with her arm.

Cynthia smiled and kissed me on both cheeks before allowing Maxwell and Portia to escort her to the parking lot. Watching her shuffle away between them, I felt a horrible sense of dread. Cynthia looked small and frail. It was the first time that I ever allowed myself to see that side of her. I always thought of her as a powerhouse of a woman who did and could do anything. For the first time, I let myself wonder how the Farm would survive without her support and the support of her foundation. It wasn't a pretty image.

FIVE

THE NEXT MORNING BEFORE the break of dawn, the reveille star-tled Tiffin and me awake, causing us to tumble onto the floor in a giant heap of human, corgi, and blankets.

I scrambled into a sitting position, and the corgi yelped as I sat on his paw. "Sorry, buddy." He scowled at me. I picked up Tiffin and placed him back on the top of my bed and tucked my blankets and sheets around him. He snuggled down into his lit-tle nest and then wasn't the slightest bit concerned about all the commotion outside.

The reveille came again, and I massaged my temples. "War waits for no one," I muttered.

I found a fresh Barton Farm polo shirt and a pair of rela-tively clean jeans and threw them on. When I stepped out of my bedroom, I found Dad downstairs in the living room giving himself an insulin shot in the belly. Dad was a type 1 diabetic. On the coffee table beside his blood sugar meter sat a mug of coffee and a copy of *North and South*. "Quite a ruckus you have going on out there." He put the syringe away.

Hayden's tabby cat, Benjamin Franklin, watched Dad's movements with his one good eye. I wouldn't be surprised if Frankie didn't plot to steal one of my father's syringes. The wily feline was notorious for stealing small pieces of property and burying them in his litter box. My watch was his latest victim. I could not bring myself to wear it again.

"That's one way to describe it," I said with a yawn. The clock in the kitchen read five thirty. I groaned. I had a long day ahead. Another hour of sleep would have been appreciated. The conversation I had with Maxwell the day before came rushing back to me, and I felt sick to my stomach.

"Coffee?" Dad asked.

My tummy rolled.

"How does your son sleep through that noise?" Dad asked.

"It's a trait he inherited from his father. Eddie can sleep through a foghorn going off in his ear."

Dad frowned. He was not a fan of my ex-husband.

The bugle went off again, and I was actually relieved to hear it. I didn't want to get into another argument with Dad about my son's father.

I grabbed my notebook from the coffee table and slipped it into the back pocket of my jeans. "I'm going to do a quick walk around."

Tiffin ran to the door and shook his tailless rump at me.

I laughed. "You can come too." I lifted his leash off of the peg by the door but didn't attach it to his collar.

It was before dawn, and the sky was just beginning to lighten over the treetops to the east. A white-tailed deer leaped out of the woods and ran behind my cottage. I wondered if she was disturbed by the early-morning wakeup call too.

Despite the lack of light, I could hear the rustle of the soldiers and their families starting their day. I walked through the maple tree grove that hid my cottage from the view of the rest of the Farm.

Children played quietly in their night dresses, and women started campfires. Tiffin lifted his long nose in the air as the first whiff of bacon floated our way. Next to a gas lantern, Abraham Lincoln trimmed the edges of his beard with a straight razor in front of a round mirror tacked to a tree trunk.

A few feet away, our second famous reenactor, Walt Whitman, scratched lines into a leather-bound diary with the stub of a pencil. His long white beard dipped onto the paper as he wrote.

Tiffin ran ahead of me, looking back every few leaps to make sure I continued to follow him. He took the responsibility of herding, even if it was just herding me, seriously.

As much as I loved the reenactors being there to draw a crowd to my small living history museum, I was happy to cross the street and stroll around the sleepy deserted village. My interpreters wouldn't report to work for another three hours. As the Bartons' three-story brick residence came into view, I could imagine what it must have been like nearly two hundred years ago when a growing family of eight lived in the home. In my mind's eye, I saw the boys in the family frightening their sisters with frogs and crickets hidden in their pockets. I imagined their mother admonishing them and their father trying to hide his smile behind his newspaper.

To me, those moments—the day-to-day lives of people who called the valley home—were what Barton Farm was really about. The battles and politicians were important, of course. They changed history and lives with their outcomes and laws. Those touched me as a historian, but they didn't touch me as person in the same way the small details of daily nineteenth-century life did.

The small details and the children who should know about them were the reasons I had to do everything within my power to keep Barton Farm open, even if it required me to speak to Cynthia directly about the Farm, the foundation, and her illness. Cynthia was kind, but she was a proud woman and would not be happy that I knew of her failing health.

The first building on the village side of Maple Grove Lane was the barn. I waved to Jason as he guided one of the cows into the pasture with a rough rope. The interpreters called Jason "Barn Boy" since he was seldom seen outside of the barn. He was a quiet kid who studied animal husbandry at a technical college in a neighboring county. What he lacked in social skills, he made up for in his connection with the Farm's animals. They all adored him. Even my pampered corgi Tiffin preferred Jason to me.

The shy teenager simply nodded to me in return.

Tiffin ran toward the barn to greet his friend, and Jason knelt down and hugged the dog.

I smiled and headed toward Barton House. Outside the house sat a spinning wheel that one of the interpreters had forgotten to put away the night before. Luckily, it had not rained or the wheel could have been damaged. I would have to remind the staff to lock all the artifacts inside their assigned buildings before they left each night. I made a note in my notebook before returning it to my pocket.

The sky was lighter now, and in the dim light, I could make out the tent covering the brick pit. To my surprise, I saw what looked like the pit's tarp sitting in front of Benji's worktable. That was unusual. Benji never left the pit uncovered at night. If she did, the mud would dry out, and it would take her half the morning to get it into brickmaking condition again.

I sighed and made another note. We were having an unseasonably hot June, and I was sure the exposed mud was dried solid. Benji would have to saturate the pit before the Farm opened and stomp it for a good twenty minutes if she had any hope of showing our guests how to make bricks today.

As I drew closer to the pit, I saw movement. I wondered if it was possible one of our barn cats had cornered a defenseless chipmunk or mouse in the mud. But I saw the form was much larger than a chipmunk or a cat ...

A blond man squatted inside the pit.

"Excuse me, sir, what are you doing? You shouldn't be over here. The village doesn't open until ten."

The man stood, and when he did I saw another person in the pit. That person wasn't moving. Fear clenched inside of my chest, and I took a step back.

I focused on the second man's feet. They were the size of bread loaves and bright red. The inflated toes were bordering on grotesque, and I had to look away.

The first man, the live one, stared at me. "This isn't what it looks like."

What does it look like? my brain asked. It looked like a dead body. My mouth felt dry.

"I saw him down here," he said, "and I hopped in to see if I could help, but he was already gone."

"What happened?" I asked, fully aware that my voice was two octaves higher than normal.

"Bee stings, I think. I got stung a few times myself."

"Bees?" A shiver traveled up my spine. Against my better judgment, I stepped closer to the pit and peered at the man's face. I saw my worst fear. "He was allergic."

"You knew him?"

"Yes, I knew him. It's Maxwell Cherry." Shaking, I reached into my pocket for my phone and called 911.

SIX

AFTER I HUNG UP with the police, I watched the man look at Maxwell more closely. "You should get out of there." My voice shook.

He nodded and climbed out of the pit.

"You probably shouldn't have gone into the pit with him in the first place. The police won't like it." I heard my mother-hen voice come out as it always did in times of stress. The present situation certainly qualified.

"I'm a paramedic. I was just checking his vitals to see if I could help." He ran a hand through his blond hair, and mud clung to his bangs. Something about the image struck me as familiar. I shook the thought away and concentrated on the situation at hand. Poor Maxwell.

I bit my lip. "Could you help?"

He shook his head. "No, I think he's been dead for several hours."

Beside the pit, I saw Maxwell's dress shoes. His black socks were rolled up into a ball and neatly tucked into the right shoe. His trousers were rolled up to mid-calf. If I didn't know better, I'd think it looked like Maxwell had tried to make bricks in his suit. "What was he doing here?" I said, mostly to myself.

"Hard to tell. Is he supposed to be in the village?"

"No," I replied.

I felt the paramedic watching me. "Then what's his connection to Barton Farm?"

My gaze flicked to his face.

"Sorry, I'm used to shooting off questions when I arrive on a scene. Just force of habit, I guess."

In the early morning light, I saw that his eyes were a dark chocolate brown. I looked away and concentrated on Maxwell in the pit. I swallowed hard and willed myself not to throw up. I'd seen a dead body before. I had even picked out the casket for my mother's funeral when I was only eighteen. My father had been too broken up to do it. However, I'd never seen one like this, so out in the open, so recently gone. *Damage control, Kelsey,* I told myself. *Damage control with a capital D.*

"I'm Kelsey Cambridge. I'm the director of Barton Farm."

"I know," he replied.

I bristled. "I'm at a disadvantage then. What's your name?"

"Chase Wyatt." I saw a flash of a dimple when he smiled.

"I need to make another call." I stepped a few feet away.

I supposed the bugler had been a blessing in disguise because if I had gotten up at my normal hour, Hayden would be with me on this farm walk. He loved to accompany me on my

38

early-morning rounds, and he was especially excited this weekend with the reenactors on Farm property.

Tiffin galloped to me from the barn, but Jason didn't appear. I wouldn't be surprised if my shy farmhand hid throughout the morning. As I listened to my cell phone ring, I clicked on Tiffin's leash. He whimpered and strained against it.

"Sorry, Tiff," I whispered. "I can't have you jumping into the brick pit."

My father answered the phone with his usual jovial tone.

"Dad, I need you to do me a favor. You need to keep Hayden inside the cottage for a little while."

"It's a beautiful day and the rapscallion is up and ready to see the encampments."

I sighed and knew Hayden would never be satisfied with being cooped up in the cottage with so much excitement going on. "Fine, but keep him on that side of the road, where the reenactors are. Under no circumstance are you to bring him into the village."

"Why? What's going on?" My father's voice lost some of its jovial quality. "Are you all right?"

"Yes, I'm fine, but there's been an accident," I said. Against my will, my eyes traveled to Maxwell's glassy face. "And someone's been hurt … " my voice trailed off. *Hurt* was putting it mildly.

"What? Who is it?" Dad asked. "Did one those would-be soldiers shoot himself in the foot?"

I caught the paramedic watching me. "I can't talk right now. I'll tell you everything when I get home."

I heard sirens approaching. Tiffin sat up straight on high alert.

"Are those sirens?" my father asked.

"Yes. I have to go now. Just keep Hayden on that side of the road."

"Okay, honey. Call if you need anything."

"I will," I promised.

The ambulance and two police cars following it ignored the PEDESTRIANS ONLY sign that marked the pebbled path leading from Maple Grove Lane into the village. I winced. I didn't want to be around when Shepley, our cranky gardener, saw the damage to his lawn.

A New Hartford police officer in a navy uniform walked up the path with a deliberate stride. "Are you Kelsey Cambridge?"

"Yes."

"Where's the body?"

"Maxwell Cherry. He's—"

"Hey, Sonders," Chase said from behind me.

"Chase, hey man, how'd you get here so fast?" the officer asked.

The two men clasped hands, and Chase said. "I found the body. Not pretty."

"Give me the lowdown." Officer Sonders bypassed me and went directly to Chase for the play-by-play of our gruesome discovery. I watched them walk away with a pang of irritation. I know that shouldn't have bothered me. Chase was a paramedic after all. He would know the information the police wanted to hear. Even though it should not have bothered me, it did. The Farm and what happened here was my responsibility.

40

The two paramedics and a second officer waved at Chase as they surveyed the brick pit.

I stood on the pebbled path wondering what to do as a man dressed in a Confederate uniform crossed the township road. I stopped him.

"I'm sorry. The village isn't open yet. There's been an accident." I looked around. Shouldn't a police officer be guarding the road, so something like this didn't happen?

"I'm Chief Duffy, New Hartford police chief."

"I'm so sorry, Chief Duffy." I felt my face grow hot. "I didn't recognize you in your uniform."

The chief finger-combed his sideburns, which were reminiscent of Union General Ambrose Burnside's magnificent whiskers. Considering how large and signature Burnside's sideburns were, the chief must have grown his purposely for the reenactment. They were truly a sight to behold. Why he, who reenacted as a Confederate general, would want to emulate a failed Union general I did not know.

"It's the sideburns," Chief Duffy said. "The sideburns throw everyone off. It's been nice to be a part of the reenactment incognito. I suppose the jig is up now. Where's the body?"

I pointed. "In the brick pit. An ambulance and two officers are already here."

"Oh good, Chase's here too, I see. He must have gotten a call about the incident while camping on the other side of the road too."

I cleared my throat. "I found Chase when I discovered the body."

"So you mean *he* discovered the body. He's the one I should talk to, then?" He leaned over and patted my stoic dog between the ears.

I ground my teeth. "No, that's not what I mean. I discovered the body, but I also discovered Chase crouching over Maxwell."

"Maxwell?"

"Maxwell Cherry. He's the one who had the accident."

Chief Duffy whistled. "So," he said with an appeasing tone, "you discovered the body second then. Is that a fair statement?"

"Yes." I took a step closer to the chief and lowered my voice. "I found Chase's behavior suspicious."

"You can't be implying that Chase had anything to do with this. He's a paramedic, one of us, one of the good guys."

"Just because he's a paramedic doesn't make him innocent. I asked him what he was doing standing over Maxwell's body."

The chief looked me up and down. "He also happens to be my nephew."

"Oh," I swallowed. "Oh."

The chief leaned in. "And what did Chase say?"

"That he was checking for vitals and seeing if he could help."

The chief shrugged. "See, what did I tell you? He's one of the good guys. Now, I'd better check into this. One of my officers will be over in a few minutes to question you. Stay around the brickyard please."

I held out my hand to stop him. "Sir, I hate to bother you about this now, but what do we do about the reenactment? Should we cancel it for the day?" Even as I said it, I felt my heart drop. It was Friday, and with clear skies predicted, it promised to be one of our busiest days of the reenactment, if not the best attendance the Barton Farm had ever seen.

"You can't cancel the reenactment," Chief Duffy said in horror. "The boys have been waiting for this for months."

"I don't want to cancel it, but—"

"I'll tell you what. Since the battlefield and camps are on the other side of the grounds, I don't see any problem with leaving that side open. I have to get my bearings to see how serious this is, but why don't you simply close the village at least for part of today?"

I agreed.

Another police department car arrived. This one drove over the corner of Shepley's wild flower garden near the road. Two more officers got out.

"There are some more of my boys now. You stay right here. An officer will be along shortly to get your statement," the chief promised.

SEVEN

Twenty minutes later, I was still waiting for one of Chief Duffy's officers to talk to me. I called Laura at home and explained what happened.

"Maxwell Cherry is dead, and he died at the Farm?" Laura's voice was breathless in my ear.

I took a deep breath. "Yes."

A new car pulled onto the lawn. An African-American man who looked like he doubled as a bodybuilder jumped out of the car with a medical bag.

"I think the medical examiner just arrived," I told Laura.

"The medical examiner? Are you serious? Was he murdered?"

My chest tightened. "What? Why would you ask that?"

"Well, he was found in the brick pit. Can you imagine him climbing in there voluntarily?"

I couldn't but said, "That doesn't mean he was murdered. The police haven't said he was." I shivered as I watched the giant medical examiner look down into the brick pit.

"But you never know. Maxwell wasn't exactly universally liked."

I bit my lip, wondering if I should tell Laura about my argument with Maxwell the day before. Instead I focused on the Farm. "I need your help."

"Of course. Anything."

I wrapped Tiffin's leash more tightly around my right hand as he tried to pull me toward the brick pit. "Call all the interpreters and tell them the village will be closed for today. If they'd like to come in to work to help with the reenactment, that would be okay. It's not required though."

"I hope I have all their phone numbers," she said slowly.

"I gave each employee a list of contact numbers for the staff."

"I know you did," she replied. "It's here somewhere. I just have to find it. Don't worry about the staff, Kelsey, I'll call them."

"After you do that, call the visitor center staff. I need the opposite from them—I need them to come in early. If we need to close the village side of the Farm, we'll have to figure out how to handle ticket sales. It doesn't seem fair to charge our guests full price if half of the museum is closed."

"I'm on it. I'm sure Judy will have a great solution."

I knew she was right. Judy was a retired accountant and our resident math whiz. She would have a solution for the ticket sales in no time, probably even before I got back to my office. "Thanks, Laura."

"Any time." She paused, and I could almost hear the wheels turning inside her head. "How are you?"

Tears pricked the back of my eyes. "Okay. It's not how I wanted to start my day, but I'll be fine. Maxwell is another story." I thanked her and ended the call. I watched the medical examiner unzip the body bag and shivered. He hadn't spent much time examining the body. Maybe Maxwell's bare swollen feet and severe bee sting allergy made the cause of death self-explanatory. One paramedic and one police officer spread the bag on the grass parallel to Maxwell's body in the pit.

"Hey, are you all right?"

I turned toward the voice. Chase had his hands in his jeans pockets and he rocked back onto his heels.

I nodded. "Yes, I'm fine."

He looked concerned. "Was Maxwell a friend of yours?"

"Not exactly, but he was a relative of a good friend." My chest tightened. *Cynthia*! The thought struck me like a jolt. How is possible that I hadn't thought of her until that moment? Who was going to tell her? The police? How would they tell her?

I left Chase balanced on the heels of his sneakers and headed straight for Officer Sonders. The officer snapped digital photographs of Maxwell's socks and shoes sitting beside the pit. He glanced at me. "Do you know why he may have taken off his shoes?"

"If he wanted to get the mud ready to make brick, that's what he would have done. It's much easier and more effective to knead the mud and clay with bare feet. What I don't understand is why he may have wanted to make bricks, especially in the middle of the night without any Barton Farm staff around to assist him."

Officer Sonders nodded thoughtfully.

"I'm so sorry to interrupt, but who's going to tell his aunt?" I asked.

He lowered his camera. "Is she the next of kin?"

"I suppose so. Neither of them have any other family that I know of."

"If she's the next of kin, the chief will inform her." He gave me an apologetic smile.

"She's not well. The news might be a shock and have an effect on her health."

His smile faded. "What's wrong with her?"

"Congestive heart failure."

He made a note. "Don't worry. We'll keep that in mind when we speak to her. Do you mind waiting over by Chase?"

I shook my head.

When I was back on the path next to Chase, he said, "You don't remember me, do you?"

I gave him a blank look in return. "Have we met before?"

He flung his right arm over his head and his left over his chest and made an "I'm dead" face.

"You're the dead guy!" I exclaimed, then slapped a hand over my mouth. I glanced over at the brick pit, but no one seemed to have heard me.

Chase laughed. "I don't think I've ever been called that before, but yeah, I'm the dead guy."

"Where's your uniform? I thought you guys stayed in character all weekend."

"My uncle is the big history buff. I just do these reenactor gigs for him." He grinned, showing off a dimple in his left cheek. "Not really my thing. Wearing that itchy wool uniform and playing dead for forty-five minutes in the smoldering heat while people step on you doesn't hold much appeal."

I eyed him. "Your uncle, the police chief."

Chase folded his arms. "He told you, did he?"

"Is there any reason he shouldn't have?"

"Nope." He rocked back and forth. "Not one single reason."

I looked way and concentrated on Chase's coworkers, who rolled Maxwell into the body bag.

"I've been meaning to ask you—" Chase began, but the other officer who arrived on the scene with Officer Sonders approached us. He introduced himself as Officer Sullivan.

"I'm ready to interview you now."

Thirty minutes later, after repeating my story four more times, Officer Sullivan released me to go back to the other side of the Farm. Tiffin and I headed in that direction. To my surprise, Chase followed us.

"I'm all done too," he said. "Can I walk you back to your cottage?"

"My cottage?" I asked, alarmed. "How do you know where I live?"

"Don't be freaked out that I know you live in a cottage on the Farm. All the reenactors know that. You told us in the opening meeting yesterday before the visitors arrived."

Despite trying to fight it, I shivered. "Yes, I suppose I did." I told myself I was overreacting. "That's not necessary. I'd rather be alone. I need time to think."

"No problem." He flashed his dimple again before walking ahead of me back to the Union camp. Why did he fight for the Union if his uncle was the general of the Confederate Army? I walked at a much slower pace, and Tiffin didn't seem to mind. It gave him more time to survey the area. The herding dog was always on constant surveillance of his farm.

As we crossed the street, I wondered how I would tell the reenactors to stay on their side of the Maple Grove Lane. When I approached the reenactor camps, though, I realized that I needn't worry. Chase stood on top of a picnic table and announced to the crowd the village was temporarily closed because of an accident.

"What kind of accident?" one woman in a blue cotton dress shouted.

Chase made eye contact with me as he answered. "Unfortunately, I can't answer that." He hopped off the picnic table and jogged toward me. "I hope I didn't overstep my bounds. I figured the sooner we told the reenactors not to walk over to the village, the better. Chief Duffy will station an officer on the path just in case anyone tries to cross the street."

"It's good to see you have everything under control," I said in a clipped tone.

Chase winced.

I shook off my irritation. "I'm sorry. It's been a long morning, and it's not even opening time yet. I really do appreciate your help."

"Anytime." There came the dimple again.

I unlocked the employees-only door on the side of the visitor center and let myself inside. Judy was already at the ticket window. She waved me away. "Don't you worry about a thing. I'll handle the tickets. Laura told me everything. Why don't you go in your office and rest a little?" she said in her grandmotherly voice.

Too tired to argue, I did as I was told.

Inside my cramped office—which consisted of full-to-bursting book shelves, a large desk, and one armchair—I turned on my eight-year-old desktop computer, a hand-me-down from the Cherry Foundation. It slowly came to life. I logged into my email account and saw I had a message from my ex-husband. The subject line said "Big News." I didn't like the sound of that, not the tiniest bit.

Against my better judgment, I opened the email and noticed right away that it wasn't addressed to me individually, which was a relief. My relief quickly turned to anger.

Hi all! Great news. I'm engaged! I'm getting married to my lovely bride-to-be, Krissie Pumpernickle.

He went on to tell the readers how wonderful Krissie was.

I clenched the mouse until I heard the crack of its plastic case giving under the pressure. I released the mouse. I needed it to keep working; I didn't have the money in the Farm's accounts to buy a new one.

Married? How could he be getting married? I knew that Eddie had been dating other women since our divorce, but I had no idea any of those dates were serious. And who was Krissie Pumpernickle? This was the first I had heard of her and her ridiculous name.

I stared at the computer, trying to process what I'd just read. Why should I be surprised Eddie would tell me such earth-shaking news in an email? It was his modus operandi to avoid conflict, one of the many contributing factors in the demise of our marriage. Instead of addressing our problems like I wanted to, he ran away from them.

My thoughts flew to my son. Reading that my ex-husband was getting married in a mass email was painful enough for me. Like it or not, Eddie was Hayden's father. Eddie's marriage to this Krissie person would impact my son's life. It set my teeth on edge that I knew nothing about her. What if she didn't like Hayden? What if she didn't like children at all?

I switched off the computer. I couldn't face any more bad news just then. I stood and walked out of my office. In the great room, I found Judy speaking with Chief Duffy and a woman I didn't know, who was wearing jeans and a blazer over a white Oxford shirt. Underneath her blazer, I saw just the edge of a revolver in a shoulder harness and silver badge clipped to her belt. Despite her attempt to look masculine with her clothing choices, she was all woman and had a curvy figure that I instantly suspected she wished there was a better way to mask. Her auburn hair was pulled severely back from her face in a tight knot at the top of her head. It made my scalp hurt just looking at it, but if the female officer found it painful, she didn't show it.

I smiled at her and Chief Duffy, but my smiled faltered when Judy shot me a worried look.

"Kelsey, just the person we've been looking for." Chief Duffy pointed to the woman. "This is Detective Brandon."

I nodded to her, but the hair on my arms stood up. Why would the chief need to call in a detective if Maxwell died from bee stings?

I looked from the chief to the detective and felt my stomach tighten. "You were looking for me?"

"Yes." The chief gave me a half smile. "We'd like ask you a few more questions in private about Maxwell Cherry's murder."

I gasped. "Murder? I thought it was an accident."

Chief Duffy grimaced. "It doesn't look that way."

My mind flashed back to Chase leaning over Maxwell's body in the brick pit. Could he have been lying to me? Maybe he hadn't been trying to help Maxwell after all.

"You and Mr. Cherry had an argument not long before he died," the detective said. Her voice was low and husky, as though she did burlesque shows as a side job.

Judy's pale green eyes grew to the size of cake pans.

"Yes, we had a disagreement," I said and straightened my shoulders. A supermodel cum police detective wasn't going to intimidate me. "How would you know that?"

The detective lips curved into a smile. "We have a witness who said he noticed the two of you arguing yesterday afternoon about the future of the Farm."

"Who is your *witness*?"

She shook her head.

The chief's tone was casual as he asked, "What was your disagreement about?"

"Am I being questioned in an official capacity?"

He nodded. "Yes."

"Do I need a lawyer?" I asked as a shiver traveled up my spine.

The chief looked apologetic, and he tucked his thumbs in his belt loops. "It wouldn't hurt."

EIGHT

I STARTED TO WALK away. I needed to process what the chief had just said. Murder? How could it be murder?

Detective Brandon's hand shot out, and she grabbed me by the upper arm, pulling me back. Her fingers bit into my skin.

I wrenched my arm away. "What do you think you're doing?"

The chief scowled at the detective. "No need to get rough there, Candy," he said.

The detective's first name was Candy? I had never heard a more inappropriate name for a person in my entire life. She was nothing close to sweet like candy.

I rubbed my arm. "We can talk in my office."

Judy watched us. "Are you okay?" she mouthed at me before I turned to lead the officers into my private office. I didn't bother to answer.

Inside my office, I sat in the chair behind my desk, which was a nineteenth-century partners desk far too large for the space. When I typed I had to hold my keyboard on my lap and it was completely impractical for the digital age. I adored it.

The chief sucked on his teeth. "You're not under arrest or anything like that. You are welcome to have a lawyer present. Course that might make us think you have something to hide."

I move a huge stack a papers from the middle of my desk onto the floor. "I don't have anything to hide."

"Good to hear." He pointed at the wooden armchair across the desk from me. There was a pile of museum catalogs on it. "Mind if I sit?"

I jumped out of my seat and grabbed the catalogs off of the chair. "Please do." I set the glossy magazine on another pile of catalogs behind my desk. The entire pile immediately toppled over like a waterfall tumbling over a cliff. I sighed and turned away from it. One of these days I would have to make the time to organize my office, but the day my benefactress's heir died on Farm grounds was not going to be that day.

"Thank you," he said as he eased himself into the chair. "Can you tell me where you were last night between eleven at night and three in the morning?"

I crossed my legs and shook my right foot under my desk. "Was that when Maxwell was killed?"

He nodded. "Yes. The coroner will be able to make a more precise time window after the autopsy, but that's the window he gave me to work with."

Detective Brandon stood in the corner of the office. When she leaned against the bookcase, the door to the metal key box attached to the bookcase swung open, and I saw all the keys to every door or gate on the Farm. She scowled at me as she closed the small door. If I were nicer, I would tell her the key box wasn't her only concern and that the bookcase was unstable and might topple onto her, but after she nearly yanked my arm out of its socket, I wasn't feeling helpful. I returned my attention to the chief.

"Maxwell died late at night," I said, "but he died of bee stings, right?"

The chief nodded encouragingly. "Yes, he did."

"That doesn't make any sense to me. How? Bees are less active after dark. When we have a problem with a wasp nest on the grounds, we always wait until nighttime to deal with it."

The chief smiled at me as if I were his star pupil. "I had wondered the same thing. Whoever knocked Maxwell out with the insulin was smart enough to agitate the bees so that they attacked."

I splayed my hands on my desktop. "Insulin?"

"Your father is diabetic," Detective Brandon said, not asking a question but stating it as a fact.

I looked from one to the other, from the chief's placid face and Burnside sideburns to Brandon's sleek hair and deep frown lines. I had made a mistake. When the chief asked me if I wanted my lawyer present, I should have said yes because as far as they were concerned, they had the murderer in their sights, and it was me.

"Kelsey?" The chief asked, "Is your father diabetic?"

"Yes, type one." This was bad. This was very bad.

"And he lives with you?"

"Uh, only during the summer. During the school year, he's a college drama professor and lives in housing near campus."

"But he's living with you right now?" This came from Brandon. The tiniest of smiles curled the corners of her mouth. I wished I could smack the expression off her face.

I uncrossed my legs and sat up straighter. "Yes, he's living with me at the moment."

Detective Brandon all but rubbed her hands together. "So you have access to his needles and insulin."

"Yes, but I would never kill anyone. That's what you want me to confess, isn't it? That I shot Maxwell with insulin and let the bees finish the job?" I stood up.

Detective Brandon pursed her lips. "We will have to search your cottage and interview your father to see if any of his insulin is missing." She paused. "You aren't the only suspect from your house."

I put a hand on my desk to steady myself. "My father? That's the most ridiculous thing I have ever heard. My father had never even *seen* Maxwell until yesterday, and as far as I know, the two men weren't even introduced. He would have no reason to hurt him or anyone else."

Detective Brandon pushed off of the bookcase. It wobbled for a few seconds but held. "Not even to protect his daughter from losing her job when the museum closed?"

"He doesn't know about the conversation I had with Maxwell. I didn't tell him or anyone else. If you don't believe me, ask him. He won't have a clue what you are talking about."

"We will," the detective promised.

"I think that's been enough questions for the moment. The reenactment opens in few hours, and I have a lot of work to do to make sure we're ready for the crowds."

Detective Brandon frowned. "You still didn't answer the chief's original question, Ms. Cambridge. Where were you between eleven p.m. and three a.m. last night?"

I glared at her but knew that it would only look worse for me if I refused to answer. And the truth really was that I had nothing to hide. "I returned to my cottage for the night close to eleven fifteen. Usually I get home long before that, but this is an unusual weekend with nearly a hundred and fifty reenactors, including their families, camping out on the grounds. I waited to go home until most of them had retired for the night. Although when I walked to my cottage, there were several who stayed awake late into the night talking around their respective camp fires. I hope you question the reenactors to find out if anyone saw anything suspicious in the middle of the night."

"I already have officers talking to them." Chief Duffy pushed himself out of his chair as if he was ready to leave.

Detective Brandon wasn't as eager to go. "Did anyone see you at home?"

"You mean an alibi?"

"Yes."

I frowned but answered her question. "By the time I got to the cottage, Hayden was asleep, but my father was up practicing his lines for his next performance. He has a part in the local community theater."

The chief gave a sideways smile. "What's the play?"

"*Hamlet*. Dad's playing the ghost of Hamlet's father."

The chief chuckled. "If I know your father, that's a role he can really get behind."

I found myself smiling back. "My father hopes to come back as a ghost himself someday and haunt the valley. He thinks it will be great fun."

"Then what happened?" Detective Brandon asked. Clearly, she wasn't a patron of the arts.

I stooped to pick up some of the fallen catalogs. I dropped them on my desk. "I went to bed and fell right to sleep. I was exhausted. The first day of the reenactment drew a much larger crowd than we expected. The bugler woke me up in the morning close to five. I decided to get up and take a walk around the property. Not long after I crossed Maple Grove Lane, I found Maxwell in the brick pit with that EMT leaning over him."

I couldn't help but notice that Detective Brandon sneered when I mentioned Chase. My eyes slid to the chief.

"Candy doesn't care much for my nephew," the chief said under his breath.

The detective snapped her notebook closed. "We'll need to talk to your father as soon as possible, Ms. Cambridge."

"He's with my son. I'd rather you not talk to him about murder in Hayden's presence."

"We would never," the chief said.

Maybe the chief wouldn't, but I wasn't so sure about the detective. Would it work in my favor that she didn't like Chase?

The chief's cell phone rang. He removed it from his belt. "Duffy. Right. We'll be right there." He slid the phone back into his general's jacket. It wouldn't do for any of the reenactors to see him with a cell phone, but I supposed his job required him to be reachable at all times. "The medical examiner wants us back at the scene while he loads up the deceased."

I winced. *Loads up* sounded like the chief was ready for a cattle drive, not to move a dead body.

The chief stepped through my office door. Detective Brandon hesitated before she went through. "I will get to the bottom of this murder, Ms. Cambridge. It would serve you well to either help me or get out of my way."

NINE

I KNEW SEVERAL LAWYERS. The problem was most of them worked with Cynthia and the Cherry Foundation. It probably wouldn't do to have one of them represent me since the heir apparent Maxwell was the murder victim. They weren't my only option … unfortunately.

Still standing behind my desk, I slipped my phone out of the back pocket of my jeans and scrolled through my contacts until I came to a name I didn't want to call.

"Hu-llo?" a groggy voice answered.

"Good morning, Justin," I said cheerily.

"Who's this?"

"Kelsey, your former sister-in-law. Are you awake?"

"No." The response was muffled, like it was spoken into a pillow.

"Well, wake up! I have a situation, and I need you at Barton Farm pronto."

There was some indecipherable mumbling on the other end of the line.

"Justin!"

"What?" he yelped. "I think you busted my eardrum."

"Too bad. I need your lawyer self to come here. I have a bad situation. Someone has died on the Farm. I need legal counsel."

Sounding more awake, he said, "Legal counsel? Doesn't the Cherry Foundation have an army of lawyers? Call one of them."

"I can't. The situation is—" I searched for the right word. "Sensitive."

"I'd think the Cherry Foundation lawyers would be all ready for sensitive situations. Call one of them for help. I'm tired."

"Justin, wait! Don't hang up. I can't call the Foundation lawyers because Maxwell Cherry is dead."

"What?" he cried sounding wide awake. "Maxwell Cherry? You've got to be kidding me."

"I wish." I leaned against the edge of my desk.

"What happened?"

"He was murdered," I said.

He swore. "Why are you calling me? This is a little out of my realm. I'm in environmental law." There was rustling sound over the phone like Justin was trying to untangle himself from his bed sheets.

"I realize that," I said, "but you're all I have right now. And I need a lawyer ASAP. The detective on the case thinks I did it."

The battle with the bed sheets stopped. "What? Why?"

I went on to give him the short version of the circumstances surrounding Maxwell's death.

He swallowed. "What's your alibi?"

61

I told him the same thing that I had told the chief and the detective just a few minutes ago.

Justin nodded. "That sounds like a decent alibi."

"Gee thanks." I drummed my fingers on the desk.

"You should be all right if your father can vouch for you being there."

"I could have left the cabin in the middle of the night without him knowing. His room isn't by the front door."

"I suggest that you not share that with the police."

"Right." I began to pace.

"Kel, I can't. I have a tennis match today and—"

"Justin Cambridge, you *will* get your behind out to Barton Farm right now, unless you want me to tell your mother what *really* happened to her precious Tiffany lamp."

He groaned. "All right, all right, Kel. You don't have to be so harsh. I don't know what I'll be able to do for you. I just barely passed the bar last month. I hope you don't expect much."

I didn't, and I was doomed.

I slid my phone back into my pocket as I walked down the short hallway from my office to the visitor center's main lobby. I checked my watch; it was a few minutes after eight. The good news was that the Farm didn't open until ten. That gave me two hours to do damage control.

Judy came out of the gift shop with Tiffin close at her heels. "We have everything in order for the discounted tickets for today's reenactment. Don't you worry about that."

I made a note in my ever-present notebook. "Thanks, Judy. I knew that I could count on you."

She gripped her hands in front of her. "Yes, well, one problem solved, another shows up."

"What happened?" My pen was poised to take notes.

She grimaced. "Shepley."

Her one word answer was enough. My irate gardener was always a problem. "What is it this time?"

She pursed her lips. "He's throwing a fit because he can't get to his gardens."

I could imagine. "Why wasn't I radioed?"

She shrugged. "Whoever reported it telephoned the gift shop, and I didn't want to interrupt you while you were in your office with the police. I told Ashland, who just got here, to take care of it."

"I'd better get over there. Shepley will eat Ashland for breakfast." I tucked the notebook into my back pocket and straightened my polo shirt.

Judy reached over to squeeze my hand. "Everything will get straightened out, Kelsey. You'll see. This will all be a bad memory soon."

If only I could believe her. I gave her a weak smile as I snapped on Tiffin's leash. We left the visitor center through the employee entrance beside the gift shop.

Outside, the sun was fully up now. Most of the reenactors sat outside their tents, tucking into breakfast and polishing the barrels of their rifles or bayonets for the upcoming battle. Others shaved in cloudy mirrors tacked on the trees or propped on makeshift tables. The men shaving used straight razors. I had to respect their commitment to stay in character, as that shaving looked dangerous.

"Mom!" Hayden cried as he ran out of the Union camp. "I met Santa Claus!"

Santa Claus? I didn't remember Santa registering. Then my father walked out of the camp followed by the Walt Whitman reenactor. I chuckled. With his full white beard and round tummy, the reenactor did indeed have a remarkable resemblance to Santa.

"Hayden, that's Walt Whitman, not Santa. He's a poet."

My son furrowed his brow. "He said that he was Santa too."

The reenactor smiled. "At Christmastime, I have been known to pitch in at Santa's workshop at the mall."

"Ahh," I said.

"I had a very nice time talking to you, Roy," he said to my father. "I'm happy to practice lines with you whenever you like. I don't have much stomach for the battles. Being a nurse during this terrible war can be so disheartening. The boys coming into the hospital are in a bad shape. It would be nice to worry over Shakespeare's timeless poetry as an escape."

Dad grinned. "I'll stop by your tent later today."

"Very good." Walt tipped his hat and went on his way.

I handed Dad Tiffin's leash. "Can you take Tiff for me?"

My corgi gave me a pouty face, but I couldn't be worrying about my dog while I spoke with Shepley. Dad took the leash from my hand, and Hayden dropped to his knees hug the dog. The pair rolled in the dirt.

"Are you going to tell me why the police are here?" my father asked quietly.

"There's been an accident."

"I've heard that from everyone in the encampment, but no one really knows what is going on other than that they aren't supposed to cross the road into the village."

"Maxwell Cherry is dead. He died in the brick pit."

Dad gasped.

"Shh, you'll attract attention," I said, pointing to Hayden and Tiffin still locked in a boy/dog bear hug.

"Mr. Renard?" a voice said behind me on the path.

I turned to find young Officer Sonders, who was first to arrive on the scene.

My father wiggled his bushy eyebrows. "Yes?"

"May I speak with you for a moment?"

My father straightened to his full height. That wasn't too impressive at five-five, but his booming voice more than made up for his lack a stature. "What does this concern?"

Officer Sonders appeared a little taken aback by my father's reaction. "Well, I ... the chief asked me to ask you a few questions about Mr. Cherry."

Dad placed a finger to his chest. "What would I know about Mr. Cherry?"

"Dad," I pleaded. "Just answer his questions."

My father's theatrics had grabbed Hayden's attention, and he was no longer rolling in the dirt with Tiffin. "Why do the police want to talk to Pop-Pop?"

I screwed up my face.

"Pop-Pop, did you steal a car? Dad told me you stole a car once."

My face turned bright red, but my father was unfazed by his grandson's question. "Your father shouldn't have told you that. However, I'll tell you the entire story when you're old enough to drive yourself. At that time, you'll see that my little indiscretion was completely justified."

A headache began to form on the right side of my temple.

Officer Sonders swallowed. "Is there somewhere we can do talk, Mr. Renard?"

"I suppose so. We can go to the cott—"

"No," I said a little too quickly, but I didn't want any police inside my cottage until Justin arrived. "Use my office. It's just inside of the visitor center there. It's unlocked, just walk in."

Officer Sonders frowned. I knew that he would report back to the police chief that I didn't want him in my cottage. I'd just made myself more suspicious, but I planned to protect my home and privacy from this investigation as long as I could, even if it was an act of futility.

"Hayden, why don't you and Tiffin go into the visitor center and hang out with Judy?" I said.

"Okay," my son said. Judy carried Jolly Ranchers in her skirt pockets, and Hayden knew that.

After I released Hayden and Tiffin into Judy's capable hands, I continued on my way to Shepley's gardens. I hoped that the scene hadn't become much worse since I had been delayed so long. I tried not to think about the conversation Dad and Officer Sonders were having in my office. Was it a good thing or a bad thing that I didn't get a chance to tell Dad about the insulin? At least now he would act genuinely surprised when he heard the news—but he was an actor, and the police knew that. Would they believe his reaction even if it was real?

TEN

AT THE END OF the pebbled path, where it met the pavement on Maple Grove Lane, another police officer stood guard. I hoped his steely presence would be enough of a deterrent for both the reenactors and the tourists, but I knew how curious the tourists could be. People were constantly trying to get a look behind the scenes in areas of the Farm that were supposed to be off-limits to guests. If the officer couldn't be there all day, I would set one of my seasonals on the job.

I started across the street.

"Ma'am? You can't go over there," the young officer said.

I hated being ma'med, even if I was a mother. "I'm Kelsey Cambridge, director of Barton Farm. I was told there was an issue with my gardener."

The officer had to be six-three, over a foot taller than me. I couldn't have seemed like much of a threat. "Oh," he said, stepping back. "I'm supposed to let you through. The chief said so."

I nodded and marched across the street.

I slowed as I stepped onto the pebbled path on the other side of the pavement and saw all of the commotion around the brickyard. The medical examiner stood by the ambulance taking notes. Apparently he had the ability to tune out distraction while he worked, because Shepley stood the length of a volleyball court away in front Barton House yelling at Ashland.

My assistant teetered back and forth on her feet, shaking her head, but she didn't even try to argue back.

"I have every right to check on my bees!" the gardener cried. "You can't keep me from them because Maxwell Cherry was dumb enough to get stung."

Barton Farm's gardener was a small man with a slight hump on his back that was put there from years and years of bending over flowerbeds. A long gray ponytail tied back with a piece of garden twine hung down between his shoulder blades. Red suspenders over his Farm polo held up his jeans. A mysterious scar crossed his left cheek from the edge of his nose to his ear, giving him a piratelike quality. In my imagination, he was one of Captain Hook's men and got into a sword fight with Peter Pan. Shepley was tiny but fierce. I bet Peter Pan needed extra pixie dust to escape him.

Two police officers stood nearby, and neither of them looked like they were going to come to Ashland's rescue.

"What's going on here?" I asked.

Ashland visibly relaxed when I appeared. "Kelsey, thank you for coming. Shepley is upset—"

"Damn right, I'm upset. These Neanderthals won't let me around the side of the house to check on my bees."

One of the officers twitched at being called a Neanderthal, but still neither said anything. The headache that had begun to form across the street started to pulse behind my right eye.

Ashland cringed. She was way out of her depth when it came to Shepley. *Don't send a girl to do a woman's job,* I thought.

Shepley pointed at the police with a dirt-encrusted fingernail. "You have no respect for this property. If you don't move out of my way, I'm going to push you over."

One of the two large officers folded his arms and glared down his nose at Shepley. "I'd like to see you try."

Shepley took a step forward as if he were ready to step up to the challenge. He was half the size of the policeman. Ashland kept rocking back and forth in her sneakers, which looked like clown shoes at the end of her spindly legs.

"Shepley," I began.

Shepley turned his dirty fingernail on me. "This is all your fault." His eyes were barely visible slits from squinting into the sun. Shepley would never be so weak as to wear sunglasses or sunscreen to protect his eyes and skin.

I scowled in return. Like many of the problems at the Farm, I had inherited Shepley. He was a talented gardener, perhaps the best in the county, but he was impossible to get along with. As long as he was alone with his plants, all was fine. If he had to make human contact, look out.

In front of Barton House, summer flowers bloomed in a small garden. Shepley's main garden was on the other side of the village, and it boasted even more flowers and rows and rows of vegetables. In this smaller bed, daisies, snapdragons, and irises bopped their heavy heads in the light breeze. Dozens of bees buzzed around us. I swallowed at the image of Maxwell's swollen feet and hoped that I would someday be able to erase it from my memory completely.

One of the officers swatted at a bee.

"What are you doing?" Shepley bellowed. "Don't hit one of my bees. Do you know how precious honeybees are? That they are in decline?"

The officer blinked.

Chief Duffy joined us. Still in his gray Confederate trousers and sixteen-button frock coat, he chewed on a stick. "Shepley's right," he told his officer. "The bees are in danger. No swatting."

The officer licked his lips. "I don't want to get stung, sir, especially since these bees killed the victim."

Shepley's eyes narrowed. "Are you allergic to bees?"

The officer shook his head.

"Then you have nothing worry about. That guy died because he had a bee allergy."

The chief removed the stick from his mouth. "You knew that Maxwell had an allergy?"

The gardener sucked on his teeth. "Everyone working on the Farm did. The man had a hissy fit when he was buzzed yesterday afternoon. A grown man squealing in the middle of the village gets attention."

I hadn't realized so many members of my staff had witnessed Maxwell's bee dance. I couldn't decide if it was good or bad news that more people knew about Maxwell's allergy.

Chief Duffy nodded at this. Not for the first time, I wished I knew what the police chief was thinking. As harmless as he appeared in his reenactor uniform, I was beginning to recognize the chief was a shrewd man.

"Now, Shepley," the New Hartford chief of police said. "We have an investigation going on into the death of one of your colleagues. To best solve the case, we can't have people walking around the village unsupervised until we've processed and secured the scene. Since your bees were the perpetrators, that puts your hives off limits."

"Maxwell Cherry wasn't my colleague," Shepley spat. "The man was a lowlife with no respect for nature or for history. He shouldn't even be able to walk these grounds. He spoils them with his twenty-first-century materialism."

The chief pointed his stick at him. "That's quite an impassioned speech."

Shepley squinted at him. "I'm not going to leave my garden. I have too much to do. Do you think these plants tend themselves? I don't care if you'd tell me the president was shot dead in my hollyhocks. I must tend to my garden."

Duffy removed a gold pocket watch from the pocket of his coat and checked the time. "I see we're not making much progress here, and I, frankly, don't have the time to argue with you. The day is warming up more by the second and we need to get the body to the morgue. So I'll let you into your precious gardens if, and only if, one of deputies stays with you. But the bees are still off-limits."

Shepley sneered. "If that's the way it has to be, then fine." He pointed a crooked finger at the two officers in his way. "Now move."

The deputies parted, and Shepley swore as he stomped back onto the green toward the main garden, which was about a football field away from Barton House. Adjoining the main garden, the iron fence around Shepley's prized medicinal garden loomed. He turned and said over his shoulder, "I'd say the bees did us a service offing Maxwell Cherry. The man didn't even recycle," he said, as though this was a grave observation of Maxwell's character.

"Shepley, please don't make this worse than it already is," I called.

He glared at me. "I won't forget this. We were just fine until you came along and wanted to change everything. If it weren't for you, we wouldn't have all these reenactors here this weekend, trampling my flowerbeds and killing people."

Shepley was wrong. The Farm wasn't "just fine" before I became director. The number of guests each year was steadily falling, and the Farm would have gone under without Cynthia's generosity. The previous director, who had been in the post for nearly thirty years, saw no reason to change anything about Farm operations. What visitors expected thirty years ago and what they were willing to pay for in today's world of multimedia overload did not match up. Unfortunately, not all of my employees were on board with my plans. Shepley was one of the old guard who thought it was enough to sit back and wait for the tourists to come to us.

Self-sufficiency was my ultimate goal for the Farm. I didn't want us to dependent on Cynthia's money. *And for good reason*, I realized as I thought of Maxwell's threat. I grimaced. Maxwell was about to take the money away before he died. No wonder I looked like such an enticing suspect to the chief.

I placed my hands on my hips. "Maxwell's death has nothing to do with the reenactment, Shepley."

"How would you know?" he spat.

I *didn't* know. It was wishful thinking on my part, but the encounter I'd witnessed yesterday between Wesley Mayes and Maxwell over Portia didn't gel with my theory. Had the handsome reenactor been so enraged over Portia's engagement to Maxwell that he murdered his rival?

Shepley picked up his garden trowel, which was lying at the foot of a sunflower, and stomped away. One of the deputies hurried after him.

The chief sighed. "He won't be away from his bees for too much longer. The medical examiner is almost done processing the scene. You may even be able open up this side of the grounds by late afternoon."

"That's good news, Chief. Thank you." I glanced around and noticed that Ashland had disappeared at some point during my argument with Shepley. Also absent was Detective Brandon. I turned toward the crime scene and didn't see her standing with the medical examiner and the other officers. I didn't like not knowing where the detective was. My instincts told me to be wary of her.

Chief Duffy hiked up his trousers. "I forgot to mention this when I spoke to you earlier, but I'd advise you not to leave the township."

I licked my lips. "Because I'm a suspect."

He rolled the stick to the other side of his mouth. "Yep. I suppose I don't have to really order you to stick around since you live here and all."

"Do you have any other suspects?"

"Sure do. I never put all my eggs in one basket, even if that basket is looking really, really good for committing the crime."

I frowned. "I have another suspect who you might not know about."

He arched an eyebrow at me. "Trying to spread out the suspicion?"

"Of course." I folded my arms.

He smiled at my honesty. I went on to tell him about the argument that I witnessed between Maxwell and Wesley.

"That does sound promising, but I know Wesley. He's a fine reenactor. He knows his buttons. Not every reenactor can recognize the right buttons for the uniform. Wesley can."

"I don't think buttons should automatically release someone from suspicion of murder."

"No, I suppose not." He sighed as if this was a major failing of our modern society. "But he's a good one, for a Union man. I've even had him in my regiment from time to time when we were low on Confederates. I can't believe he would do such a thing. He's tentative on the battlefield and doesn't have the will to attack like some of my other soldiers do. But I'll certainly talk to him. It seems that I need to pay a visit to the fiancée, Portia, too."

I shielded my eyes from the sun with my hand. "Has Cynthia been told?"

He nodded. "I'm afraid so. I sent one of my officers to her home to tell her because I couldn't leave the scene and I didn't want her to find out through the rumor mill. My officer used to take piano lessons from her as a child. I thought it was a good choice to have someone she knew break the news."

"And how is she?"

He shook his head. "Officer Parker said that her maid took her straight to bed. It's been quite a shock. The maid told Parker that Cynthia's health has been failing in the recent months."

I swallowed. *Which is why she was preparing to turn over her foundation to Maxwell.* As much as I disliked Maxwell, my heart ached for Cynthia. She was one of the most cheerful and kind people I knew. While others may hide their fortunes away in the turbulent economy, she shared it and supported local arts and community. When she did pass away, it would be a great loss to the entire town of New Hartford.

"If the village reopens this afternoon, does that mean the Blue and Gray Ball can still be held?"

The ball was planned to be held Sunday evening. The Farm had rented large white tents, which would be set up where we now stood, in the center of the village green. The tents themselves had cost me a small fortune and then there was the period decorations and food. It wasn't easy to find a caterer who was willing to make mid-nineteenth-century fare, and the one who'd agreed wasn't cheap. Just asking the question made my stomach turn. If the ball was cancelled, it could ruin the Farm. Tickets were $75 a pop. And we expected a hundred guests at the event, in addition to the reenactors who had paid extra for the event and the Farm staff who were invited. I guessed that there would be between 300 and 325 people attendance.

The chief dropped his chew stick on the ground. "The ball has to go on. My wife has been talking about it for weeks. It's the first interest that she's shown in my hobby. She bought a hoop skirt!"

I shoulders sagged with relief. "I'm glad."

He pointed a finger at me. "I will have this case tied up by tomorrow afternoon. Because even though I like you, Kelsey, all my money is on you having done it. If I can, I'll wait to arrest you until after the ball."

I wondered if I should say thank you for that kindness.

ELEVEN

THE MEDICAL EXAMINER CALLED for Chief Duffy. The chief
tipped his hat to me and walked over to his colleague. A few
feet away from them, a crime scene tech held a dead bee up in
the sunlight to examine it. He tilted it back and forth in his
tweezers before dropping it in a small plastic evidence bag. Beyond the brickyard, I had a clear view of the barn. Jason disappeared around the side of it. I quickly looked away. I didn't want
to bring any of the officers' attention to Jason; he wasn't supposed to be in the village.

I walked along the pebbled path and made like I was going
to cross the street. Taking a quick look over my shoulder to
make sure that no one was watching me, I veered right toward
the barn. I ducked through the break in the split-rail fence.

The Farm's two oxen, Betty and Mags, who hadn't yet been
moved to the far pasture for the day, stared at me as I dashed
toward the barn door. They weren't used to having anyone

other than Jason in their space. Although the girls were known for being gentle, I didn't linger to find out how they viewed my visit.

I jogged up the dirt ramp into the barn, pausing just inside the doorway to let my eyes adjust. There was no electricity. Jason worked by sunlight and battery-powered lanterns when he needed extra light. "Jason?" I whispered. I sidestepped what looked like a dropping from one of the oxen.

Miss Muffins, our head barn cat, yowled at me and wove in and out of my legs. Many times I wished that Hayden had fallen in love with this lovely calico and asked us to take her home instead of Frankie, the terror of the Western Reserve.

I bent to scratch her behind the ear. When I straightened, I whispered again, "Jason?"

Barn Boy materialized out of the shadows of a stall. He moved silently. Many of the seasonal staff complained that Jason was creepy because of how stealthily he moved and because he rarely spoke, even when asked a direct question. Laura joked that he had been raised in the middle of the park by wolves. I told her that she was ridiculous. Besides, there hadn't been wolves living in Ohio for generations.

Jason waited and watched me. His movements were tentative around people, even me, and Hayden and I were the closest thing to human friends he had. Around the livestock he was different. I had witnessed him approach a bucking horse with a steady hand and firm stride, yet he tiptoed toward me like he expected a lashing. Jason didn't trust most people. Many times, I wondered what had happened to him when he was a child that made him so skittish. But I knew asking him would be a waste. He wouldn't answer me if I did.

"Are they gone?" he whispered finally.

Miss Muffins pranced over to him. He bent over, picked her up, and cradled her in his arms. The cat purred, sharing in the comfort Jason found by holding her.

"Is who gone?" I stepped farther into the barn, wanting to be able to read Jason's expressions, but he stood in the shadows.

"The police." His voice was scratchy from underuse. "They were in here about an hour ago. I hid in the hayloft."

"Why did you do that?" I asked.

"I—I didn't want to talk to them. I have nothing to say." He placed Miss Muffins on a hay bale and picked up a bucket of horse feed.

"A man died in the brick pit last night."

He carried the bucket to the horse stall. "I know."

"The police will want to ask you what you might have seen." I paused. "And they'll ask you to leave the barn. The chief doesn't want anyone on this side of the road until the village is reopened."

"I can't leave my barn." He said it like Shepley defending his garden, but Jason's proclamation was more earnest, as if he were physically unable to leave the barn and animals. "They won't want to know what I know."

My skin prickled. "What do you know?"

He poured the bucket of feed into a feed bag hanging just inside the horse stall. Scarlet, the Farm's mare, rubbed her nose into his palm before burying her head into her feed bag.

"Jason, did you sleep here last night?" I asked. I knew the teenager sometimes slept in the barn when one of the animals was sick, but now I wondered if it was a more regular thing.

He hung the bucket from a nail on the stall's outer wall.

I perched on the hay bale next to Miss Muffins. Even though I was half a foot shorter than Jason, I thought I might look less intimidating if I sat. "Were you here last night?"

He nodded. This conversation was going great. I bit my tongue to hold back the urge to reprimand him for not answering my questions directly. That would only make him close down more.

I set Miss Muffins in my lap, and the small cat curled up into a purring ball of fur. I stroke her back for a couple of seconds before I asked, "Did you see anything?"

He picked up a garden hose to fill water buckets for the animals. "No, but I heard something."

I barely heard his whisper over the sound of rushing water. "What?"

He released the nozzle. "I heard a scream."

My pulse quickened. "And?"

"And that was all." He picked up one of the buckets. "I figured that it was one of the Civil War people. I didn't want to go out there and see them." He wouldn't meet my eyes. "That's why I stayed last night. I knew the animals would be scared with all the noise coming from the reenactment camps."

My heart sank. Jason had had the perfect opportunity to witness the murder and clear my name, but he hid instead. I couldn't blame him. In his place I would assume any noise came from the reenactors too, although I would have investigated because I'm naturally nosey.

"What time would you say you heard the scream?"

"It was close to one in the morning. It woke Miss Muffins and me up. It woke up Scarlet and the oxen too. It took a little while for all the animals to calm down."

"Was it just one scream?"

"Yes, only one."

"Did you make out any conversation? Any other noise at all?"

He shook his head. "I thought I imagined it, like it was a dream, but when I saw the animals were awake and agitated, I knew I hadn't dreamed it at all."

"Did you notice anything else strange?" I asked.

"No. Miss Muffins and I didn't venture out to see what was going on. The scream was short, which made me think that it was one the reenactors loose in the village. I didn't want to face them."

How I wished that he had. But then again, what if Jason had seen the killer? Would he be here today to talk about what he'd heard?

"Kelsey, please don't tell the police what I told you," he begged, meeting my eyes for the first time since our conversation began. His eyes were bright green. The same shade as Miss Muffins's.

I frowned. "Why not?"

"I don't want to talk to them, the police." He started to shake. "I can't talk to them. I can't."

Miss Muffins jumped from my lap, and I got up from the hay bale. "Jason, are you okay?"

He ignored my question. "Can you promise?"

I bit the inside of my cheek and found myself saying, "All right. I won't tell them right away, but if I have no choice, I will."

He nodded. "Thank you."

"Now, you have to go home," I said.

"Home?" he murmured, like that was a foreign concept.

My brow knit together. "Yes. The police don't want any visitors or staff in the village. It might not be for very long. The chief just told me that the village might reopen as early as this afternoon. You can come back then."

"But the animals—"

"Finish feeding them and then go, but if you don't want the police to know that you've been here, you'd better sneak away through the woods and come out the other side of the grounds near the battlefield."

"I don't want to go home."

"Then go somewhere else," I said. "It won't be long. Or you can stay and help on the other side of the road with the reenactment. We can always use an extra set of hands."

Jason shivered. "I'll find someplace else to go."

I wasn't surprised at his reaction. I knew the threat of having to socialize with strangers would be far worse to Jason than vacating the grounds for few hours.

He nodded. "I'll leave just as soon as I finish the feeding."

"Good," I said, wondering all the while at Jason's strange reaction to the word *home*. I made a mental note to check his personnel file to see where he lived. Now that I thought about it, it seemed that Jason was always at the Farm no matter the time, day or night.

I turned to go. When I stepped out of the barn, I ran right into Chase Wyatt. I bounced off his chest, and he grabbed me before I fell backward through the barn's open door. He pulled me toward him, but I put my hands out and pushed myself away.

"What are you doing in here?" I demanded.

"I'm looking for you."

"Me? Why? And you can let me go now." I tried to pull my arms from his grasp and resisted the strong urge to kick him in the shin or higher.

His face flashed red. "Oh, I'm sorry." He dropped his hands. "I need to talk to you."

I tugged at end of my braid and found it still intact. "Is this about the reenactment?" I looked him up and down. "I see you're back in your medic uniform."

His blush deepened. "Preparing for battle, as it were."

I started down the path that led from the barn to the road crossing. I wanted to get Chase away from the barn and Jason as soon as possible. "The reenactment battle will happen on schedule if that's your concern. Only the village is closed this morning. The chief believes that it will reopen this afternoon."

"It's not about the reenactment or the village. At least not exactly."

I kept walking, and he caught up with me in one stride. Curse my short legs.

"I want to help," he said.

"If you want to help with the reenactment other than being a soldier playing dead, we always welcome volunteers and can put you to work. There is a lot to do to keep this event running smoothly. I'm sure my assistant Ashland has a number of places you can pitch in."

"No," he said. Now he was walking backward, so that he could look me in the eye as he talked. "I want to help you find out who killed Maxwell."

"I don't have time for this." I increased my pace, which made him walk more quickly.

The heel of his boot caught on a root, and he toppled backward flat on his back. "Oooph!"

I stepped over him and kept going.

Chase scrambled to his feet. He brushed off dirt and possible ox manure—not that I would tell him that—from his uniform as he galloped to catch up with me. "I heard the chief tell you that you were the number-one suspect. I can help you with that."

I turned onto the pebbled path and nodded at the officer watching the road as I crossed. When Chase and I reached the other side, I said, "Thanks, but no thanks."

He stepped closer to me. So close that I could smell the coffee on his breath and campfire on his clothes. "Yours isn't the only reputation and career at risk here."

I pulled up short, which made him stumble a few steps. I arched one eyebrow at him; it was a maneuver that used to drive my ex-husband over the edge. By the scowl on his face, it had the same effect on Chase. "Really?"

"I want to help you and myself."

"Yourself?" I asked. Behind him I saw the brigades lining up with their commanding officers. The lieutenants gave orders and rallied the men—and some women dressed as privates—for the battle. Both Southern and Northern infantrymen saluted their superiors. If it hadn't been for the occasional Farm employee driving by on a golf cart, I would have believed that we really had stepped back into 1863, moments before a scrimmage.

"Yes, I'm a suspect too." He searched my eyes with his chocolate ones. My eyes were also brown, but they were closer to tree bark in color. "You have to know that," he said.

"I don't know that. I thought your uncle, the chief, was certain that you could do no wrong."

Chase grimaced. "He may have said that, but I know he'll change his mind when he learns about my past with Maxwell."

"Perhaps it's not the chief you're worried about," I said, arching my eyebrow for a second time. "Maybe it's Detective Brandon."

He wrinkled his nose. "What did she say?"

"What do you think she said?"

He gave a sideways smile. "That she wished that I was in the first Confederate line in Pickett's march in Gettysburg."

I folded my arms. "Oh, and why is that?"

His smile grew broader. "Candy and I have a history."

"I bet." I started walking again.

He grabbed my arm and jerked my body backward. "Listen to me, Kelsey. We can help each other."

I gritted my teeth. "You had better let go of my arm or I'm going to break your hand. I'm small but you don't want to mess with me."

He looked down at his hand as if surprised to see it wrapped around my forearm. He dropped his hold of me.

I rubbed the place where he grabbed me. I could practically feel a bruise forming.

"I'm sorry." His brow knit together. "Did I hurt you?"

"No," I lied, holding my chin up. "Why do you need my help?"

"Because this is your turf."

"That's how I can help you; how can you help me? Because so far this is sounding pretty one-sided in your favor, and that doesn't work for me."

He sighed. "I know the reenactors. This isn't my first reenactment. My uncle has been dragging me to these events since I was in middle school. As a reenactor, I can move through the camps and ask questions without raising suspicions. Everyone is going to be talking about Maxwell's death, so if I ask some subtle questions, they'll think I'm just making conversation and passing time. Just like in real war, the time sitting around between real battles can get pretty boring."

"I'm not going to help you without knowing your connection to Maxwell."

He removed his forage cap and ran a hand through his blond hair. The hair stuck up in all directions and gave him a boyish quality that I did not trust. His playful appearance was misleading. I knew nothing about this man. He could be a stone cold killer. He was the one I found looming over Maxwell's body after all.

He sighed. "Okay, you win. All I will say is that I knew Maxwell. We were not friendly."

"I wouldn't say *that* cryptic history is winning my support." I stepped backward. "Why did you act like you didn't know who the body was?"

"I panicked. You found me in a very awkward position, and I knew Candy would be called in. She's always called in when there is a suspicious death anywhere in the county."

"Sounds to me like Detective Brandon has it out for you."

"You met her," he said. "That's a very scary position to be in."

"That's your problem, not mine. And I can't say I blame her since you were standing over a dead body and all." I watched him closely. "How did you know Maxwell?" I pressed.

"From business."

"Business? I thought you were an EMT."

"I am."

I waited. He said no more. I shrugged as if it didn't matter to me and kept walking. We were on the edge of camp now; much closer and reenactors would begin to overhear our conversation.

He stepped beside me. "Now I'm in a worse spot because the chief will think that I purposely misled him by claiming I didn't know Maxwell."

"Didn't you?" I asked.

"You aren't making this easy either." He slapped his cap back onto his head.

"I see no reason to."

"So you don't want my help? You're willing to try to solve this case all on your own. What about your son?"

"What about my son?" I snapped, jabbing him in the chest with my index finger. "Don't you dare bring him into this!"

He held up his hands as if in surrender. "Whoa, I'm sorry, Mama Bear."

"I think we've talked about this long enough." I stomped away.

TWELVE

I PULVERIZED PEBBLES ON the path as I marched back to the visitor center. How dare that cocky EMT bring Hayden into our conversation? I suddenly had a desperate need to see my son. I picked up my pace and ignored reenactors who tried to wave me down with questions. I couldn't deal with their need for gossip at the moment.

I passed the visitor center as my phone beeped in my pocket, telling me I had a new text. It was from Justin. I'M HERE was all the message said.

I made a sharp turn toward the visitor center as my former brother-in-law came of the sliding glass doors. Justin blinked in the early morning light. He was probably out late the night before at a night club or trendy bar trying to impress the ladies with his bright, shiny new law degree. Many times I wondered if Justin would ever settle down and stop being a playboy. He was handsome and smart. There was no reason he couldn't find a decent girl who had the ability to balance her own checkbook.

My pace slowed because Justin wasn't alone. My ex-husband, Eddie, was with him, and so was a young woman who I didn't know. Betraying me, I felt my heart beat pick up. Eddie, with his Gregory Peck good looks, was as handsome as ever. He was a physical therapist with his own practice in New Hartford. He wore freshly pressed chinos and a pink polo shirt with his company logo on it. But it wasn't Eddie who made my pulse race. It was the woman ten years my junior holding his hand. A ring with a dime-sized diamond on it encircled her left ring finger. Krissie. I wished I could say this was the first time I had seen Eddie holding another young woman's hand, but it wasn't. The last time, we were very much married. If hand holding was his only indiscretion I might have still been married to him.

"Suck it up," I whispered to myself. "Justin," I waved.

"Kel, there you are." Justin's face broke into a grin. The younger of the two Cambridge men was as handsome as his brother. Just a year younger than Eddie and I, Justin had taken seven years to get through law school. I tried not to dwell on that, as I now required his legal advice.

"Wow," Justin said. "This is crazy. Are you really letting all these actors walk around with guns and swords?"

"The guns aren't loaded. The swords are blunt," I said. "And they are called reenactors not actors."

"Huh." His eyes scanned the scene. His mouth fell open. "Is that Abraham Lincoln?"

"Yep," I said as if that wasn't unusual at all. "Walt Whitman should be here somewhere too."

"Who?" Justin asked.

I sighed.

He shook his head. "Cripes, this place is out of control. I had to tell the dragon lady at the window four times that I was your lawyer before she would let me in. Thankfully, your assistant Ashland happened by and recognized Eddie."

My eyes slid to my ex-husband. "What are you doing here?" I knew my tone was frosty, but it had been a trying morning and the reenactment hadn't even opened up yet.

Eddie frowned, and I noticed the flash of annoyance cross his face. Someone who didn't know him well would have missed it, but I knew Eddie better than anyone. He had been my next-door neighbor and best friend as a child. We started dating in high school and we got married after college because that's what was expected, and I think it never occurred to either of us that there was another option. Our marriage was rocky, and we realized that we wanted different things out of life. Eddie wanted money, success, and prestige for his business; I wanted to preserve history and return to school, which I eventually did without his blessing. We might have gotten through it with time, work, and counseling, but then he had an affair with one of his clients. She was also married, so ours wasn't only the marriage ruined. That was three years ago, and I was over it ... sort of. Hayden was two when we divorced, so he didn't know about the affair. As far as I was concerned, he never would.

Eddie forced a smile. "Kelsey, I'd like to introduce you to Krissie Pumpernickle."

Krissie couldn't have been more than twenty-two. She was small like me, but her build was more athletic, as though she'd grown up doing gymnastics or cheerleading. Her hair was trimmed in a short pixie cut that was perfect for her tiny head and gave her a fairylike quality. She was beautiful, and I tried not to hate her for it.

"Nice to meet you, Krissie." My eyes slid over to Eddie. "I got the email. I so appreciate learning that you are getting married in a mass email. That was so kind after knowing you my entire life."

Eddie's jaw twitched.

I smiled at Krissie and reminded myself that what had happened between Eddie and me had nothing to do with her. I also felt sympathy. The poor girl didn't know what she was getting herself into. "I'm happy to finally meet you, Krissie, since until this morning, I didn't even know you existed."

"I thought you said you told her months ago," Krissie said under her breath.

Eddie pursed his lips together.

Ahh, trouble in paradise. I can't say that I wasn't the tiniest bit pleased by that. If Krissie was going to marry Eddie, she would have to get used to it—he was notorious for keeping information to himself. It was something that we argued about on a regular basis.

"Are you guys interested in touring the encampments? You've never shown an interest in history."

Eddie frowned. "Justin told us about the situation." He paused. "I don't think this is a safe atmosphere for Hayden, so Krissie and I wanted to take him home."

This was just what I was afraid of when I saw the email about their engagement. Krissie, the-wife-to-be, was looking for ways to start building a custody case against me. I would not have it. I would not let some other woman raise my son.

"Why?" I asked through gritted teeth.

"Justin told us Maxwell Cherry is dead, possibly murdered. You have to agree with me that this isn't the best place for a five-year-old."

"Hayden isn't in any sort of danger. My father is with him and he doesn't even know what's going on. He wants to be here for the reenactment. Are you going to be the one who tells him that he has to leave?"

Eddie frowned. "If I know your father, he's out there showing Hayden the crime scene."

I glared at Eddie. As much as I knew about him, he knew just as much about me. It was terribly annoying.

Krissie patted her pixie hair. "As a mother, I would want to be one hundred percent sure that my son was safe."

"Are you a mother?" I snapped.

"I'll be a stepmother very soon."

I closed my eyes for a brief moment and counted to ten.

I held up my hand. "I'm far too busy to stand here and fight with you about this. I'll find Hayden for you, and you can ask him if he wants to stay here or go with you. You're welcome to stay here at the reenactment if you want to keep an eye on him."

"Maybe being here during the day is fine, but at least let him stay the night at my house," Eddie said.

I bit my lip. As much as I hated to admit it, Eddie was right. I wouldn't have time to watch over Hayden between the reenactment and the murder. My father meant well, but he was easily distracted and consumed with his play.

The reenactors had a bonfire planned for that night for Farm staff. I knew Hayden would be heartbroken to miss it, but I'd rather he be safe. And for all his faults as a husband, Eddie was a good father.

My shoulders sagged. "All right." I hated the thought of Hayden spending any time with Krissie, but I guessed it was something I would have to get used to. She would be his step-mother after all. It was so hard to me the fathom. But then, if I didn't want Eddie to remarry, I shouldn't have divorced him. "Does Hayden even know about Krissie?"

"I've met him several times," she said in answer to the question I had asked of Eddie. "We went to the Indians game last weekend."

I ground my teeth. Eddie had introduced my son to this new woman and hadn't even told me about her.

"You're doing the right thing for Hayden, Kel," Krissie said.

The way that she said "Kel" put my teeth on edge. Yes, Justin and Eddie used my nickname, but they had known me all my life. I just met Krissie two minutes ago.

"It's Kelsey," I said. "And I am so glad that I have your approval."

Krissie frowned, and Eddie sighed. Maybe this is why he hadn't mentioned her to me yet. Eddie knew me well enough to know how I would react.

Krissie gave me a sympathetic smile. "We understand you're under a lot of stress right now."

She didn't know the half of it.

"I'm heartbroken for Cynthia too," she said.

"Do you know her?" I asked.

"Of course. I would never have made it through college without Cynthia. Her foundation gave me a scholarship. Cynthia treats all the scholarship recipients like they're her own children. Maybe it's because she doesn't have any children of her own." Tears gathered in Krissie eyes. "I hate to think of her grieving for her nephew, even if he was one of the most disagreeable people I had ever met."

At least Krissie and I agreed about something.

Eddie wrapped an arm around his fiancée. "I really have Cynthia to thank for meeting Krissie."

The young girl gave her husband-to-be a watery smile.

"How's that?" I asked. I really didn't want to know the answer. Maybe I just liked to torture myself.

Krissie beamed at Eddie. "I'm a physical therapist too, and I had a college internship at Eddie's office. That's how we met."

While we had been talking, Justin wandered away. He now stood with a young woman in a mid-nineteenth-century floral dress. The girl laughed at something Justin said. Eddie and I shared a look. It was amazing how his brother could sniff out the prettiest girl in every situation.

"Why don't I go rescue that poor girl from Justin's clutches, and he and I will find Hayden for you? You can check out the camps while you wait. It won't take long."

Eddie looked as if he wanted to protest, but Krissie said, "I would actually like to take a look at the camps while we're here."

"All right," he finally agreed, folding his hand around hers.

I walked up to Justin and smiled at the girl. "Justin, let's go."

He smiled at me. "I've just been having a wonderful conversation with Maggie here. Did you know that she's been to thirty-one reenactments?"

"Maggie, how old are you?" I asked.

She bit her lip. "Sixteen."

"Well, Justin is almost thirty. I think this conversation is over, don't you?"

Maggie's face turned bright red, and she hurried back to her camp. I started in the direction of my cottage. "Come on, Justin."

Justin caught up with me. "Cripes, Kel, I was just talking to the girl."

"Then it's not a big deal that I interrupted you."

He met my stride. "Am I in trouble?"

"Yes," I hissed as we passed a reenactor washing tin dishes in a wooden tub. "What is Eddie doing here?"

He rubbed the back of his head. "Aww, Kel, he called me right after you did, and I may have let it slip about Maxwell Cherry buying the farm." He grinned as if to see if I enjoyed his pun.

I glared back.

"When I got here, he and Krissie were already in the parking lot. I couldn't get into the Farm because of your dragon lady at the front. He was able to get us in." He held up his hands as if in surrender. "And before you ask, I didn't know that he was going to bring Krissie. She's new to me too. I just met her last week."

My brow wrinkled. Even though I didn't like it, I could guess why Eddie kept his girlfriend-now-fiancée secret from me; but why wouldn't he have told his brother, his best friend? When Eddie and I were married, there was rarely a day that went by when I didn't see my brother-in-law. Justin even lived with us for a couple of years while he took his time through law school.

We stepped into the sugar maple grove, and I stopped. We could still hear the rumbling of conversations and practice shots from the encampments, but we could no longer be seen by any of the reenactors. "Before we reach Hayden, let me tell you what's going on." I gave him a brief description of the morning's events. I ended with, "So now the chief thinks I killed Maxwell because he threatened to remove funding from the Farm when Cynthia gave him control over the foundation's money."

He kicked a stone from the middle of the path. "You are in big trouble."

"I don't see how that observation helps me in any way."

"From that one semester in law school when I took criminal law, I would say we need to build some reasonable doubt in the chief's mind about your guilt."

"I've been trying to do that. There's another excellent suspect." I told him about Chase.

Justin nodded. "He sounds promising. I like it that the detective seems to hate him. That helps. But you lose points since he's the police chief's nephew."

"I need you to have my back on this."

He gave me a sideways smile. "I always have your back, Kel. You know that, even where my brother is concerned."

97

I started walking again. My cottage was set far back in the sugar maple grove. Another plan I had for the Farm was to produce and sell maple syrup. That had been one of the main agriculture operations for the Barton family, and most of the trees in the grove were ones that Jebidiah Barton planted himself. There were so many opportunities to make the Farm self-sustaining, and I could feel all those plans slipping away with Maxwell's murder.

The cottage came into view. It was a little bit larger than the traditional cottage and built in a Cape Cod style with whitewashed siding and navy blue shutters. One of Jebidiah's descendants built the cottage around 1930 and used it strictly as a hunting cabin during the summer before the surrounding woods became a state park. At that time, the cottage had the bare essentials: a potbelly stove, dry kitchen, and feather mattresses on rope bed frames.

Before Hayden and I were able to move in, the Cherry Foundation covered the expenses to have the home brought up to the twenty-first century, which included running water, an interior bathroom, and Wi-Fi. I didn't take my passion for history as far as wanting to use an outhouse in the middle of winter.

The front door of the cottage banged against the siding. I winced when I thought about the dent the doorknob must have left in the siding. Hayden flew down the walk, Tiffin on his heels. The corgi's belly skimmed the grass beneath his feet.

Justin held out his arms and his nephew threw himself at him. Justin caught him as if the thirty-five-pound child weighed no more than a pillow. Hayden's uncle swung my son upside down. I bit my tongue to hold back the reminder to be careful. Tiffin barked encouragement.

Dad came through the front door. Again he was sporting his reenactor-light ensemble. He wore a colonel's jacket over jeans and had a cow horn tethered to his belt. A slouch hat, which resembled a modern-day cowboy hat, sat crookedly on his head.

"Are you coming to see the reenactors?" Hayden asked his uncle. "Mom didn't tell me that you were coming."

"She didn't tell me either," my dad said, arching a bushy eyebrow. I got my talent for eyebrow-raising from my father. It was well-suited for the stage.

"Your dad is here too," I said.

Hayden's face lit up. "Really? He never comes here."

"Kelsey," my father began, but before he could finish, Detective Brandon stepped out of my cottage followed by Officer Sonders. He held a syringe inside an evidence bag.

THIRTEEN

"What's going on?" I asked, looking from my father to the officers and back again.

Justin set Hayden back on the ground.

My father licked his lips. "After Officer Sonders finished interviewing me, the detective showed up with a warrant to search the cottage."

Justin stepped forward. "May I see this warrant? I would also like an inventory of everything that you took from Kelsey's home."

"Who are you?" the detective asked Justin.

"I'm Kelsey's legal counsel, Justin Cambridge."

Her eyes flickered when Justin said his last name, but she made no mention of it. She'd find out in her own time that he was my former brother-in-law. Actually, I wouldn't be surprised if she knew already.

"Can you please tell me what you took from the house?" Justin asked, sounding more grown up than I had ever heard him.

The detective removed a folded document from the inside pocket of her jacket. As she moved, her gun was clearly visible. Unlike the reenactors' weapons, hers was loaded and lethal.

Justin took the document from her hand and read it quickly. "The judge granted them permission to search your private residence, personal office in the visitor center, and the grounds for insulin, syringes, and beekeeping paraphernalia."

Officer Sonders held up the evidence bag. "We found the needle and insulin."

"That's—that's not the needle that killed Maxwell, is it?"

"No." Detective Brandon said as if this was a great disappointment. "But we would like to compare it and your father's insulin to the insulin in Maxwell's system."

I started to protest, but my father jumped in. "Kelbel," he said, using his pet name for me. "Just let them take it. If it doesn't match the needle and insulin that was used on Maxwell, we'll be able to put this all behind us."

But what if it matches?

Justin handed the document back to the detective. "You were certainly quick on getting a court order."

"When someone like Maxwell Cherry dies in our little town, it gets the attention of the county courts." She slipped the paper back into her inside jacket pocket. I noticed a scratch on the inside of the detective's wrist as she replaced the paper. She caught me looking at it. Her eyes narrowed. "Your cat did not welcome us into your home."

I take back every bad thing I ever said or thought about Frankie.

Hayden and Tiffin were running around the yard in circles. I wished I had the kind of energy and freedom from worry as my two boys did. "You searched my house in front of my son." I felt my body tense up.

"We were sensitive, knowing the boy was there. We didn't say anything in front of him that might be damaging to you."

I balled my hands into fists. Justin stepped lightly on the toe of my sneaker. It was a warning to keep my temper. I took a deep breath.

Overhead two squirrels chased each other through the trees. Tiffin sat on his back paws and barked at them. The squirrels knocked a maple leaf from its branch, and it landed at the detective's feet. She ignored it.

"We appreciate your cooperation during this investigation. If you really are innocent as you claim, you have nothing to worry about."

I wondered at how Chase and the detective could have ever been a couple. She seemed too rigid for him. Granted I hadn't known Chase for long, but in the short time I'd known him, I pegged him as someone who owned a whoopee cushion and knew how to use it.

"I don't have anything to hide," I said. "If you need that needle and some of my dad's insulin for tests, then take it," I continued, as if she needed my permission.

She nodded. "Very well. I hope you and you ex-brother-in-law will continue to cooperate." She waved at Officer Sonders, and the pair headed down the path.

So she already knew who Justin was. She already knew everything about me.

After the police officers disappeared into the trees, Justin whistled. "Jeez, Kel, what did you do to her?"

"Nothing. Absolutely nothing. She took one look at me and hated me."

He brushed his hair out of his eyes. "Let's hope she hates her ex, Chase Wyatt, more."

Hayden and Tiffin galloped over to me. "Can we go see Dad now?" Hayden asked. "I still can't believe he's here. He says the Farm is a waste of money."

I bit the inside of my lower lip. *Don't react, don't react.* "We'll go find him now. He's here with Krissie. Do you remember Krissie?"

"Oh, yeah, Dad said that she was going to be my new mommy, but I already told him that I had a great mommy and didn't want another one." He threw his arms around my legs and hugged me.

I shot Justin a look over Hayden's head.

He raised his hands in surrender. "Don't look at me like that. He's just my brother."

I sighed and knelt in front of Hayden. "I'm going to have to work extra-long today, so you'll get to stay with Pop-Pop and Dad, okay?"

"Will Krissie be there too?"

"Yes."

He sighed. "Okay, but I don't like her. She's always talking to me like I'm a baby. I'm not a baby. I'm a big guy, and I'm going to kindergarten next year. They don't let babies into kindergarten."

"No, they don't," I agreed. I kissed him on the top of his head.

My father grunted. I knew he didn't like the idea of spending the entire day with Eddie. Where I forgave Eddie—well, sort of forgave Eddie—for the affair, my father had never even tried.

"Justin, can you take Dad and Hayden to the camps and find your brother? I need to take a shower and clear my head."

"Sure," Justin said good-naturedly.

Tiffin seemed torn as the guys started down the pebbled path. Dad and Justin walked, but Hayden took the path at a skip. His blond hair bounced on the top of his head.

"Go on, Tiff," I said.

The dog gave me one last look, then raced down the path after his boy.

I picked up the leaf that had fallen at the detective's feet and twirled it in my fingertips. I carried it through the white picket fence that marked the edges of my front yard, and before entering the cottage, I tossed it on the ground.

In my tiny living room, I chewed on my thumbnail and ignored the taste of blood. If the chief believed that I or, worse yet, my father was behind Maxwell's murder, I had no choice but to prove him wrong. An arrest for me could cost me much more than my job and the Farm's survival. It could cost me Hayden. It would give his father cause to press for full custody. That wasn't something Eddie had shown interest in before. He and I both seemed happy with the arrangement that we came to together outside of the court. We always had been on the same page when it came to how to raise our son, but that was before Eddie got engaged. Krissie's appearance in our lives could change everything.

I knew that I had to talk to Eddie and find out everything that I could about Krissie. I sighed. I thought my biggest problem this weekend would be keeping the reenactors from fighting over hard tack. Murder and a new stepmother for my son had never been in the realm of possibilities.

I headed to the shower. I had mud from the brick pit encrusted on my polo shirt and under my fingernails. I would feel better when I was clean; at least that's what I told myself.

Frankie met me at the top of the stairs, appraising me with his one good eye.

I leaned down to pet him. "Thanks for scratching that mean police detective."

The tiger cat arched his back and hissed.

I retracted my hand. "Okay, cool. We'll go back to ignoring each other. That's fine with me."

He ran down the steps.

Twenty minutes later I was showered and dressed in clean clothes. With my trusty notebook in the back pocket of a fresh pair of jeans, I was ready to face the rest of the day. I glanced at my watch. 9:45. The Farm doors would open in fifteen minutes.

I was tightening the rubber band at the end of my long French braid when my radio crackled as I hooked it on my belt. "Kelsey, come in?"

I immediately recognized Ashland's timid request.

I removed the radio from my belt. "What is it, Ashland?"

"We need you at the battlefield."

I headed to the door, still talking into the radio. "Is something wrong?"

"You have to come and see for yourself."

Not another dead body, please. One of those was more than enough for me.

Outside the cottage, I ran down the path through the maple grove back to the main part of the Farm. As I broke through the maple trees, I heard shouts and cries coming from the battlefields. The encampments were empty. I saw a line of gray and blue backs facing me. Everyone was staring at the field. I elbowed my way through men standing shoulder to shoulder, just as they would have in battle. The method of attack was the greatest contributing factor to the high number of casualties during the Civil War. That old Napoleonic style of attack wasn't suited for the rifle used during the war, a rifle that was accurate at two hundred yards. As I pushed my way through, I muttered apologies.

Finally, I fought through the ranks and reached the split-rail fence that encircled the battlefield. In the middle of the field, Chief Duffy and three of his deputies stood in a semicircle around two men, one in blue and one in gray, wrestling in the middle of the field. I climbed over the fence. "What's going on here?" I asked anyone who would listen.

The chief shook his head. "There's a dispute over a musket."

"Why don't you try to stop them?" I demanded.

He pointed at one of his officers. "Parker tried."

The young officer held a tissue to his bloody nose.

The Confederate soldier laid a blow on the Union soldier, whose face I could not see. The soldier in the blue clothing reeled backward and landed flat on his back, holding his chin. It was Wesley, Portia's ex-boyfriend.

The Confederate bent over and ripped the musket out of Wesley's hands. "Don't touch what doesn't belong to you, Yank."

The Rebel soldiers in the infantry line cheered and whooped.

I stepped forward and helped Wesley to his feet.

He rubbed his chin. "Thank you." His complexion was bright red. He stomped away, and the audience started to break up.

"Chief, did you interview Wesley?" I asked.

"I did." Duffy chewed on a new stick. "He said that he didn't know about Maxwell's death."

Detective Brandon joined us. I wondered where she came from, as I hadn't noticed her before. She pursed her lips. "We have interviewed him, Ms. Cambridge. At this time, we have no reason to take him under arrest, but rest assured that we are keeping an eye on him and everyone"—she gave me a pointed look—"who may be involved in Maxwell's murder."

Out of the corner of my eye, I saw Hayden slip under the fence and run toward me. "Mom, the camps are so exciting! Can we have a reenactment next weekend too?" Hayden jumped in place.

I shivered at the very thought and scanned the crowd for Eddie or my father. I wished they had taken Hayden somewhere else during the fight. I didn't want my son seeing two grown men behaving like children.

The chief looked down at Hayden. "Who's this?"

I wrapped a protective arm around Hayden's shoulders. "This is my son, Hayden."

Chief Duffy scratched his impressive sideburn. "You enjoying the reenactment?"

Hayden nodded eagerly. "Yep. My mom planned the whole thing. She's really good at making plans."

I felt Detective Brandon watching me. Just because I could plan an event, it didn't mean I could plan and execute a murder, but I couldn't say that with Hayden standing there.

The chief tipped his hat at us. "Well, I hope you will be watching our battle. It's sure to be exciting."

There had already been too much excitement at the Farm for one day as far as I was concerned.

Eddie hopped over the fence and joined us. Thankfully, Dad and Krissie stayed on the other side. I didn't see Justin. I hoped he wasn't flirting with that sixteen-year-old girl again.

Eddie put a hand on Hayden's shoulders. "H, you can't run away from Krissie and me like that."

Hayden looked up at his father. "But I was going to see Mom."

"Who are you?" Detective Brandon asked.

Eddie's eye grew wide when he looked at the police detective. I suspected he noted her beauty. His reaction made me feel bad for Krissie and better for myself. Other women would always catch Eddie's eye. I hoped the twenty-two-year-old physical therapist knew what she was getting herself into.

"I'm Edward Cambridge. Hayden is my son."

The detective looked at me. "Did you invite the entire family to the occasion, Ms. Cambridge?"

I clenched my jaw. "Eddie's here to look after Hayden since I have to work."

The detective opened her mouth, but the chief interrupted her by clapping his hand on Detective Brandon's shoulder. "You had better head out, detective." He dropped his hand. "Or you will be late for that interview in town."

The detective scowled. Clearly, she didn't want me to hear that. What interview did she have in town? Who was it with? It had to be related to Maxwell's murder. That was the biggest case in the town, possibly the biggest case the county has ever seen.

The detective left, and the chief returned to his men. Apparently the murder of a prominent heir in the community wouldn't keep him away from his reenactment weekend.

FOURTEEN

THE FARM OPENED AT ten o'clock sharp, and visitors began pouring into the encampments. The battle wouldn't be until two in the afternoon, but the visitors would have plenty to look at in the camps until then. Many of the reenactors allowed the Farm guests inside their tents and answered their questions about life during the Civil War. Over the noise, I heard Abraham Lincoln begin the Gettysburg Address. Despite its repetition, I never tired of hearing it.

I climbed over the fence, and Eddie handed Hayden to me over the top rail before climbing over himself. I tickled Hayden before setting him on the grass next to his grandfather.

Eddie dusted off the back of his pants. "We had better head home. I have several appointments with clients today at my office. Are you ready to go, H?"

Hayden's eyes grew to the size of duck eggs. "I don't want to leave. I want to see the battle. I promised the general that I would stay."

Eddie pursed his lips together. "Buddy, your mom and I think it would better if you spent some time with Krissie and me since she'll be so busy with the reenactment."

Hayden turned to me with tears in his eyes. "Mom, you promised that I would get to see the camps and battle."

I squatted in front of my son. "I know I did, Hayden, but Dad and I both think it would be better if you spend the night at his house."

"Do we have to go now?" His blue eyes filled with tears.

I looked up at Eddie.

My ex-husband sighed. "I have to go. I have to work and can't stay here all day. I suppose you can stay until I get home from work."

My father grinned. "I'll stick with him. You'll enjoy seeing the encampments with your gramps, won't you, Hayden?"

The five-year-old grinned. "Yes! I'll stay with Pop-Pop."

Eddie didn't look like he was keen on the idea but didn't know how to get out of it without earning a tantrum from our son.

"I can stay too," Krissie said. "I can keep an eye on Hayden. We will have a great time, won't we, Hayden?"

Hayden stepped closer to Dad.

"Krissie, I would hate to leave you here all day," Eddie said.

"I don't mind," she said quickly. "It will give me a chance to get to know Kelsey better."

A muscle in my jaw twitched. "Now that that's settled, I need to get to work. Stay with Pop-Pop, okay, buddy?" I hugged my son before returning to the visitor center.

I was just walking toward the employee entrance when Laura called my name. I turned around and met her under a maple tree that overlooked the Union camp. Since the village was closed, she wore a Farm shirt instead of her period costume.

"Did I just see Eddie leaving the encampments?"

"Probably." I let the door close after us and ran a hand over my tired eyes.

"And did I see your father and son walk into the camps with a stunning young woman just now?"

"Yes," the word came out like a whimper.

"And she is?" Laura dug her fist into her hips.

"Eddie's fiancée."

Laura's mouth fell open. "What?"

"You seem more upset that Eddie is engaged than that I'm a murder suspect."

She waved away my comment. "The murder thing will go away. This stepmother-for-Hayden thing could go on for a while."

"A while?" I forced a laugh. "You don't think Eddie's second marriage will last forever?"

"Considering his track record, no."

I scowled because that track record was also a reflection of me.

She backpedaled. "Not that *your* next marriage won't last. Speaking of marriage, did you see the Union camp's medic?" She fanned herself. "He can take my temperature any time."

112

I glanced across the battlefield. "I've met him."

Just then Chase turned and caught me looking and smiled. Crud.

"That's the guy I found standing over Maxwell's dead body. I don't think he's a good candidate for whatever you are about to suggest."

Her eyes twinkled. "Who said that I was pointing him out for your sake? I might want to get to know him first."

"Fine." I shrugged. "Go ahead. He's just a murder suspect to me."

"Uh-huh." Her mouth quirked into a half smile.

I glanced at my watch. The visitors kept coming out of the center. I was surprised by the number. There seemed to be twice as many as had been there at this time yesterday. Tomorrow being Saturday, the crowd would be even larger. I couldn't let this incident of Maxwell's death dampen all that I had achieved with the reenactment.

"I don't think I stand a chance," Laura said. "Blondie over there won't take his eyes off of you. I think you have an admirer."

"Not likely. He wants to help me find out what happened to Maxwell."

"Even better. That would require a lot of alone time."

"Laura, I have work to do, and I'm a murder suspect. Can we leave the matchmaking for another day?"

"I'll just say one more thing. Then I'll drop it for now."

I sighed. "What?"

"The divorce has been final for three years. It's okay to let yourself date again. Have some fun. I'm not asking you to get married." Her face softened. "Not every guy is like Eddie."

I squeezed her hand. "I know you're only saying this because you love me, but I'm not going to throw myself at the first handsome man who smiles at me."

She sighed. "I wish you would." She smoothed her hair, which was pinned back for her interpreter outfit even though she was in modern clothing. It would allow her to make a quick change in case the village opened sooner than expected. "If you aren't interested, I may take a crack at him."

"Crack away," I said. "Just be on the lookout for a syringe."

"A syringe?"

"That's how Maxwell was killed." I went on to tell her about the brickyard and the bees.

"That's so cold, even for Maxwell." She placed a hand on her chest. "Do you think he felt the bee stings?"

I shook my head.

"That's something to be thankful for." She headed toward the Union camp.

I was about to enter the visitor center for a second time when Ashland, gasping for breath, came running at me. I grabbed both of her arms to steady her. I should have my studious assistant take some strength-training classes. One of these days, she was bound to snap an ankle on those spindly legs of hers.

"Thank you." She took a breath. "Everything seems to be going smoothly. I went out front and told the crowd waiting in line that the village end of the Farm was closed, but they could

114

purchase tickets for the reenactment at a reduced rate. They seemed to be satisfied with that."

I made a checkmark in my notebook next to *adjust ticket prices*. "Great. I have a research project for you."

"Oh?" She perked up. Ashland loved research. Someday I could see her with her PhD, poring over archives in the basement of some obscure library somewhere, searching restlessly for one fact. As much as I relied on her, I knew living history work was not her forte because it involved the living. Ashland did better with people long dead.

"I need you to research all the nonprofits in the county that the Cherry Foundation funds. The foundation might support others in different parts of the state or even country, but we'll start closer to home."

"But why?" she asked.

"The police think I killed Maxwell because once he got control of Cynthia's money, he planned to remove funding from Barton Farm."

She turned gray. "He can't do that."

"He could and he was going to. Barton Farm can't be the only nonprofit that Maxwell planned to leave hanging. Maybe someone from one of the other operations that the foundation sponsored killed him."

She started writing furiously in her little blue memo notebook, which was identical to my own. I hid a smile, flattered that Ashland wanted to mimic me. She was the perfect person for this research job.

Another idea struck me. "Oh, and cross-reference that list with the reenactor roster. Look for last names that match or anything that shows someone from one of the organizations the Cherry Foundation funded would be here on the grounds with the reenactment. It's a long shot, but it's the best I've got."

She made another note. "What if there is no possible way someone from one of those organizations was on the Farm?"

"That means it was either a reenactor"—I thought of Chase—"or a Farm staffer. But the motive will be much less clear."

She gasped. "No one on our staff would do such a thing."

"That's what I would like to believe."

"It must be a reenactor then," she said with more conviction than typical.

"That would be my preference." *As long as it wasn't Chase*, I mentally added. For some reason, I wanted the EMT to be innocent. I didn't dare search my feelings to guess why, and I wouldn't dare mention that to Laura. She would never let me hear the end of it.

FIFTEEN

Between Judy at the ticket counter and Ashland in the field, I didn't have anything to worry about where the reenactment and Farm staff were concerned. The reduced ticket rate appeared to appease visitors that the village was closed, and Ashland reassigned the village staff who'd elected to come into work throughout the Farm.

I considered joining Hayden, Dad, and Krissie in their tour through the encampments, but something nagged me. Wesley Mayes, the spurned ex-boyfriend of Maxwell's fiancée, was accused of stealing something from another reenactor two times in as many days.

I went in search of the Union reenactor.

The Union camp was on a half-acre of land and had only been on the Farm for two days, but as I walked through it, it seemed like the reenactors had been there for weeks, just like they would be in the middle of a siege. The high-ranking officers had tables and chairs set outside their tents with maps spread out that described the terrain. The privates sat on the ground on fallen logs they dragged to the camp from the maple grove, or on their folded jackets. They swatted at flies that buzzed through their camps as they chewed on raw coffee beans. Others sipped coffee from tin cups. The liquid was so black, it was a wonder it didn't burn holes in their stomachs.

I went up to one of privates. "Good morning."

He picked a piece of coffee ground out of his teeth. "How do you do, ma'am? How can I help you?"

"Fine. I'm looking for Wesley Mayes's tent."

"Ol' Wesley." He pointed behind him. "Over there yonder."

I glanced at the dirty white tent he pointed out. Many of the reenactors purposely dirtied the exterior of their tents in order to make it more realistic to the time. In 1863, a private could go a very long time between baths. The smell must have been suffocating. Some of the reenactors followed suit and didn't bathe during the reenactments. I hoped I didn't have any reenactors like that on the Farm property. I didn't want to scare any visitors away with the smell.

Thanking the private, I headed to Wesley's tent. A lady reenactor and two children, also in nineteenth-century dress, stood outside the tent beside Wesley's. The children were making cornhusk dolls. I smiled at them.

"Wesley?" I called. There was no answer, so I peeked inside. Wesley lay on the mat on the ground he used for his bed, and Krissie Pumpernickle sat cross-legged on the grassy floor beside him. They weren't touching, but it was clear the two were deep in a private moment.

I gasped and walked backward. When I reemerged from the tent, I found the woman and children from the neighboring tent staring at me.

Krissie popped out of the tent. "Kelsey, this is not what it looks like."

I folded my arms. "What does it look like?"

She smoothed back her bangs as Wesley walked out of the tent. She didn't answer.

"What are you doing in his tent?" I asked my voice was sharper than I'd intended.

"Oh!" Krissie blushed. "I was just saying hi to Wesley. We used to go to school together."

I narrowed my eyes. "Where's Hayden?"

Krissie's blush deepened. "He's with your dad. I wouldn't leave him alone." My face must have shown my disbelief because she said, "Really, I wouldn't. And I hope, Kelsey, that you aren't getting the wrong idea."

"Why would I get a wrong idea?"

"Eddie doesn't need—"

I held up my hand. "I have no desire to say anything to Eddie. Whatever relationship the two of you have is none of my business." I paused. "Unless it affects Hayden, then you had better believe I will make it my business."

Her red face began to fade. "Thank you, Kelsey. You don't know how much that means to me. We would never do anything that would hurt Hayden."

"I hope that's true." Before she could protest, I pointed to each of them. "You two went to school together."

Krissie nodded. "That's right. College. I haven't seen Wesley in years. He and Portia are a couple of years older than me and already graduated. It certainly was a shock to see him dressed up like a Civil War hero."

Great, she wasn't even out of college yet.

"I ran into her and invited her into my tent to talk," Wesley said. "That was all. We couldn't reminisce about school in front of the other visitors; I can't drop character in front of them. The tent was the only place we could speak freely."

I wasn't sure I was buying their story, but it would have to do for now. I had other pressing business to talk to Wesley about. "I'd like a moment with Wesley," I said.

"All right," Krissie murmured, but she didn't move.

"I want to talk to Wesley alone, Krissie."

"Oh! Right, I'm sorry." Her face flushed again. She gave Wesley a side hug. "It was nice to see you again, Wes. We'll have to pick a time to catch up a bit more."

He smiled. "We will. And thank you." He turned to me. "We can talk in my tent."

I ducked back into the tent. "You seem to entertain a lot of ladies in here."

He sat on a camp stool. "Not really. You and Krissie are the only ones who have been inside here. What do you need to talk to me about? Is something wrong?"

Was something wrong? What a ridiculous question when a dead body was discovered on the other side of Maple Grove Lane. I held back any sarcasm.

"The police said that they told you about Maxwell's death."

"I heard about it. I don't know what it has to do with me."

"He was about to marry your ex-girlfriend."

He shrugged. "So what. I'm over that."

"You didn't seem over it yesterday in the village."

He stiffened. "I had been blindsided. I knew nothing about the engagement then."

This was sounding a little too similar to my own situation for comfort. "What did you do after you saw Maxwell and Portia together?"

"I came back to my tent and got drunk. It made me feel better."

I frowned. "There isn't supposed to be any alcohol on Farm grounds. I could kick you off of the property for drinking."

He laughed as if I were joking. I wasn't but didn't see it worth the time to go over the Farm rules. Besides, if I kicked Wesley out of the reenactment I would never learn if he killed Maxwell or what his real connection to Krissie was.

"What happened after you got drunk?"

"I went to sleep. I sort of remember some of the guys helping me into my tent, but it's fuzzy. I was wasted. I didn't wake up until the bugler set off around five. I could have killed that guy. I had an awful hangover and a splitting headache. Have you ever heard a bugler go off when you had a headache?"

Actually, I had, that very morning.

He shook his head. "It was terrible."

"So you slept all night? You didn't get up at all?"

"You mean, 'You didn't get up in the middle of the night and kill Max'?"

"Well, yeah."

He scowled. "No. I think you can go now."

"In a minute." I folded my arms. "You've only been here two days, but there are already two instances of Confederate reenactors accusing you of stealing their possessions. Why's that?"

"Because they're Rebs."

I cocked an eyebrow. "Really? That's the best answer you have?"

He scowled. "For some reason, the last couple of days, I've found Confederate gear in my tent. Before I can find out who it belongs to and return it to the owner, the Rebel comes stomping into my tent because he *heard* I took a canteen, rifle, whatever it was." He blew on his bangs, which drooped into his eyes. "The Rebs always want to challenge me to a duel. We're in the middle of the Civil War here, not the American Revolution."

"You don't know how those items get into your tent?"

He glared at me. "I just told you that."

"You didn't take them by accident?"

"How would I take something from the Confederate camp by accident? I'm telling you, I'm not taking this stuff. Someone is putting it in my tent."

"Why would someone do that?"

"I don't know. To play a practical joke, to get back at me."

"Get back at you for what?"

He removed his forage hat and threw it on his mat. "If I knew, I'd put a stop to it."

"Could this be related to Maxwell's death?"

"I don't see how." He frowned as if genuinely frustrated. "I can't say that I'm not happy that Maxwell's dead, but I had nothing to do with his death. Do you believe me?" he asked.

"I don't know what to believe, but I will give you the benefit of the doubt. For now."

"I guess that's all I can hope for."

"It's more than you can hope for," I corrected.

SIXTEEN

AT TWO ON THE dot, cannon fire exploded with a boom that shook the trees in the valley. The Confederates gave the rebel yell as they made their charge across the battlefield. I watched from the fence rail along with more than seven hundred visitors. Even though I knew it was a reenactment, the cries of the men as they fell touched me. Grown men and women in board shorts and Capri pants watched the battle with rapt attention. Children covered their eyes and peeked out between their fingers. No one spoke. A shiver ran down my spine. This is what I had wanted when I presented the idea of the Civil War reenactment to Cynthia and the board of trustees. I wanted history to come alive. I wanted visitors to be able to put themselves in the shoes of the men and women living one hundred and fifty years ago. When people remembered the past, then and only then could they learn from its mistakes.

Then maybe something like the Civil War would never happen again. I believed a true student of history would hate war more than anyone else.

Amidst the smoke from the rifles and cannons and the scent of gunpowder on the wind, I picked out Chase Wyatt in his medic's uniform moving from man to man in his brigade, checking on the wounded and dead.

The Union general called the retreat after about thirty minutes of hard fighting, and the Union men began to pull back, carrying what men they could off of the field. They'd lost this battle, but they would win the one tomorrow. With a reenactment, you could plan the outcome; it was in real war that you couldn't.

The visitors broke into whoops and applause. Some booed. We were in the North after all, and most of my visitors were Yankee sympathizers to the extreme. Tomorrow, when the North won, there would be great cheers, which is why I asked for the North victory to be on Saturday, when I thought we would have the most visitors.

I pushed off from the fence.

The chief came up to me on the path and sighed. "I hate to see my boys fighting without me, but I suppose a murder investigation should come first."

"I suppose," I said.

"The crime scene techs are finished across the street. The brick pit will have to be closed for the remainder of the week, maybe beyond that too, but you can open the village."

I removed my radio from my belt. "Great. We still have a few hours left. I'll call in the staff."

He nodded. "You do that." He turned to go.

"Chief, have you found any more suspects?"

"Something I'm not lacking for in this case is suspects. My roster is full to bursting with suspects."

I wanted to ask him what he meant by that, but my radio crackled. "Hey Kelsey," Laura's voice came over the device. "The village is open. Want me to call in the staff?"

"I was just about to radio about that. Can you call Judy and have her do it? I'd like you to get over to the village."

The radio crackled again. "Will do. Ten-four."

I rolled my eyes. Laura loved saying *ten-four*. I thought the fact that I gave her a radio had gone to her head.

I waited until Laura radioed back that she was in position and then went into the visitor center and used the PA system to announce that the village was open. I decided to continue to sell discounted tickets for the rest of the day. Until more seasonal workers took their positions, the village would not be fully opened, which meant that some the buildings would remain closed until they arrived. We couldn't have visitors wandering around the historical artifacts unsupervised.

I took a deep breath. Everything would be all right. Other than the murder and a scuffle, the second day of the reenactment was going well.

Hayden ran up to me. "Mom! The battle was so cool! I want to be a soldier."

Tiffin ran behind him with his tongue hanging out of his mouth.

Like any mother, I shivered. That would be the last thing I would want my son to choose, but he had a lot of time to change his mind. Last week he wanted to be a minion from *Despicable Me*.

Krissie smiled at me. "I called Eddie and told him that the battle was over. He's on his way here to pick us up."

Hayden grabbed onto my jeans. "Mom, do I have to go? I want to stay here with you and Pop-Pop. What about the bonfire tonight? I want to roast marshmallows."

I winced. I had hoped that Hayden would have forgotten about the bonfire. My father's bushy eyebrows knit together as they waited for my answer.

"I want you to stay too, buddy, I do, but a man got really sick in the village this morning, so I think it would be better if you go with Dad tonight. You, Pop-Pop, and I will have our own bonfire next week after the reenactors are gone. Then we won't have to share our marshmallows."

Hayden cocked his head and considered this. He was protective of his marshmallows. "You promise?"

"Of course." I hugged him.

"Is he okay?" Hayden asked.

"Who?" I asked.

"The man who got sick. Is he okay? I hate being sick. I'm real sorry anyone else got sick."

My heart melted at my little guy's compassion. "Ummm... they took him to the hospital," I said, which was technically true since the morgue was inside of the hospital.

"I hope he gets better. It's no fun being sick. Remember when I had that cold? It was terrible. I'd hate for anyone to feel that bad."

Tears sprang into my eyes. I hugged my son, turning my face away from him so he would not see the tears. "You are a special little guy. Do you know that?"

"Well, duh, you tell me that like every day."

"Then it must be true," I said.

I walked with Dad, Hayden, and Krissie through the visitor center. Now that the battle was over, many of the visitors were leaving. They spoke excitedly about the encampments. "I hope we can come next year," I heard a girl tell her father. She had the same gleam in her eye about history that I'd had as a child. I had to keep Barton Farm open for children like her and for children who didn't know anything about American history. They needed to hear it.

Eddie's luxury SUV turned into the circular drive of the visitor center. He got out. "Did you have fun today?" he asked.

"It was great!" Hayden said. "I still don't know why I have to leave."

Krissie gave me a light squeeze. I didn't hug her in return but awkwardly patted her back. "I'm so happy that I got to meet you finally after all this time."

Yes, after all this time that I didn't even know about. I bit my tongue.

Eddie put Hayden's backpack into the back seat of the SUV. Hayden gave Tiffin a hug good-bye, and Eddie lifted our son into his booster seat.

"Eddie, you really missed a great day," Krissie said. "I think you, Hayden, and I should come back tomorrow to see more of the action."

I bit my tongue from asking if she wanted to come back to reunite with her old college buddy, Wesley Mayes.

Hayden wriggled in his seat while Eddie tried to buckle him in. "Can we? I want to come back! I won't even ask to watch a show tonight if we can come back."

Eddie turned and looked at me, raising both of his eyebrows.

"I would love it if you all came back." I smiled. "Saturday promises to be an even more exciting day than today. There'll be two battles: one in the morning and one in the afternoon."

Hayden clapped his hands. "Yes!"

Eddie looked at his fiancée. "If that's what you really want, honey."

"Definitely." She flashed her white smile to me. "We're all going to be part of the same family and this gives us all a chance to be together like a family."

"Umm, yeah," I managed.

My father snorted, and I elbowed him.

"Oomph," he mumbled.

Eddie stepped away from the car door. I leaned inside the car and smoothed Hayden's hair away from his brow and kissed the top of his head.

"Can I have my backpack?" he asked.

I reached across him and handed him the bag. He rooted around in it until he came up with his plush Spider-Man. "I had to make sure I had Spidey."

I patted Spider-Man on the top of his head. "I'm glad he's safe. Be good for Dad, okay?"

"Okay." He pulled more toys from his bag as I shut the door. They would all be on the floor of Eddie's SUV in a matter of minutes, and Hayden would complain that he couldn't reach them until Eddie pulled the car over to the side of the road to pick them up. He'd hand Hayden the fallen toys just to hear them all fall to the floor minutes after he started driving again. I swallowed the lump in my throat.

"I guess we'll see you tomorrow," Eddie said. He and Krissie climbed in the SUV and drove away. I waved at Hayden as they went, but he was too busy with his action figures to pay any attention to me.

Dad wrapped his arm around me. "I hate to see the squirt go, but this is for the best. You don't really want him to be exposed to the investigation, and if there is some crazed reenactor running around killing people, it's best to have the boy as far away from that as possible."

"You're right."

My father pulled on the end of his beard. "Is it just me or is that Krissie too nice? There's something artificial about her. As an actor, I'm a student of human nature, and I can tell when people are playing a part. She's not doing a very good job of it either. I certainly wouldn't cast her in anything."

"I thought it was just me because she…" I trailed off.

Dad's brow knit together. "Because she's going to marry Eddie?"

I shrugged. The answer was obvious and didn't need a response. "Maybe she was nervous. I mean, I would be pretty nervous about meeting my fiancé's ex-wife, especially if the marriage ended on as bad of terms as ours did."

"You're giving her too much benefit of the doubt."

"Can you give someone too much of that?"

"Sure you can." He paused. "You know, Kelsey, it wouldn't hurt you go out on a date now and again. I'm not saying you should get remarried, but go out and have some fun. You spend all your time worrying about Hayden, me, and this farm."

"I like worrying about Hayden, you, and Barton Farm."

"I know you do, but there is more to your life than being a mom and daughter, and working."

I wasn't so sure about that. First Laura and now my father? What was wrong with being single? I had Hayden. He was all I needed. I sighed because I knew both of them only said this because they loved me and wanted me to be happy. Maybe I had been happier before the divorce, before I knew about the cheating, but I didn't have the weight of Barton Farm on my shoulders then either. The responsibility contributed to my overall stress, but I refused to give it up until I was forced out. In the two years since I had become director, I had come to love the Farm and fell more in love with history than ever before.

"Just think about what I said." Dad tweaked my right ear like he had when I was little girl. "Now, that Hayden's gone, I'm going to head back to the cottage for a bit to practice my lines." He grinned. "Hamlet, can you hear me? Bahhhaha!"

I chuckled. Dad's ability to make me laugh was one thing that I could count on.

Tiffin sighed and followed me back into the visitor center. He was always blue when his boy was away. I glanced down at him. "I miss him too, Tiff."

Ashland ran up to me, dodging Abraham Lincoln as she went.

"Careful there, dear lady. Don't you know that we are at war?"

She ignored him. "Kelsey." She waved at me.

I walked over to her. "Ashland, slow down. What's wrong?"

She took a deep breath. "I did what you asked me to. I researched the nonprofits that the Cherry Foundation supports in the county: there are seven of them."

"Seven?" I had hoped that there weren't that many.

She nodded, still out of breath. "I emailed you the list."

I removed my cell phone from my pocket and saw that I did in fact have a new email from her. It came in the middle of the battle, which explained why I hadn't hear my phone ping when it arrived. "It's a start." I scrolled through the names. Barton Farm was one of the seven, so that took the list down the six. Maxwell wouldn't remove money from a children's hospital; that would make him look bad, and Maxwell had been all about appearances. So I knocked another off of the list. That left me with five. Five wasn't too bad. However, with the reenactment going on, I didn't know how I could be driving all over Summit County looking for these organizations and questioning people about Maxwell. Right away I knew a couple of them would have no interest in the reenactment.

"I found something else," she said.

"What?"

"You asked me to cross-reference it with the reenactors. I'm working on that. There are a lot of them, and I haven't found anything so far. I am about halfway through the all names on the Union and Confederate lists." She chewed on her lip.

"Ashland, spit it out," I ordered.

"I took a break from all the reenactors and cross-referenced the Farm employees with the organization list, and I found a connection."

"What?" I asked. "A connection other than the Farm itself?"

She nodded. "Number three on the list."

"New Hartford Beautification Committee?" I asked.

"Right." She paused. "Shepley is on the committee. In fact, he's the head of it."

SEVENTEEN

A BEAUTIFICATION PROJECT WAS just the sort of organization that Maxwell would find a waste of money. "I need to talk to Shepley."

"I thought you would say that. Should we tell the detective and chief?"

I shook my head. "I don't want to involve Shepley if it really looks like he had nothing to do with this. If I see any evidence that he knows anything, I'll tell the detective. Let's go."

She hesitated. "You want me to go with you?"

"Of course. Now, come on."

We walked across the grounds and despite my nervousness about having a second confrontation with Shepley in one day, I smiled when I saw a group of reenactor children teaching visiting kids how to play with a hoop and walk on stilts. The modern kids' parents snapped photograph after photograph. Good.

I hoped they shared those photos with friends and family, so that we would attract even more visitors to the Farm.

As we passed the brickyard, I could not help but look. The area was blocked off with crime scene tape, and there still was a tech there taking samples from the mud in the pit. If they already knew Maxwell's cause of death, I wondered what the hoped to find in the mud pit.

Ashland shielded her eyes from the brick pit. My assistant clearly didn't have the stomach for murder.

We walked through the rows of vegetables in Shepley's main garden. Next to it, near the edge of the forest, was his pride and joy: his medicinal garden. A six-foot-high iron fence encircled it. Shepley had started it two years ago with a grant from the state of Ohio. The purpose of the garden was to show the flowers and herbs pioneers used for medicine in nineteenth century. Many farmers like Jebidiah Barton had such gardens because until the area was settled and civilized, they did not have a local drugstore close by and sometimes there wasn't even a doctor. However, science had since learned that many of the plants can also kill a person if not taken in the right way, which is why the iron gate to the medicinal garden was locked when Shepley was not tending to it.

Inside the garden, Shepley yanked dandelions and other weeds from around wilted lily of the valley leaves. By this time of year, the tiny bell-shaped flowers had come and gone. He separated the dandelions from the other weeds. He always said they were good for salad; I took his word for it. Bent over his work, Shepley's back appeared even more humped in shape. I winced. It must have been painful for him, but I had never heard him complain—at least, I had never heard him complain about aches and pains. There were many other things about the Farm he complained about.

Shepley straightened up. "What do you want?"

"You really shouldn't greet your supervisor like that," Ashland murmured, but it was loud enough for Shepley to hear.

I glanced at her in surprise. Maybe this weekend would make her grow some backbone.

Shepley snorted and resumed weeding.

I stepped forward. "We need to talk to you about Maxwell."

"Why would I want to talk about that rat?" Shepley dropped a handful of leaves and stems into his bushel basket. It was half full. "The man is scum."

"Do you think that because he planned to remove funding from the New Hartford Beautification Committee?"

A dandelion dropped from his hand. "What do you know about that?" He scooped up the dandelion.

"I know that you have an initiative to bring more native plants back into the town." I paused. "And I know Cynthia signed on to support it with Cherry Foundation money. If Maxwell removed funding, the initiative wouldn't be able to go forward. Unless you have another source of funding I'm not aware of."

The gardener spat tobacco juice an inch from my shoe. "Sounds to me that you know all you need to know. Now leave me alone with my plants."

There was no tobacco use allowed on the grounds, but I chose to ignore it because I wanted information. "How did Maxwell feel about Cherry Foundation money going to your group?"

Still bent over, Shepley pulled the bushel basket farther down the garden row. He stopped in front of a huge lavender plant. "How do you think the little weasel thought about it?"

"He didn't like it," Ashland said.

The gardener snorted. "No, he didn't like it. In fact, he told me that he was going to stop it. He had no respect for plants. I can't deal with a man like that."

"When did he tell you this?" I asked.

He shoved the wad of tobacco into his left cheek with his tongue and looked like a black-toothed chipmunk. "The swine told me about it just yesterday."

I wrinkled my brow. That night Maxwell was dead. "I was with Cynthia and Maxwell the entire time they were on the grounds. I never saw you."

"You weren't with them the entire time. I was inside of the church when he, Ms. Cynthia, and some girl came inside. I was just trying to catch my breath and get out of the sun for a spell. The church is a nice place to do that. It's peaceful. Typically tourists respect it and don't speak too loudly inside.

"While Cynthia and the girl admired the church, Maxwell pulled me aside and told me his plans. I would have decked him right there if Ms. Cynthia hadn't been in the room. He must have known that too." He held a weed so tightly in his hand that it bent in half under the pressure of his grasp. "I had planned to talk to Cynthia sometime when Maxwell wasn't around and tell her what her nephew planned. Maybe that would change her mind and make her leave her money to someone better, not that I know who that might be. Whoever killed Maxwell did me a favor because now I won't have to do that. I'd buy him a beer if I knew who he was." He spat a string of tobacco over the basket. "Can you believe he called some of my herbs *weeds*? He's the weed as far as I'm concerned." He ended his speech by calling Maxwell a foul name I had never heard before. Working with Shepley had certainly expanded my vocabulary.

"Where were you last night?" I asked.

He narrowed his eyes so small that they were just dark lines on his face, Mr. Magoo style. "I don't have to answer your questions about my whereabouts after work hours."

"You'll have to answer Detective Brandon's questions."

"Send her over here and make her ask me, but I have nothing more to say to you."

"Okay, I will," I promised.

Ashland hurried after me when I stomped from the medicinal garden and out through the larger garden as well. "Are you really going to tell the detective about Shepley?"

I slowed my pace. "I might the next time I see her."

"Do you think he did it?"

My shoulders drooped. "No. It's too hard for me to believe Shepley would keep it a secret. He would be too proud of himself over it."

"That's what I think too."

"Was he the only Farm employee with a connection to one of the Cherry Foundation's nonprofits?" I asked.

"The only one I found so far. I'm still working on the list."

I gave her a sidelong glance. "If I didn't know better, I would say you were enjoying this."

"Oh, no," she said quickly. "I wouldn't enjoy someone dying."

I patted her arm. "Relax. I meant you're enjoying the research into the crime."

She relaxed. "I guess I am. It's very interesting to see everything the Cherry Foundation supports."

I agreed. "There's something else I need you to look into for me."

"Sure," she said eagerly. "What is it?"

"Jason," I said as we passed the barn.

"Barn Boy?" Her brow shot up.

I frowned. "Yes, and please don't call him that."

"I'm sorry." She hung her head.

"I think he's been living at the Farm. I'm worried about him. Can you pull his personnel file? I want to confirm his home address."

"Living at the Farm? Is he allowed to do that?"

I shook my head. "I think he's been squatting in the barn. The question is why. First, I want to make sure he's okay, then I will try to convince him to sleep somewhere else."

"Do you think something's wrong at his home?"

I shook my head. I didn't want to share my fears with Ashland, not until I knew all that facts about Jason's home life.

"Was he here last night?" she asked.

I nodded. "Yes, and he heard a scream in the middle of the night close to one in the morning."

Ashland froze. "He did?" She shivered. "How terrible."

"It must have been Maxwell." I chewed on my lip. "Just before he died."

"He must have been terrified. Did he go out and investigate the scream?"

I shook my head as we crossed the street and stepped onto the pebbled path on the other side. "No. He assumed that it was a couple of reenactors causing trouble, and he didn't have the nerve to face them."

"Well, it was probably smart that he didn't approach them. He could be dead now too." She made a note in her notebook.

It was my turn to shiver at the thought of what might have happened to Jason.

"I'll pull his personnel file," she said. "I'll do it right now."

"Great. I'm going to leave the Farm for a bit."

She stopped midstride. "Where are you going?"

"On an errand," I said. "I should be back in an hour."

EIGHTEEN

ALL DAY I HAD felt a need to go visit Cynthia, but fear that I would intrude on her grief made me wait. I knew that she would have her house staff with her, but who else was visiting her and giving her comfort during this time? As far as I knew, Maxwell was her only family. After Ashland ran back to the visitor center to hunt for Jason's personnel file, I went in search of Laura.

I found her eating cornbread with Chase Wyatt in the Union camp. I turned to go before she spotted me, but I was too slow.

"Kel, over here!" she called.

Reluctantly, I joined them.

With a smile, Chase held up a square cast-iron pan to me. "Cornbread?"

"No, thank you," I said curtly.

He shrugged and cut out another hunk for himself.

"Chase and I were having a nice visit, and I told him all about you," Laura said.

My face grew hot. "Laura, can I talk to you?" I nodded to Chase. "Enjoy your cornbread."

His smile broadened. "Oh, I will. I make the best cornbread in camp. I don't usually share it, but then again, I don't usually get nice company like Laura."

Laura stood from the camp stool and brushed cornbread crumbs from her skirt before following me away from Chase.

When we were out of earshot, I hissed, "What were you doing with him?"

"I wanted to check him out before I encouraged you to go out with him. As your best friend, that's my job."

I looked heavenward. "I appreciate your concern, but really it's not your job. It's not anyone's job."

She shrugged. "I made it mine." She paused. "He's a really nice guy, Kel. I think you should date him after this whole murder investigation is over."

Oh right, we still have the little issue of a murder that has to come before my love life.

I threw up my hands. "Laura, what makes you think that he wants to go out with me?"

"Oh, I know he does. I can tell. He was very interested in you and asked a lot of questions."

I started in the direction of the visitor center. "That just means he wants information—information he can feed his uncle the police chief, so he can get whatever supposed heat from the investigation off of himself and onto me."

She shook his head. "He seemed genuine."

I rolled my eyes. "Whatever he may feel about me is a moot point. I'm not interested. Besides, he could be married.

Sometimes reenactors remove their wedding rings, either because their character wasn't married or because he didn't have a wedding band."

She grinned. "So you noticed he's not wearing a wedding ring."

I scowled.

"For your information, he's not married. I asked. Don't worry, I asked all the pertinent questions. He lives in New Hartford. Has been engaged once but never married. Doesn't have any kids. He's been an EMT for the town for over ten years."

I groaned. "I'm over this conversation. Can we talk about something else?"

She shrugged. "Okay."

"Can you be in charge for a bit? I'm going to visit Cynthia."

Her face fell. "Do you want me to come with you?"

I shook my head. "No, I'll be all right. I don't know if she'll be up for to too many visitors. I don't even know if she will be up to seeing me."

"Where's Ashland? Shouldn't she be in charge while you're gone?"

"Technically," I smiled, "she is. But you know that any one of those reenactors could push her over. I need someone tougher to take care of things while I am away. I won't be gone long."

"Hurry back. You don't want to miss the bonfire."

"I'll be back long before the bonfire." Before I left her, I said, "Please, I don't want to hear anything more about Chase, okay?"

"Okay," she agreed.

My car was in the back corner of the parking lot beside the carriage house. It was an old sedan, a hand-me-down from my father. It was all I could afford on my salary at the Farm. Thankfully, the job came with a roof over my head or I would never make ends meet. Eddie paid child support for Hayden, but I had opted out of alimony. I was determined to make my own way. At the time I made that decision, Laura told me that I was crazy for turning down the money. Sometimes I agreed with her, but I would never tell her that.

Cynthia's home was the largest estate in the valley and sat within the park's limits. Since her property was there before the state park was established in the 1980s, she got to keep it. With the park surrounding her land on all four sides, she had the good fortune of not having to worry about any crazy neighbors bringing down her property values. Her only neighbors were the trees, birds, and animals of the forest.

A curved road was the only way in or out of the estate. Either side was lined with trees that bent toward each other over the road, making a broad leaf canopy. The only break in the canopy was the beginning of Cynthia's driveway.

Maxwell had also lived with his aunt on the sprawling property, which was big enough for him to have his own wing. That must have made his death that much more difficult for Cynthia. Despite the size of the property, she was accustomed to seeing her nephew every single day.

The mansion sat well back from the road. Oak trees lined either side of her driveway. I pulled around in front of the house, a Tudor replica that was four stories high. I had seen houses like this when Eddie and I spent our honeymoon in England. I pushed those memories of happier times with him aside. He was getting married now. It would be best if I filed those memories in a drawer and threw away the key.

I rang the doorbell and waited. Nothing happened. Perhaps Cynthia went to stay with friends. I knew that Maxwell was the only family she had. I was just reaching for the lion-head knocker when the door opened. I dropped my suspended hand.

Cynthia's butler, Miles, opened the door. I was willing to bet Cynthia was the only person in New Hartford with a butler. Miles wore a gray suit and a sour expression. He was dressed down when compared to Carson from *Downton Abbey* but for rural Ohio, he looked like he was ready for Wall Street.

"Good afternoon, Ms. Cambridge. How can I help you?" he drawled.

"I would like to see Cynthia, if she's feeling up to it."

Miles eyed me. "Ms. Cherry is indisposed at the moment. Since you're coming from Barton Farm, I presume that you know why. She is devastated by the murder of her beloved nephew. It's been a terrible shock for the entire house." He started to close the door.

I stuck my foot over the threshold to stop him. "Can you at least ask her if she is up to seeing visitors?"

Miles's scowl deepened. "Please wait here."

I yanked at the end of my braid while I waited. It was a nervous habit left over from my childhood. When I realized what I was doing, I dropped my hair. It reminded me of Portia, who had constantly played with her hair when I met her. Where was she today?

The door opened again. Miles stepped back into view. "Ms. Cherry would like to see you."

"Thank you," I said meekly.

I stepped into the home. The front door opened into an entryway that was twice the size of my living room. In fact, I knew that I could fit my entire cottage inside the front hall and have room to spare. The floor was some type of mosaic. Instead of staying in keeping with the Tudor exterior, the best way to describe Cynthia's home was *eccentric*. I knew each room represented a different region of the world, and the entry was an homage to the Middle East.

Miles led me to the solarium. Since the solarium faced west, the force of the late-afternoon rays spilled into the room. While the entry was Middle Eastern, the solarium was appropriately decorated like the tropics. Large potted palm trees and succulents dominated the space. The furniture was in keeping with the Caribbean colors of peach, cream, and turquoise.

Cynthia sat in a sunny spot on a chaise longue. Despite the heat, she had an afghan wrapped around her shoulders and a second one tucked around her legs. I could have been wrong, but I thought that she was shivering. Was being cold a symptom of congestive heart failure, or grief?

The wall of windows she faced overlooked the Cherry estate. A great blue heron swooped down and stole a koi from Cynthia's lake. "How dreadful. Miles, please ask the gardener to find a way to scare the herons away from the pond. I hate the idea of losing any more fish."

"Of course, ma'am." Miles bowed.

"And please have a tea tray brought up for Ms. Cambridge and me. Something sugary. I have no intention of eating healthy on this day."

He nodded and walked backward out of the room.

I had almost expected him to say "my lady" and was disappointed when he did not.

Cynthia untangled one of her arms from the afghan and held out her left hand to me. "Kelsey, it was good of you to come. It's been a most terrible day, and I'm happy to see a friendly face."

I squeezed her hand. "How are you?"

She patted a tissue to the side of her red nose. "I'm all right. But any time I think of poor Maxwell, I burst into tears. He was the only family I had, you see."

I sat on the edge of the ottoman at her feet and squeezed her hand. "I know that. It must be so hard."

"I've outlived all of them—my parents, my sisters and brother, my nieces, and now my nephew. It doesn't seem fair that I would have the burden of being the last person standing. No one wants to be the one left behind. Everyone wants to be the first to go, so that you can avoid the sting of separation."

I didn't know what I would do if I lost Hayden before I died. I shivered. I couldn't even entertain the thought.

"I keep expecting Maxwell to march into the solarium for our afternoon tea and complain about something or other. I know he could be difficult at times. But every day, he took the time to sit down with me, sip a cup of tea, and tell me about his vision for the Cherry Foundation. Some of his ideas I didn't agree with, but I was happy that he was so impassioned for the responsibility that he was willing to spend time with his elderly aunt to talk about it."

I chewed on the inside of my lip. Maxwell had been a greedy and selfish person, but his aunt still loved him, reminding me that everyone leaves someone behind to mourn him when he dies. If he doesn't, then the life—as well as the death—is a true tragedy.

Miles returned with the tea tray. There was a Royal Doulton teapot in the middle of the tray with two teacups and saucers. It also had silverware that was surely made with real silver. I wouldn't expect Cynthia to dine on anything less.

Cynthia thanked Miles, and he walked backward out of the room again. It was a wonder that he was able to do that without running into a palm tree. I would have taken them all out by that point.

"I'm so very sorry about Maxwell," I said as I poured her a cup of tea. My words sounded empty. I was sorry. I was sorry for Cynthia. I was even sorry for Maxwell. He may have been a ruthless business man, but no one deserved to die that way.

"I know that Maxwell wasn't well liked. He was a shrewd person. Very few people got to see his softer side. I did. Portia did." She covered her face with her hand. "Every time I think of the poor girl, it brings me to tears. She and Maxwell had their whole lives in front of them. I'm ashamed to say that I was already daydreaming about having children on the estate again." A tear fell onto her lap.

I focused on making my own tea in order to give her a moment to compose herself. I added cream and sugar to my cup. Considering the surroundings, I thought it was appropriate to take my tea the British way. "Have you seen Portia today?"

She nodded. "Of course I have. She was in the breakfast room this morning and then at luncheon. Although neither of us felt much like eating."

I nearly dropped my teacup. "She lives here."

"Why, yes." She shook her finger at me. "It's not what you think. I would not stand by any hanky-panky in my home."

I choked on my tea with the unwelcome mental image of Maxwell and hanky-panky.

"But the house has several wings. It seemed silly for Portia to keep throwing away her money to rent an apartment when they were engaged. She lives in the east wing, where I am, and Maxwell lived in the west."

"Is Portia here now?"

She nodded. "I imagine she's in her suite. She only came down for the meals because I asked her to."

I sipped my tea. I wanted to ask about the future of the foundation and, by extension, the future of Barton Farm, but I couldn't bring myself to do it. Cynthia relieved me of that worry.

She set her tea still untouched on the small glass table beside her. "I know my mind should not be whirling with practicalities now, but it cannot be helped. I have so many affairs to put in order. I have called my lawyers and they will be here in droves tomorrow."

"Because of the foundation?" I asked.

She nodded. "All of it was to go to Maxwell to be used as he saw fit. He understood my vision for how the foundation should operate. He would have done the right thing."

Maxwell may have understood her vision, but I doubted he planned to carry it out.

Cynthia picked up her teacup from the side table between us but did not sip from it. "Now I don't know who will take over

149

the foundation. I don't have any more family, not even a distant cousin."

"I'm sorry, Cynthia." I wrapped my hands around my teacup.

"Thank you," she murmured. "There are Maxwell's businesses to worry over too, though I suppose most of those will go to Jamie."

"Who's Jamie?" I set my own teacup on the table and selected a pink petite four from the tray.

"Jamie Houck is—was—Maxwell's partner at the investment firm. I'm surprised you haven't seen him. He's an avid reenactor. Maxwell said all he had spoken about for weeks was the reenactment at Barton Farm."

Maxwell's business partner was a reenactor. That meant he would have been on the grounds at one in the morning last night when Jason heard the screams. That meant he was a viable suspect. The more suspects there were, the better it was for me to put doubt in the chief's head about my own guilt.

"Is he on the Union or Confederate side?"

"The Confederate, I think. At least when I saw him on the battlefield yesterday his uniform was gray. I didn't bring it to anyone's attention because Maxwell and Jamie had a small disagreement earlier this week. I wanted us to have a nice visit without any disturbances."

Maxwell and Jamie had had a disagreement just that week! It was too good to be true. I was already trying Jamie for the murder in my head because, of course, Maxwell's business partner would know about Maxwell's allergy to bees. I frowned. But how would he have access to insulin? Unless he or someone else he was close to was diabetic. Had he purposely framed me because he knew my father was diabetic and I would be the number-one suspect?

"You seem to be lost in thought."

I shook my head. "I'm sorry."

"You must have so much on your mind about the reenactment and now Maxwell's death. Has it had a big impact on the Farm?"

"The chief closed the village for the morning, so we sold tickets at a lesser rate today. But he allowed us to have it reopened by midafternoon."

"I'm glad. Chief Duffy is a good man, and he will find out what happened to my nephew."

"So Jamie was unhappy with Maxwell. Was anyone else?"

She ran her fingers over the edge of the afghan. "I don't think so. His argument with Jamie wasn't anything the two boys wouldn't have patched up eventually. I'm sure it had to do with real estate. It was their latest venture."

I asked my next question carefully. "Did he tell you if he planned to change or remove the funding from any of the organizations that the Cherry Foundation supports?"

The afghan fell from her shoulders. "Take funding from? Maxwell would never do that."

If Cynthia didn't know about him removing funding from Barton Farm, I wasn't going to tell her and tarnish her memory of her nephew, however misguided that memory may be. Maybe Portia knew more about her fiancé's business dealings.

"How many organizations does the Cherry Foundation support?"

She was thoughtful. "Too many to count. I love to give away money. My father always said that you will never regret giving someone a gift. I believe that. All my contributions to nonprofits are gifts. My father made a fortune in the tire industry. It is my privilege to give it away."

"Did Maxwell feel the same way?" I asked. I knew that her heir did not. He constantly complained about the thousands of dollars she poured into the Farm with little, in his eyes, return on the investment.

"Oh, yes. Maxwell was a giver too."

I bit my tongue and fought the urge to correct her. Maxwell hadn't been a giver; far, far from it.

"It's hard to know what to do now. I relied on Maxwell for advice."

"You don't have to think about the Foundation now. Take care of yourself." I brushed crumbs from my lap.

"But so many depend on the organization. Decisions cannot wait until I have recovered." She pulled the afghan back over her shoulder. "I was considering donating to the New Hartford Beautification Committee's wildflower project. It was a plan to reintroduce native wildflowers to portions of the state park and town. It was in conjunction with the park rangers of course, but all the seeds and planting equipment had to be donated."

"This was the project that Shepley is involved with?" I tucked the afghan in behind her, so that it wouldn't slip off again.

"Thank you." She nodded. "And yes, Shepley is in charge of the project. It sounded like a wonderful program and Shepley has the expertise to support it."

"Have you changed your mind?"

She shook her head. "No, but it's difficult to make any plans for the future now. I have to rethink everything." She frowned. "I'm not well, you see."

I squeezed her free hand.

"I fear my time is close," she whispered.

"No, Cynthia, don't say that. You have years ahead of you."

She shook her head. "I need to get my affairs in order. To-morrow, my lawyers will help me do that. My father always said to keep your ducks in a row. I don't want to leave a mess behind for whoever might come after me."

My chest tightened at the thought of losing Cynthia. She was like the eccentric favorite aunt I never had. It was difficult to think of Barton Farm without her. I didn't even know if the Farm could survive without her.

She squeezed my hand. "You've been a treasure to me, Kelsey. I know Barton Farm is in good hands with you at the helm. And don't worry. I will make sure the Farm is taken care of. I won't let anything happen to it, even after I'm gone."

I held back tears. "Thank you." It just showed what kind of person Cynthia was that she thought of the Farm and of me in the midst of her grief. I had to find out who killed Maxwell not just to save myself and the Farm, but for Cynthia. This selfless woman deserved closure, and I was the one who would give it to her.

Cynthia's maid stepped into the room. "Ma'am, your bath is ready. A nice soak in the tub will do you a world of good."

Cynthia nodded, but her spirits were still down. "Thank you, Marguerite. That sounds lovely." She started to remove the

153

blankets wrapped around her body. I stood and tried to help her.

The maid hurried over and stepped between Cynthia and me. "I will help her."

I let my hands fall. Marguerite helped Cynthia to her feet. In her pink tracksuit, Cynthia looked even smaller and frailer. She said that she didn't have much time, and seeing her sway back and forth in Marguerite's arms, I had to agree—no matter how painful it was to admit.

The woman led Cynthia to the door and looked back at me. "I will ring Miles for you."

"No need," I said. "I'll show myself out."

She nodded and led Cynthia from the solarium. I walked down the hall, heading for the front door until I could no longer hear their voices, and then I went in search of Portia Bitner.

NINETEEN

CYNTHIA HAD SAID THAT Portia's room was in the east wing. How would I find the right door in a house so large? And I knew if Miles found me wandering the mansion, he would have me thrown out.

Footsteps clicked on the tile in the front hallway. Portia herself appeared, then pulled up short when she saw me. Her eyes were bloodshot, her nose red, and she didn't have any makeup on. In grief, she was somehow more beautiful. Maybe I misjudged her. As hard as it was for me to believe, maybe this beautiful young woman really had loved Maxwell.

"Wh-what are you doing here?" she asked.

I raised my eyebrows at her reaction. "I was checking in on Cynthia."

Her face cleared. "Yes, of course you would. That was kind of you."

"I'm so sorry about Maxwell."

She gasped and covered her mouth. "Thank you. That's very kind of you."

"Cynthia said that you live here."

She blushed. "Maxwell and I live in separate wings. When the lease was up on my apartment earlier this year, Maxwell thought it was prudent for me to move into the mansion before the wedding. There is plenty of space. I could go a whole day without seeing him. He was a very busy man." She covered her mouth with her hand. "But now I don't know how much longer I'll be staying here. Poor Maxwell. How can I think of myself at a time like this? Who could have done such a horrid act?"

"Wesley?" I asked

She dropped her hand. "He would never."

"He seemed pretty upset yesterday about Maxwell." I folded my arms.

"He wouldn't." She shook her head back and forth like a toddler. "Did you tell the police about that?"

"I had to."

"Wesley wouldn't hurt anyone."

"He was there as part of the reenactment."

"I—I have to go."

"Wait," I said. "Did you see Jamie Houck at the reenactment yesterday?"

She turned. "Jamie?" Her eyes grew wide. "Yes. He's the one you should be talking to the police about." She combed her long black ponytail with her fingers. "If anyone wanted to hurt Maxwell, it was him."

I could tell Portia liked the idea of Jamie being the killer instead of Wesley. "Why's that?" I asked.

"He and Maxwell had a terrible fight last week." She tugged on her hair. "I was at Maxwell's office waiting to go to lunch with him when Jamie stomped inside. He slammed Maxwell's door, and I heard them screaming at each other. It was awful."

"What where they screaming about?"

She dropped her ponytail. "It sounded like a real estate deal that went bad. Maxwell and Jamie were buying land for development."

"What kind of development?"

She shook her head. "I don't know. Maxwell always told me not to worry about it when I asked. He told me that he would make sure I wouldn't have to worry about anything ever again." Tears fell from her eyes. "What am I going to do now without him?"

Again, I wondered how this young woman attached herself to Maxwell Cherry and became so dependent on him. I tucked a flyaway hair behind my ear. "I know I didn't memorize the entire of roster of reenactors who are at Barton Farm this weekend, but I can't recall ever seeing the name Jamie Houck."

"Maxwell told me that he uses another name when he's reenacting because he doesn't want any of the reenactors to ask him for money."

"What's the name he uses?"

She shook her head. "I don't know."

Behind me, someone cleared his throat. I turned to find Miles glowering down at me. "Ms. Cambridge, did you lose your way when leaving the house?"

I smiled brightly. "Nope. I was sharing my condolences with Portia."

"Very good," he said. "But as this has been a difficult day for the entire household, I must ask you to leave."

"Sure thing." I looked back to say good-bye to Portia, but she was already gone.

———

As I drove back to the Farm, I drummed my fingers on my steering wheel. How was I going to find out which reenactor was Jamie Houck in disguise? At least I knew to start with the Confederates since Cynthia saw him the day before in a gray uniform. I wished that I had gotten the chance to speak to her again after talking to Portia. Cynthia might have known his nom de plume when reenacting. But I couldn't disturb her again. I would assign the task of discovery Jamie's identity to Ashland. She would enjoy it.

By the time I turned into the Farm's parking lot, there was a long line of cars leaving through the main exit. The Farm closed at five o'clock, and it was only a few minutes till. I parked my car beside the supply shed and sighed. At least I wouldn't have to worry about the visitors on the grounds again until ten o'clock the next morning. As long as the reenactors didn't start brawling again, I could concentrate all my efforts on trying to find out who killed Maxwell.

The first order of business was to find Ashland to see what she had learned about the other nonprofits and Jason, and to give her the new research assignment.

I entered the visitor center from the side entrance and found Judy at the ticket counter, counting the money from the cash drawer. When I approached, she held up a finger and kept counting. After she finished the stack of fives, she looked up. "We did very well today, Kelsey, even with selling the tickets at a discount. I've never seen ticket sales like this before. It's hard to believe that Saturday and Sunday promise to be even bigger days."

I smiled. "At least that's something that has gone right this weekend. Is Laura here?"

"She just radioed from the village. She is doing the rounds to make sure all the buildings are locked up tight."

"That's great. It gives me one less thing to do."

Judy sniffed. "I'm happy that Laura is pitching in like that, but it is my opinion that Ashland should be the one checking the buildings. She is the assistant director. She's been cooped up in your office all afternoon playing on the computer. It's no wonder the girl is as pale as a sheet."

"Don't worry about Ashland," I said. "She's doing some re-search for me."

Judy frowned but said nothing more.

I went to my office to find Ashland, but despite Judy's com-plaint that Ashland had spent the entire afternoon in my office, my assistant wasn't there. I picked up the radio that I had left on my desk before going to Cynthia's and radioed her.

"Kelsey, I'm glad you're back," her voice crackled through the radio.

"Meet me near the Union camp," I said.

I passed a few straggling visitors heading to the exit as I went out the sliding glass doors into the Farm. Ashland was al-ready waiting for me at the Union camp.

As the reenactment was officially over for the day, some of the reenactors had removed their flak jackets and cartridge boxes. They leaned their rifles against the trees and hung their coats from them. They sat on camp stools in their white undershirts and suspenders. Dirt marred their shirts and faces, but they were smiling. It had been a good day for history.

Ashland smiled. "This really is amazing, Kelsey. Having the reenactment on the Farm was a stroke of genius."

I tried not to beam at her praise and failed. "Thanks."

"How was your errand?"

"Informative," I said "I went to see Cynthia."

Ashland shivered. "Cynthia? Why?"

I frowned. "I wanted to tell her I was sorry about Maxwell." I told Ashland what I had learned.

Her brow wrinkled. "Jamie Houck. There is no one by that name on the reenactor roster. I memorized it."

Of course she did.

In front of us, reenactors removed their powder bags and rifles from their shoulders and dropped them in front of their tents.

I shielded my eyes and scanned the men for Chase. "He's reenacting under a fake name."

"How very strange," she murmured.

"I want you to find out which reenactor he is." I dropped my hand.

"I can do that. I'll take a copy of the reenactor roster home and work on it from there."

"Are you coming back for the bonfire? Everyone on the Farm's staff is invited. It should start around eight."

A strange look crossed over her face. "I don't think so. It's been a long day. I think I just want to go home."

I was about to ask her if she was all right when my father walked up to us in his costume for Hamlet's father's ghost, which consisted of tights, a black robe, and metal breastplate. The drawn on eye circles and smattering of fake cobwebs in his hair and across the front of the breastplate gave him the perfect "I'm dead" look. Dad held out his left arm and recited, "*Murder most foul, as in the best it is; But this most foul, strange, and unnatural.*"

"I have to go. I'll grab that roster." Ashland fled.

Dad put a hand to his chest. "Does she not appreciate Shakespeare?"

I gave him a look. "Considering this morning's discovery, you walking around spouting off about foul murders is a tad insensitive."

"Bah," my father said and adjusted a piece of cobweb on his breastplate. "It shows that Shakespeare is timeless and that foul murder is a universal problem still today, even in our happy little museum bubble."

I couldn't argue with him on that point. "I'm guessing tonight is dress rehearsal."

"Yes, and you still plan to be there tomorrow night for the opening performance?"

I smiled. "Don't worry, I'll be there. Laura is coming with me."

"Very good." He sighed. "I do wish you would relent and let Hayden to come along too. I want our boy to see my big performance."

"He's a little young for Shakespeare. Let's wait until he's at least through kindergarten."

"I suppose that's all right." He whipped his cloak over his shoulder. "I'm off to the theater!" With that, he strutted away, chest and chin out.

Walt Whitman walked by me carrying a dish of rice and beans. "Perhaps that reenactor is off by a few centuries?"

I didn't bother to respond.

TWENTY

As the sun began to dip in the west, the reenactors built a large bonfire in the middle of the two encampments. They skewered hot dogs and marshmallows with their ramrods and held them over the flame. A Southern private strummed a banjo. Brown jugs were passed back and forth. The reenactors told me there was no alcohol at the reenactment, but I suspected that some of those jugs held much more than water. And Wesley Mayes had gotten wasted last night on something a lot stronger than apple cider. After the day I had, I was tempted to ask for a swig.

The fire cast shadows on the planes and grooves in the reenactors' faces. I almost felt like I was stepping back in time to the Civil War. It was hard to believe the battles were only a hundred and fifty years ago. In the grand scheme of human history, that was like last week.

Abraham Lincoln stood silhouetted by the flames and was yet again repeating the Gettysburg Address.

In the firelight, it was hard to make out the soldiers' features and tell one from another. Their uniforms were similar and that made it difficult to find someone too. I stepped through the Union camp, looking for one particular soldier: Wesley Mayes, the person I thought had the most reason to want Maxwell dead. There was much that was left unsaid from the conversation we'd had that afternoon. I found him, but he was not alone. Chase Wyatt was with him.

Wesley sat on a log on the edge on the encampment. He held a pipe in his right hand. In his left was another brown jug. By his erratic movements, I knew it didn't hold root beer. No one liked root beer that much.

Chase scooted over on his log to make enough space for me to sit. It was either that or the ground. I couldn't stand over them like a dictator.

I perched on the log. The space was small and it was impossible to keep our legs from touching. I tried to ignore the fact that my left leg was pressed up against Chase's right one.

Chase held out a metal plate to me. "S'more?"

I took one. A string of marshmallow trailed from the plate. With as much dignity as I could, I pulled the cracker away.

Chase winked at me. "Wesley here was just telling me about Portia."

Wesley took another swig of from his jug. "Portia. I was never good enough for Portia."

Chase watched the fire about fifty yards away from us. "Wesley says he was the one who introduced Portia to Maxwell. Isn't that interesting?"

That was interesting.

Chase put his lips just inches from my ear. I would have moved away, but then I would have fallen off of the log. "The guy is smashed. If you have any questions for him, you'd better ask them fast before he passes out."

"How did you know Maxwell?" I asked Wesley.

"He was my boss." He almost dropped the jug but caught it at the last second. "I was a clerk in his office while I was in college. Portia was my girl." He whimpered.

"What exactly was Maxwell's business?" I asked.

Wesley wiped spittle from his cheek. "He's a venture capitalist. He invested money in stuff to make more money. Making more money is always priority number one."

"What did he invest in?"

"Mostly property."

"What kind of property? Where?"

"All over. His big project was the new mall that's supposed to happen on Kale Road."

I wrinkled my brow. "That's the one that's been under construction for almost four years."

He nodded. "Two of the big chain stores that said they would anchor the new mall pulled out because of the economy. Without the big anchors, the little boutique and smaller shops dropped out too. The anchors claimed the new mall was too close to the Chapel Hill and Summit malls since it's sort of in between the two."

165

"Did he lose money?" I swatted a mosquito that buzzed my ear.

Wesley laughed bitterly. "He lost hundreds of thousands, maybe a million. Maxwell was the top investor."

Chase whistled. "How did he keep his business from going under?"

"He laid off about half the office two years ago. I left on my own because I saw the writing on the wall and I'd just finished college. Thankfully, I was able to get a job at a bank. And he always has his aunt to fall back on. I guess he could just ask her for money. She has buckets of it."

"Do you know what Maxwell's financial situation is now?" I dug the toe of my sneaker into the grass.

"No, but I know that the ground where the new mall is supposed to go is still torn up and there's no building going on. I assume if he had the money or a buy-in by a new anchor store, construction would have started by now. It's midsummer. Starting construction too late in the year would be a mistake. Everything will screech to a halt when winter comes."

It sounded like it already had.

"Does the name Jamie Houck mean anything to you?"

Beside me, I felt Chase watching me.

"Houck was his business partner. They bought real estate together."

"Do you know what he looks like? Have you met him?"

Wesley shook his head. "I heard the name around Maxwell's office, but they always met somewhere else. I never saw him. He could be here for all I know."

Interesting he would say that since according to Cynthia, Jamie was somewhere in the reenactment.

"How exactly did Maxwell meet Portia?" I asked, steering the conversation away from Jamie Houck.

"I brought her to my last work Christmas party. It never even occurred to me that she would leave me for Maxwell. The guy was like thirty years older than her. It's just more proof to me that money was more important to her than love."

"Did Portia need money?"

"Everyone needs money." He took another gulp from the brown jug.

"Sure they do," Chase said. "But not everyone is willing to marry for it."

Wesley raised his jug. "It was definitely for the money. Portia may look like she has money, but she has nothing. Many times I paid her portion of our rent or for all the groceries. I'll never see any of that money now," he said bitterly.

"When did you leave Maxwell's office?"

"About a year and half ago."

"And when did Portia dump you?" Chase asked.

"Six months ago. She claimed it was because she wanted to pursue her career and couldn't have any distractions, but now I know that was a lie. She was probably already with Maxwell when she dumped me." He lifted the jug to his lips. "I'm so stupid. I will never trust a woman again."

"Not all women are like Portia," Chase said. "There are a lot of kind and honest women out there."

"Let me know when you find one, because I don't know any."

Chase bumped my shoulder. "I have one sitting right next to me."

I shifted to the edge of log. How could he even say that about me? He didn't know me. He didn't know anything about me. How did he know I was kind and honest after two days?

"After you quit the investment firm, did you ever see Maxwell again?" I asked.

He shook his head. "No. Not until I saw him yesterday with Portia on his arm. Why did she come here if she wanted to keep it a secret? She knew I was a reenactor. I've been doing this since I was a kid. She came here to hurt me." He took another swig from the jug.

She did know, I thought. That was why she didn't want to tour the encampments when she first arrived on Farm grounds. I tried to recall if Maxwell acted like he recognized Wesley. I couldn't remember, but at the time I was more worried about whether or not Wesley was about to deck Maxwell than with observing Maxwell's facial expression.

Chase leaned on his knee and put his cheek in his hand. "Is there any hope for you and Portia now that Maxwell's out of the picture?"

"No." A tear fell from his cheek into the dirt. "She doesn't love me anymore."

"Are you sure?" Chase asked. "Maybe she didn't want to marry Maxwell. You said it was for the money. How do you know she doesn't love you?"

Wesley raised his jug. "She'll find another sugar daddy," he said bitterly.

"What did you do after Portia left the Farm yesterday?" Chase asked.

He laughed. "I got hammered. It was the only thing I could do. This morning, I woke up with the mother of all hangovers."

At least that matched the story he gave me earlier that afternoon.

"Have you ever had a hangover at a Civil War camp?" Wesley asked Chase.

"Nope."

"I don't advise it."

"Maybe you should lay off the hard cider or you'll be in the same place tomorrow."

"Ehh," Wesley said and took another pull from the bottle.

My hand fell from my lap and knocked into Chase's. For half a second he hooked his fingers around mine. I jerked my hand away and jumped out of my seat.

Chase's face was neutral like nothing had happened, and he stood up. "I think you should hit the sack right now. If you wait much longer, you won't be able to lift your rifle tomorrow. We've got two battles, remember?"

Wesley shrugged as if what happened tomorrow didn't matter to him.

"Let's go, big guy." Chase lifted Wesley up on his feet and slung Wesley's arm over his shoulder like he weighed no more than Hayden. Then I remembered that Chase was an EMT. He was an expert at picking up people. I nudged my foot against a tree root as an idea crept into the back of my brain. If he was an expert at moving people and strong enough to carry Wesley, who was much taller and heavier than Maxwell, he would have had no trouble dropping Maxwell into the brick pit with the bees.

The problem was I didn't want Chase to be the killer. I was beginning to like him. Still, I knew I shouldn't trust myself where men were concerned. I had loved Eddie and look how that had turned out.

I left off toying with the tree root, stood, and dusted off the back of my jeans, then swatted at two more mosquitoes that dive-bombed my face.

"Kelsey, if you would carry his lantern, we can make it back to his tent," Chase said.

I picked up the gas-lit lantern and led the way back into the encampment. The sun had set while we talked. Above the trees, a blue and purple cloud bruised the western sky. There was still a large crowd of men, women, and children around the bonfire, cooking hotdogs and toasting more marshmallows. The acrid smell of campfire hung in the air, reminding me of summer camp as a child.

In the encampments, all of the white tents on the Confederate and Union side looked identical, and although I had been to Wesley's tent during the day, I lost my way after twilight.

"How do we know which tent is his?" I asked.

"I know," Chase said. He made a sharp turn down a row of white tents and paused at the one at the end. It was the closest tent to the village part of the farm. In the middle of the night, Wesley had a clear path to the village. He could slip away and no one would have been the wiser.

He could slip away and commit murder.

Chase helped Wesley to the mat in the middle of the tent. Pieces of white cotton sheet made up the bed. It didn't look particularly comfortable, but it must have been better than sleeping on the bare ground.

Wesley snored as Chase swung his feet on the bed. He removed the other soldier's boots and set them neatly at the end of the bed. Again I was struck with how dedicated to detail the reenactors were. The inside of the tent was spare. It held the mat and a small folding table, and two more rifles. I wondered how many of those rifles he had brought to the reenactment.

Chase waved me out of the tent, carrying Wesley's cider jug. As most of the reenactors were still at the bonfire, it was quiet around the tents. A faint hoot from an owl came from somewhere in the trees. I couldn't make out exactly where the bird was.

Chase dumped the remainder of the jug in the grass. "That was an informative conversation."

The smell of alcohol burned the inside of my nose. I held up the lantern, so I could better see his face. In the firelight, I noticed that his eyes weren't just chocolate brown, as I had believed. Golden flecks peppered his irises.

I lowered the lantern. "I hope you didn't get poor Wesley drunk just to get that information. He's going to be miserable tomorrow. He was miserable today."

"He probably will be, but I'm sure someone has some aspirin hidden somewhere in his camp that they can give Wesley to take the edge off. And I didn't get him drunk." He smiled. "He was already halfway there when I found him and more than willing to talk about Portia. For him it was like a therapy session. I didn't even charge him. It was a deal all around."

I wasn't so sure. Would Wesley regret what he told us about Maxwell and Portia tomorrow? Then again, would he even remember?

"I visited Cynthia today," I said and then mentally kicked myself for telling Chase that.

"How is she?"

"Distraught," I said, realizing that it was the perfect word to describe my friend's grief.

"I'm sorry. You're close to her?"

I nodded. "She's the Farm's benefactress, but she's also like an aunt to me. She's done so much for Hayden and me to make our lives on the Farm better. She went way above the call to make sure we were happy here. I love how much she cares for the Farm and takes my opinions and suggestions into account. I hate for her to be going through this."

Chase set Wesley's jug beside the entrance to the tent. "I knew I was right back there."

"What do you mean?" I folded my arms.

"When I said that you were a kind person, you are. You're concerned about Cynthia when obviously Barton Farm has a better chance of survival now that Maxwell is dead."

"Don't let your uncle hear you say that. He's already convinced I killed Maxwell. I'm surprised they haven't arrested me yet."

"That's because Candy is set on proving I'm the killer." He sighed. "She would love to arrest me. She fantasizes about it, I'm sure."

"What is the deal with the two of you?"

He didn't say anything for a couple of beats. "She's my ex-girlfriend."

"I guessed that much, but why does she hate you so much?"

He shrugged. "I broke it off."

"Why did you do that?" I heard myself ask even though it was a deeply personal question, one I had no right to ask an acquaintance, which Chase certainly was and would most likely always remain.

"We grew apart and wanted different things. We were about to get engaged and had the talk about kids. She doesn't want any; I love kids. I knew if I married her I would be okay with that for a few years, but I would eventually resent her if I didn't have children. I didn't want it to come to that, so I ended it."

"I didn't expect such an honest answer."

He grinned. "I'm a pretty honest guy. You'd know that if you'd let me help you find out what happened to Maxwell."

"I don't know."

"I hope that I proved here that I can be helpful."

"I don't know that Wesley would have been that forthcoming with me," I admitted. "I saw him earlier today when he was sober, and he barely said a word about Portia."

"So you admit that I was helpful."

"I guess so." I shrugged.

"Are we a team?"

I chewed on lip. Maybe Chase was right, maybe I did need his help getting down to the bottom of Maxwell's death. He could get closer to the reenactors than I could, but could I trust him? This wasn't a game. My freedom and possibly the custody of Hayden were at stake.

He held out his hand. "Let's shake on it."

I stared at his hand for a long moment.

"Come on. It won't hurt."

I shook his hand, and he held mine much longer than anyone making a pact would have.

"Are you going to tell me why you're asking about Jamie Houck?" Chase asked.

I frowned.

TWENTY-ONE

THE MORNING AFTER THE conversation with Wesley, I wanted to see the property that Maxwell planned to save with Cynthia's fortune, and I wanted to do it without Chase. I'd agreed to work with him to solve Maxwell's murder, but I didn't have to tell him everything. Since I was keeping secrets, I could only assume he was too.

Vacant lots, empty homes, and struggling cash advance businesses dotted Kale Road. Several fast food restaurants languished on the street, but there was little else.

I rolled to a stop next to the largest vacant lot. An eight-foot-high chain-link fence surrounded the three acres. When I was a child, there had been two rundown apartment complexes there. They were eventually condemned because of asbestos in the buildings. They stood on the property until four years ago, when they were knocked down and the land was cleared.

I turned and drove down the side street. There was the gate entrance. The gate stood wide open. The lock was cut and dangled from the chain link. Maybe someone planned to rob the construction site. It seemed to me the only thing you could make off easily with was a rock or a pocketful of dirt. I drove through the open gate. The grounds looked like the surface of the moon. Ten- and twelve-foot-high piles of dirt and rubble were scattered haphazardly around a bulldozer, which appeared not to have moved in months.

It was hard to believe a mall would be successful in such a place and on such a forgotten street. It would have to take a strong will and a lot of money to make it happen. I had to respect Maxwell for wanting to bring construction here to revitalize a struggling part of the town. What a gamble it must have been.

As I sat surveying the bleak scenery, a black sedan with tinted windows pulled up alongside my car. The driver's-side window powered down. The man behind the wheel wore an Oxford shirt and sunglasses tinted the same dark shade as his windows. "Can I help you?"

The no trespassing sign was clearly visible on the fence. Crud. I shouldn't have even turned into here.

"Sorry," I said. "I was just turning around."

"Nobody is supposed to be in here."

"I know, I'm sorry."

"You shouldn't be here. This is a construction site."

"The gate was open, and I needed to go back the way I came. I thought this was a quick and easy place to turn around. Again, I'm sorry. I'll be on my way."

A look of annoyance passed over his face. "One of our demo guys must have left it open. I will have to report it."

"Is this your property?"

He removed his sunglasses for a better look at me. "I'm the foreman."

"Is construction starting again on the property?" I said, trying to act casual. "I live nearby and would love a mall so close to home."

His face relaxed. "Do me a favor and tell your councilman that. Maybe then I can get my permits."

"Did the town council shut down the work site?" I smiled. "I'm sorry, that was an intrusive question."

"That was part of it. There were bigger reasons the job site shut down." He gritted his teeth. "Much bigger. We thought that all that was behind us. Construction was about to start on Monday. Now, I don't know. Things have changed."

"That's too bad. Do you mean Maxwell Cherry's death?"

"What?" he snapped. "Who are you exactly?"

"Oh, I'm Kelsey," I said, hoping that I wouldn't regret giving him my real name. "What did you say your name was?"

"I didn't, and it shouldn't matter to you if you were really here to turn your car around. How do you know Maxwell?"

"I don't know him well. His aunt is a friend. I visited her after I heard the news."

He nodded. "Cynthia is a good lady, much better than the rest of us." He said this like it was significant. Did he not consider himself a good person? "I think our conversation is over, and I will ask you leave. Now."

I started my car. "Sure." I waved as if we were old friends. "It was nice to see you."

I could feel the man's eyes through my rear window as I pulled out onto the side street.

As a drove out of the fence, I passed a police car. Detective Candy Brandon was in the driver seat, and she saw me.

My heart rate picked up. I hadn't technically done anything wrong. Okay, I trespassed on the construction site, but I was there with the foreman.

But Detective Brandon wouldn't see it that way. By now, she must know the construction site's connection to Maxwell Cherry, and seeing me having a conversation with his foreman just made me a whole lot more suspicious in her eyes.

As if to prove my point, I saw flashing lights in my rearview mirror. I wasn't speeding. I didn't have a taillight out. I was a murder suspect.

Detective Brandon rolled her cruiser to a stop behind me and got out of the car. She took her time walking up to my window. She wanted to make me nervous.

I powered the window down and waited.

She leaned on the roof of my car.

"Something wrong, detective?" I asked.

"I have to say I was surprised to see you at Maxwell Cherry's construction site this morning."

Her face was so close to me, I could see the freckles on her nose. I bet she hated those freckles. They made her cute. Detective Brandon wasn't someone to relish being considered cute. She would consider it a liability.

"Errands," I said, gesturing to the groceries in the back seat of my car. "I wanted to get my shopping done before the Farm opened this morning. We have two battles today, and tomorrow is the Blue and Gray Ball." I smiled. "I know the chief will be there since he's a reenactor, but will you be attending the ball? Consider yourself invited. Just keep in mind, nineteenth-century ball attire is required."

She frowned. "I can't say I have ball attire that would work for any century."

I opened my mouth again, but she interrupted me. "Who were you talking to at the job site?"

I ran my hand over the steering wheel. "The job's foreman. He just happened to drive up when I was turning around."

"Am I supposed to believe that?"

"Yes," I said. "Because it is true."

She pursed her lips. "I will check your story out with the foreman."

"I'm sure you will."

"I hope you're not playing detective."

"Whatever would give you that idea?" I asked.

She pushed off the car and folded her arms. "Take my advice: leave the investigating up to the police."

"You got it," I lied.

She frowned. "I have another piece of advice for you too. Stay away from Chase Wyatt. He's trouble."

I dropped my hands to my lap. "Why would you talk to me about Chase?"

"I've seen you two speaking at the Farm. The guy is slick and he'll be able to make you believe what he wants." She squinted as a cloud moved out of the way of the sun.

"Is that what he did to you? Did he make you believe something?" I asked before I could stop myself. As soon as the question was out of my mouth I regretted it. *Way to go, Kel. You just made her hate you more.*

She glared at me so hard that all of the cuteness I saw earlier in her face disappeared. "I know him. I'm sure he promised you all kinds of things. Don't believe him or you will be sorry."

Sorry because of Chase or sorry because of you? I wasn't brave enough to ask.

She turned to go. "You leave the Farm again, you tell me."

I snorted as she walked back to her car. Like I was going to tell her every time I left the Farm. Not happening.

In her car, Detective Brandon gunned her engine and sped in front of me. Her cruiser disappeared around a corner.

I didn't head straight back to the Farm. There was another address that I wanted to check on first. As I drove, I kept an eye on my rearview mirror. I half expected to find Detective Brandon had doubled back around to follow me. She either wasn't following me or she was so good at it that I didn't see her.

I pulled into one of the fast food parking lots and idled. I picked up the personnel file that Ashland had pulled for me the day before. The tab read JASON SMITH. I opened the file and skimmed his application. It was sparse. I hired him when I saw him work with the animals at the county fair. I had a gut instinct that he was the right one for the job. I had little else to go on other than a two-year vocational degree in animal husbandry.

He was also the only one who was willing to take the dismal pay I was able to offer. I typed his home address into my GPS on the dashboard.

"Address not found," the automatic voice said.

I frowned and typed in the address again.

"Address not found."

The address on Jason's application didn't exist, at least as far as some satellite orbiting the Earth was concerned. Maybe it was new construction or something and just not in the GPS yet. But I knew that wasn't true because Jason's application was two years old.

The application said that Jason lived on Route 15. I knew where that was, so at least I could get close enough to where his home should be to confirm my suspicions. I told the GPS to find a store near Route 15. It came up with a drugstore. It was a start.

I ran my hands back and forth over the steering wheel. I shouldn't be away from the Farm in the middle of the reenactment. Too much could go wrong when I wasn't there. But then again, if I didn't find out who killed Maxwell, the Farm was doomed anyway.

I turned onto Route 15. The drugstore came and went. Beyond it there were three car dealerships. The businesses fell away. There were no houses, duplexes, or apartment buildings on the street. Unless Jason lived on the top floor of one of the car dealerships, I could not see how he lived there at all. That didn't add up anyway because the dealerships had a different number of digits than the house number he'd written down.

Time to face facts. Jason didn't live on Route 15. Jason lived in the barn on Barton Farm. The question was, what was I going to do about it? Since his application was two years old, it proved that he had been lying about his living situation for at least that long and maybe living at the Farm just as long.

Hayden and I lived on the Farm grounds too. How had Jason been able to avoid me after hours for all these years? I knew the barn was in the village on the other side of the road, but still, Hayden and I would often go for walks in the village after hours.

My shoulders drooped. How long had this young man needed a place to live and hide?

TWENTY-TWO

I GOT BACK TO the Farm just as the first cannon fire broke out for the morning battle. *Boom*! The blast reverberated through the valley.

"Kelsey," Benji waved at me when I stepped onto the grounds.

"How's it going?" I asked.

She frowned. "Not good. I don't know what I'm supposed to do. My brickyard is still closed, and the cop the chief put over there told me that it will remain closed for the rest of the weekend. I can't even get my supplies and move my brickmaking talk somewhere else. Who wants to hear about brickmaking without a demo? This is such a pain."

"Well, the circumstances were unexpected," I trailed off.

She knocked one of her many braids over her shoulder. "They got the dead guy out. What more do they need? The bees did it. I'm real sorry about that, but I have a job to do."

Ten yards from us, a whoop went up from the battlefield as the Rebels made a run at the Union soldiers. The Union line hid behind the hay bales made to look like trenches—I wouldn't allow the reenactors to dig up my pasture land for real trenches.

She threw up her arms. "What am I supposed to do?"

"I'll let it be your choice. You can either work in the visitor center directing people and handing out Farm maps, or you can join one of the other crafters."

"I guess I can go to candle making. But that is so boring." She pretended to hold a dip stick in her hand. "Dip. Drip. Dip. Drip. Yawn."

I smiled. "You'll survive. It won't be forever," I reassured her.

"I'll head there now."

I held up my hand. "Wait a second. I wanted to talk to you anyway. Before you left work on Thursday, what was the state of the brickyard?"

"Do you think I left it a mess or something? Because I've worked here seven summers, and I always take care of my station." She folded her arm across her chest.

"Relax." I rolled my eyes. "I'm not accusing you of that. I'm just curious to hear what everything looked like before I found Maxwell's dead body in the pit the next morning."

"Oh, well, it was normal I guess. I put all the supplies in the cupboard underneath the station like I always do.

I nodded.

"And I checked the mud for any bees or signs of bees. I didn't find any and covered the pit with the tarp." She took a breath. "I guess it's weird that he died from a bee sting when I'm sure there weren't any bees there." She shrugged. "I mean, did a whole colony wait until I left to move in? I wouldn't think worker bees were that smart."

I wrinkled my brow. That was an interesting problem. "You were stung the morning before."

"I was, but Shepley stopped over and got all the bees out."

"Shepley?" I asked. My problem gardener seemed to be coming up in a lot in conversations about Maxwell's death. "How did he remove them?"

"He used a smoker. I didn't watch too closely. I was about twenty yards away, waiting outside the Barton House. I didn't want to be stung again."

"And you didn't see any bees later in the day?

"A few came back, so Shepley came over and smoked for them again. After I got stung early that morning, I was really paranoid about them and would check the mud every chance I got. I didn't see any more after that."

Shepley. I needed to talk to Shepley.

Everything about Maxwell's death was more complicated than I could have ever imagined. Killed by bees, yes, but only after being injected with insulin and dumped into a pit that should have been bee-free. Killed in the middle of the night with hundreds of people nearby and yet not seen. His murder was either committed by someone completely disorganized or completely brilliant.

More yells rang out as the Rebels made their retreat. They had won Friday's battle, but Saturday belonged to the North.

The medics and a select number of privates on both sides went into the field to collect their fake dead. Automatically my eyes searched for Chase. Two days ago, I wouldn't have been able to pick him out from far away. Today, I recognized him immediately by the blond hair peeking out from under his kepi and from his self-assured movements when checking on the fallen members of his regiment. While others checked the bodies strewn on the ground with timidity, he did so with confidence. Checking on someone's health was something that he did every day.

Chase knelt by one of the bodies that was in the very middle of the field. He shook the body's shoulder. It didn't move. Whoever was playing the part was committed to staying in character. Chase forcefully opened his medical bag. He leaned over the man's mouth and blew air into the body.

This wasn't right. Something wasn't right. I had never seen CPR performed at a reenactment. In fact, mouth to mouth recitation wasn't even known of during the Civil War. A reenactor would not try to bring a fake dead person back that way.

Privates from both sides began to crowd around Chase and the body on the ground. I took a few more steps toward the fence that separated Maple Grove Lane from the battlefield.

"Mommy." A little girl pulled on her mother's sleeve. "What's wrong with that man?"

Her mother patted her head. "It's all part of the acting. Why don't we go into the visitor center and get some ice cream?" She turned her daughter so that she could no longer see the field.

"Okay!" her daughter cried, the body in the middle of the field forgotten with the promise of an early morning ice cream.

I appreciated that the mother lied to her daughter and used ice cream as a bribe. I would have done the same if Hayden were standing next to me. I bit the inside of my lip. Where *was*

Hayden? They should be here by now. I hoped Eddie had the good sense to distract him from the drama playing out in the middle of the field.

One of the reenactors on the field was speaking into a cell phone.

"Mom, that guy has a cell phone. They aren't supposed to have those," an annoyed teenager said. "That guy is cheating."

That was all the confirmation I needed. I climbed over the split-rail fence. As soon as my feet hit the grass, I ran toward Chase and the man. I pushed reenactors aside.

"Move, please! What's going on?"

Chase was still in middle of giving mouth-to-mouth to the soldier on the ground. He wore blue. He was a Union man. When Chase compressed the soldier's chest, I saw the man's face. It was Wesley.

"Come on, buddy," Chase said as he pumped. "Come on. Breathe."

Wesley's features were fluid, as if they could slide right off his face. I had seen the same effect on my mother right after she stopped breathing. Wesley wasn't coming back. He was dead. I placed my small hand on Chase's broad shoulder. The rough wool of his uniform felt harsh against my palm. Underneath the fabric, his muscles twitched with every compression of Wesley's chest.

"Chase," I whispered. "Chase, he's gone."

Chase shook his head and kept up with the CPR. He wouldn't give up on Wesley even if all hope was lost. Wesley's eyes remained closed. But I knew Wesley Mayes was dead, and he told me he didn't kill Maxwell Cherry. He may not have, but whoever committed that murder had struck again.

TWENTY-THREE

BEHIND US, I HEARD the wail of an ambulance. "Listen," I told the reenactors. "I don't want the visitors, especially the children, to see this. If you guys could stand in a line and block the public's view of Wesley, I would greatly appreciate it."

They fell into a line that would have made Generals Grant and Lee proud. All stood erect, shoulder to shoulder. Occasionally, I saw a tear fall from an eye. Wesley had been a member of their community, their friend. He had told Chase and me that he had been a reenactor since he was a child, a legacy that apparently followed his parents' love of the Civil War.

Portia came to mind. How would she feel to have another man that she loved—if it could be believed that she loved Maxwell—dead? Then again, did this make Portia the most likely killer? Did she terminate men who were no longer of use to her, or did she believe Wesley murdered her fiancé out of jealousy and revenge?

Another line I had heard my father recite many times from *Hamlet* came to mind. "*So art thou to revenge, when thou shalt hear.*"

I shook my head. Portia wasn't even on the battlefield or on the Farm grounds. How could she be responsible for this?

"How did he die?" I whispered.

A Confederate soldier to my right answered me. "He just seemed to have stopped breathing. When he fell, he hit his head on this rock." He pointed at the large rock sticking half out of the ground. It was a boulder, which had been too heavy to move when the field had been turned into a pasture land for the cows and oxen or a battlefield for the reenactors.

"So it was an accident?"

On the ground, pumping Wesley's chest, Chase shook his head. "Seems a little too coincidental for my taste."

"Mine too."

Chief Duffy hurried over. "I was in the commode when I got the news and got here just as quick as I could. What's happened?"

The Confederate soldier saluted. "It's Wesley Mayes, sir. He fell and hit his head on the rock there."

"Terrible accident. It doesn't happen often, but I have heard about other reenactors dying in freak accidents like this. It's the first time for it to happen in one of my battles."

"I don't know if it was an accident, Chief," Chase said and kept pumping the fallen man's chest. "Hitting his head on the rock could certainly knock him out cold, but that wouldn't be the reason he would stop breathing."

"You think he died before he hit the rock?" the chief asked.

"He stopped breathing before he hit the rock. I don't know how long it would take him to die." He glanced behind him at the infantrymen blocking the public's view.

Chief Duffy scanned the men. "Did anyone see Mayes fall?"

"I did," said the young Confederate private who had spoken to me. He had terrible acne and his hair was plastered to his face with sweat. "He fell with the first assault."

"That means that he was lying on the field for at least half an hour," I said.

"He could have been struggling most of that time," Chase said. "Since we thought he was pretending to be dead, we didn't take any notice."

"Excuse me," a breathy female voice said.

Infantrymen stepped aside, and my assistant appeared. She gasped when she saw Wesley lying dead on the grass. Behind her, EMTs and police in uniform pushed through the line. Chase stood up and let another EMT take over pumping Wesley's chest.

"Wyatt," one of the EMTs said. "You look sharp in the getup. I'm sure the ladies are fainting dead away when they see you." His eyes slid to me.

Chase's jaw twitched, but he didn't reply.

A second EMT kicked the first in the shin. "Shut up. Wyatt, can you tell us what's going on here?"

While Chase repeated the details of Wesley's condition, I pulled Ashland aside.

Ashland paled. "It's just so horrible, too horrible for words."

I snapped my fingers in her face. "Pay attention. We have a serious situation."

She shook her head. "Right. What do you want me to do?"

"First, make an announcement that there has been an accident and we request that visitors stay out of the EMTs' and police officers' way."

She made a note in her tiny notepad.

"Then, I want you to gather together twenty or thirty reenactors. Have them go to the village and play their parts out there. Ask them to talk about the war. Hopefully most of the crowd will follow them. Have Abraham Lincoln give his speech, and send Walt Whitman over too. He can recite *Leaves of Grass* beginning to end if need be. I won't even be a stickler about the version."

"Where will we hold the speeches?"

I thought for a moment. "The steps of the church will be perfect. Call Benji up to help you. She should be in candle making by now, but she's been looking for something more exciting to do since her brickyard is closed."

Ashland looked at me with awe. "Kelsey, how are you able to make plans like this so fast?"

The hero worship on her face made me uncomfortable. "Out of necessity. Now go."

I returned to the chief's side. He and Chase were arguing.

"The reenactment will stay open," the chief said. "There is only one day left."

Chase ran his hand through his hair. "Do you want someone else to get hurt?"

"Of course not," his uncle said.

The EMT lifted the stretcher to take Wesley off of the field. I knew it was a lost effort. From the EMTs' faces, they knew it too. But they weren't going to give up. It was their job not to give up.

The police chief poked one of his officers holding a camera. "Parker, go with them and take photos of the wound on the back from every angle in case if this turns out to be foul play."

Chase threw up his hands. "*If* this turns out to be foul play?"

"Relax, my boy," Chief Duffy said to his nephew.

As relieved as I was for the finances of the Farm to hear the chief say the Farm would remain open, I wasn't positive it was a good idea either. Maybe we should count our losses and get out while there were only two dead bodies to account for.

"Sir," Chase said, "I don't think it's wise to keep the reenactment open."

"What does Kelsey think?" Chief Duffy squished his bushy eyebrows together. "This is her show. I will follow her lead."

Both men turned to me.

I watched the EMTs lift Wesley over the fence and through the crowd. He was so young, just a couple years out of college. It seemed like such as terrible waste, but if we canceled the reenactment, I would never be able to reimburse all the Blue and Gray Ball ticket sales. It was too late to get my deposits back from the caterer, or for the tent, table, and chair rentals. More importantly, a killer would get away. Wesley and Maxwell deserved justice. So did Cynthia.

"I think we need to finish out the weekend. If we ask the reenactors to cross the street, most of the tourists will follow, which will give you time to search the field or whatever else you need to do. Lincoln and Whitman can recite speeches and poetry on the church steps."

The chief smiled. "Excellent plan."

Chase shook his head and walked away. I'd disappointed him and, surprisingly, I felt worse about that than anything else.

Twenty minutes later we learned that Wesley was pronounced dead at the hospital.

TWENTY-FOUR

My plan worked. Between Honest Abe and Walt Whitman, most of the tourists crossed the street into the village to listen to the speeches and mingle with the reenactors. Those who didn't listen to the two great men speak walked through the houses and other buildings in the village. My first-person interpreters had never been so inundated with visitors in their careers, but they handled it beautifully.

I had to admit Ashland took charge of the situation and made it seem like this was the plan for the day all along. In addition to Abraham Lincoln and Walt Whitman, she convinced some of the reenactor children to play an early version of baseball on the far edge of the village near Shepley's garden. As long as no one hit a baseball through one of the original wavy glass windows on any of the buildings, all would be well.

Shepley was the only person in the village not pleased with the turn of events. Dozens of visitors walked through his flowers and raised beds admiring his work. All the while the gardener stood at the entrance, a pitchfork in his hand, looking like a cross between the Hunchback of Notre Dame and an avenging scarecrow.

Wisely, the visitors gave him a wide berth when they entered and exited the garden.

"Shepley, can we talk?" I asked.

"What are all these people doing over here? You told me that most of the folks would stay on that side of the road. Then all of the sudden it was like Moses and the Israelites crossing the Red Sea. They just kept coming."

I adjusted my radio on my hip. "There was an incident during the reenactment."

He snorted. "An incident? You seem to be having a lot of those, Ms. Director. One of the reenactors kicked the bucket, I already heard."

I winced. If Shepley knew that Wesley died, then most of the visitors must have known too. Hopefully, they'd just assume it was heat stroke. One known murder on the grounds was more than enough.

"Do you want to talk about the dead guy? Because I don't know anything about that. I bet you regret this Civil War thing now. Problems happen when someone gets too big for her britches."

"I don't want to talk to you about the reenactment. I spoke with Benji a little while ago."

The hard lines on the gardener's face softened. Benji was the one person on the Farm he didn't gripe about. It may be because she, like Shepley, would rather play in the dirt than interact with other people.

"She said that you got the bees out her brick pit for her on Thursday."

He yanked his pitchfork out of the ground. "They weren't bees."

"I saw her foot; she was stung."

"Yes, but she wasn't stung by a bee. She was stung by a wasp. A mud dauber. Bees wouldn't bury themselves that deep into the mud where she wouldn't see them until she stomped them."

"Why was everyone calling them bees?"

He jabbed the pitchfork into the grass a few inches from its original spot. "City slickers don't know the difference. Honey bees are valuable. Mud daubers are pests."

"How did you get rid of them?"

"I used the smoker to relax them and scraped away their mud tubers. They were at the south corner of the brick pit. I shot it with some insecticide for good measure after the second smoking. I hate to use the stuff, but it's really the only way to deter them."

I grimaced. I hated to think of Benji stomping on insecticide for eight hours a day. That couldn't be good for her. As much as Benji would dislike it, maybe I needed to rethink having brickmaking as a Barton Farm craft.

"The medical examiner said he died of bee stings. I saw the tech collect the dead bees."

"I know. It's like I suspected from the start. Those are my bees."

"From the hives? How did they get in the brick pit if only mud daubers were going in there?"

He yanked the pitchfork out of the earth again. "Someone put them there."

"How can you be sure the bees were from your hive?"

"I can show you." He started across the green to Barton House.

Because of his back, Shepley's pace was slow, giving me plenty of time to take in the scene around me. Walt Whitman stood on the church steps and recited the famous poem about war he'd written in 1861 at the very beginning of the Civil War.

"*Beat! beat! drums!—Blow! bugles! blow!*" he said. A crowd of roughly seventy visitors, including some children and teenagers, stood at foot of the church steps and listened.

Lieutenants and privates, both North and South, chatted with visitors in the middle of the green, showing off their carbines and revolvers. Laura stood on the front porch of Barton House, helping a girl spin wool on the spinning wheel. All would be perfect and just what I wanted for the Farm, but for the murder in the way.

I followed Shepley around the side of the house. Laura saw us. She mouthed, "What is going on?"

I shook my head.

Behind Barton House, there was another flower garden cultivated and cared for by Shepley and the three beehives at the very back of the yard. Shepley had asked for the hives last spring. Cynthia, in her generosity, donated the money from the Cherry Foundation for the construction and for the bees. After the initial cost, the hive became self-sustainable because we sold the honey in the gift shop. The visitors loved it. Many times the shop had more demand for honey than what was available.

The bees had been a success for the Farm, but that didn't mean I wanted to get up close and personal with them. I might not be allergic like Maxwell was, but I didn't want to get stung. Behind the garden shed, a large plastic crate held all the instruments of beekeeping; gloves, suits, hats with masks, serrated knives to cut the honeycomb, and a handheld smoker.

Shepley pulled out a hat from the crate and handed it to me.

My hand was suspended in the air. "Can't I watch you from here?"

"No." He scowled. "I'm not doing anything that will upset my bees more than they already are. Holding the honeycomb up out of the hives so that you can see it would do that. You either put on the hat and suit or forget about it."

I took the suit and hat from his hand.

The beekeeper suit was a white cotton onesie. I stepped into it, slipped my arms into the sleeves, and zipped it all the way up to my throat. The sleeves went well beyond my wrists and the legs were way too long. If a bee happened to make it into my suit, I was a goner; it could sting me a dozen times before I could rip the suit off. I told myself not to think about that. I donned my hat and allowed the netting to fall over my face. A thin gray film now separated me from the rest of the world.

Shepley donned his matching outfit quickly and picked up the smoker. "Let's go."

The hives were on the edge of the trees, close enough to see but far enough away that visitors didn't pester the bees, and in turn, the bees didn't sting the visitors.

Shepley shuffled toward the beehives. I took a deep breath and followed. We were within six feet, and I could already see bees flying by me in my peripheral vision. "Bees are good," I reminded myself. "Panicking will only agitate them, and then they will sting you."

"Calm down," Shepley said. "You're making me nervous, and if I'm nervous, my bees are nervous."

"Okay," I squeaked.

He lifted the lid off of one of the hives. Bees swirled around him, but they didn't appear to be particularly upset. He pumped smoke onto the corner of the honeycomb, and pointed down.

When I didn't move, Shepley glared at me. I shuffled over to him. One of the honeybees landed on my arm and just as quickly flew away.

"I thought you were tougher than this," he said.

"I am. Just not when it comes to stings or needles. I hate needles." My phobia probably came from being a child of a diabetic and watching my father give himself insulin shots in his stomach and testing his blood each day. Dad never shielded me from the realities of his disease. For that I was glad, so I knew what to do if he needed me. At times when he wasn't feeling well enough to administer the shot himself, I was able to do it for him. However, there was a big difference between being able to give a shot to someone else and being able to take a shot yourself.

Shepley pulled one of the screens out of the hive. There was a piece missing near the corner, about the size of a silver dollar. It was far enough inside that someone would have to remove the screen to see it, so if Shepley just did a cursory check on his beehive, he would have missed it completely.

He pointed. "See, here you can make out the serrated edge of the knife as it cut through the honeycomb."

"That's the honeycomb, but how did the bees get into the brick pit? Just by you picking up that piece, I can see most of them are trying to get out of your way."

Five or six bees stubbornly clung to the screen as he pulled it all the way out of the hive. "If Maxwell was really as allergic as he claimed, one sting from one of these sleepy guys would have done the job."

And Maxwell had multiple stings on the bottom of his feet.

Was I standing next to the killer? No, it didn't make sense. Shepley wouldn't have spent all this time telling me how he killed Maxwell when he could easily kept it hidden in his hive and no one would be the wiser. "Thank you for showing me this."

He slid the screen back in place and nodded. "Whoever did this was careful to avoid the queen. I hate to lose any of them, but if the queen is okay, the colony will be okay. Had the queen been killed, the entire hive would have been in chaos, and in their confusion, other bees might have even abandoned the hive altogether. Bees without a hive spells disaster." He replaced the lid on the hive. "The worker bees will fix the hole in no time. I can already tell they've made progress since yesterday."

He walked back to the shed, where we removed our bee-keeping suits. "I think I need to learn more about the circumstances of Maxwell death," I said, more to myself than to Shepley.

"Finding out who offed Maxwell Cherry isn't going to save the Farm." He dropped his beekeeping hat into the crate.

I stared at him.

"Everyone knows that's why you're spending so much time on this."

A bee buzzed by my ear and I flinched but did not move. I handed Shepley my hat. "Thank you again for showing me."

As I walked away, he called, "It's not your job to save this place."

That's where Shepley was wrong. It was my job. As I walked through the garden I saw that most of the visitors had returned to the encampments on the other side of the road or left the Farm for the day. I glanced at my watch: just a half-hour before closing. The day was quieting to the hour when only the Farm staff and reenactors would be left. I sighed.

Laura stepped out of the Barton House. She was in full character and rolling a ball of freshly spun yarn. "What's up?" she asked.

I burst out laughing at her use of present-day street vernacular.

She grinned. Apparently her question got the desired effect. "I saw you head to the hives with Shepley. What were you doing back there with him?"

I gave her a brief version of my suspicions.

"You need to tell the cops this. It sounds important." She nodded to the brickyard. "Talk to the officer over there. I swear he must being trying out for British royal guard. The guy does not move. I've been watching him all day."

"Oh?" I teased.

"Hey, he's a nice-looking guy. Most of time I have to look at Shepley stooped over his eggplants. I should have the chance to enjoy a new view now and again."

I shook my head. "Have you seen Jason?"

"Barn Boy? Nope. But I don't usually see vampires out in the light of day."

"He's not a vampire."

"You believe whatever you want. I know the truth."

I rolled my eyes and walked to the brickyard. Unsurprisingly, Laura followed me. "Hello, Officer Sonders."

"Ms. Cambridge." He nodded, first at me and then to Laura.

"Hi handsome," Laura said with a wink.

The officer turned bright red.

I suppressed a sigh. "Can I have a look at the brick pit?"

Behind him the brick pit was covered with Benji's blue tarp.

The officer shook his head. "No one is supposed to go in there. Chief's orders."

"Did you find any pieces of honeycomb when the pit was searched?"

"Honeycomb?" he asked.

Laura balanced the ball of yarn in her hand.

"Yes," I said. "From a beehive."

He gave us a blank stare.

"Was any of this in the pit?" I held up the piece of dry honeycomb that I'd taken from the ground near Shepley's beehives.

"Oh. Sure. There was a piece near the deceased's feet. The bees were making honey, I guess."

"Bees don't make honey in mud," Laura said and lowered her voice so that only I could hear. "It's a shame he's not as smart as he is good-looking."

"Near his feet?" I swallowed. Shepley was right. I knew Maxwell was murdered. I knew Maxwell had been given insulin to knock him out. I knew Maxwell's killer was smart and organized, but to put a piece of honeycomb at his feet with bees was cruel. That was done by someone who wanted to make sure that Maxwell was stung multiple times. That was done by someone who wanted to make sure that Maxwell was stung dead.

Officer Sonders stepped forward. "Hey, are you all right? You look like you might be sick. I'm going to have to ask you to step away from the crime scene if you're going to throw up."

Laura peered at me. "She's not going to be sick," she assured the police officer. "I've seen her throw up on multiple occasions and she didn't look like that. We went to college together," she added as if that was explanation enough for her knowledge.

I took a deep breath. "Can you radio the chief and ask him to bring his nephew, Chase, too?"

"The chief is dealing with the death on the field."

"Please."

Officer Sonders frowned but unhooked his radio from his belt and radioed the chief.

I inched toward the brick pit just a few feet. With the tarp covering it, I couldn't see the mud. A wasp buzzed by my ear. I ducked. It was probably a mud dauber.

The plot to kill Maxwell had been much more elaborate than I first thought. Whoever did it had to know the Farm intimately. The culprit knew that wasps were hiding in the brick pit, that my father was type 1 diabetic, and how to remove a piece of honeycomb from Shepley's hives without disturbing most of the bees.

The more I thought about it, the more it looked like someone from the Farm was behind the murder. Since the only official Farm employee suspect was me, I was looking better and better as the killer. I knew that, and Chief Duffy and the lovely Detective Brandon knew that too.

TWENTY-FIVE

LAURA STEPPED BESIDE ME. "Kel, what's wrong?"

I didn't want to share my suspicions with her that it was a Farm employee who murdered Maxwell. If I said it aloud, then it might be true, and as much as I loved and trusted Laura, I knew that she had a tendency to let things slip.

The arrival of Chase and his uncle saved me from answering. They were still both in their uniforms from the field. A smudge of dirt marred Chase's cheek. He frowned. "What's going on, Kelsey?"

I told them both about the honeycomb missing from Shepley's hive and about honeybees versus mud daubers. As I spoke, neither man reacted.

"What?" I asked.

The chief chuckled. "You must think this is our first rodeo. We knew about the honeycomb. The medical examiner caught onto that right away. He found the pieces of honeycomb. There wasn't much, just shreds of it, but I guess you have to know the different kinds of bugs in his line of work. Me, I can't tell a fly from a ladybug. Since there were only tiny pieces of the honeycomb left, we suspect most of it had been removed after Maxwell was stung."

I swallowed. That would mean whoever did this waited and watched Maxwell get stung and then removed the honeycomb. It was too horrible for words. And here I was thinking I was sharing this monumental break in the case and they already knew about it.

"Why wasn't I told?"

His face clouded. "There was no reason to tell you."

My jaw twitched. "Did you know?" I asked Chase.

He looked away. There was my answer.

Laura clicked her tongue. "Not cool, Chase. Now she'll never like you."

Chase stared at Laura and then blushed. I couldn't believe that she was making junior high jokes at a time like this.

The one thing that I had learned for certain about this conversation was that my partnership, or whatever it had been, with Chase was over. From here on out, I was going to solve this case in spite of him and his police chief uncle.

Chief Duffy beamed. "It doesn't matter anyway. The case is closed."

"You found the killer?" Laura asked.

"Sure did." He removed a plastic bag from the pocket of his Confederate coat. "Got the confession right here."

"Who did it?" Laura was asking the questions. I was too shocked to speak.

"Wesley," Chase answered.

My eyes flicked over to him. "I don't believe you."

"Read it for yourself." He handed me a piece of paper in a clear plastic envelope.

It was dated the day before.

Dear Portia my love,

I am sorry for what I have done and what I will do. I know you are hurting because of my actions and my choices. For all his faults, Maxwell did not deserve the end he received. Please forgive me and remember what I do next is to make all of this easier on you. I have forgiven you.

All my love forever,

Wesley

Laura took the letter from my hand and read it. "Whoa."

I turned to Chase. "But we saw him last night. He gave us no clues he planned to do this."

"He was drunk and depressed. That can make a man stop thinking straight."

"But—"

"I know it's hard for you to believe, Kelsey," the police chief said. "But those are the facts. It's good news for you and for the Farm. You're off the hook."

Off the hook? Okay. So why didn't I feel better about it? Because a hurting young man was dead. Whether it was by his hand or someone else's, it didn't matter; he was still dead.

Laura handed the chief back the piece of paper. "He doesn't really come out and say that he killed Maxwell in that letter. Just that he's sorry."

The chief shrugged. "We'll have our psych guys look it over from the county crime lab, but sometimes confessions aren't verbatim."

Laura frowned.

"How did he die?" I asked. "Chase said that he stopped breathing before he hit his head on the rock on the battlefield."

"He poisoned himself." The chief slipped the letter back into his pocket. "At least that's what the medical examiner believes. We won't know exactly what he used as poison until we get the toxicology report."

In my mind's eye, I saw Wesley taking swig after swing from that brown jug. Chase and I had assumed that it was liquor. Had he been poisoning himself the entire time? "The cider he was drinking last night," I said.

Chase nodded. "We already recovered the jug. The medical examiner is taking it to his lab for comparison."

"But you dumped the contents out into the grass." My tone was accusatory, but I could not help it.

His brow furrowed. "I did. I didn't even suspect that there was anything else in there other than hard cider."

"Where did you find the letter?" I asked.

Chase answered this time. "It was sitting in the middle of his pillow on his mat like it was waiting for us."

I started for the road without another word. All I wanted at that moment was to see my son. I hadn't seen Hayden all day.

Instead I had wasted my time wrapped up in this murder, and it came to nothing, other than a young man dead.

I heard running footsteps coming up behind me. "Kelsey!" Chase ran around me and jogged backward in front of me.

"Get out of my way, Chase."

"Let me explain."

I stepped around him and looked both ways before crossing the street.

"My uncle told me not to tell you about the bees."

"Great. You respect your elders. That's one point in your favor, but you are still running a deficit."

"I'm sorry. But we can still—"

"What does it matter now? Wesley did it, right?" I glared at him. "You believe that?"

"There's the letter—"

"Laura's right. It's not a real confession. This doesn't feel right."

"It's enough to end the case. Don't you want that?"

"Not if it's not true!"

"You are—"

"Dear lady, is this soldier bothering you?" Walt Whitman asked, stroking his long white Santa Claus beard.

Chase grabbed at my hand, but I shifted away from his grasp.

"Dear boy," Walt snapped. "That is no way to handle a lady." He took Chase by the arm. "Perhaps you would like to listen to my poetry to calm yourself. Have you heard of *Leaves of Grass*? I have always found that poetry gives me clarity. In 1862, when I was working in the hospital as a nurse, I found that a few lines of my verse soothed the men in their pain. You are one of the lucky ones not to have been injured in battle. We pray that there aren't any more casualties, but this war will go on for many more months, I'm afraid."

"Kelsey," Chase said, ignoring Walt's speech.

I kept walking. As far as I was concerned, Walt could have him. Yanking my radio from my belt, I radioed Ashland.

"Yes, Kelsey," she said, sounding more confident than I had ever heard her.

"Do you know if Eddie brought Hayden to the reenactment today?"

"He did," she said over the radio. "They arrived late, about an hour ago."

"Where are they?"

"I just saw them in the candle maker's shed."

I thanked her and ended the transmission.

TWENTY-SIX

INSIDE THE CANDLE MAKING shed, Eddie and Hayden watched as Benji pulled a full dip stick of light blue-green bayberry candles from her copper tub of hot wax. "I'm making bayberry candles." With her free hand, she held up a dried twig from a bayberry bush, which still had its leaves and berries on it. "The wax comes from this bush. During the nineteenth century, these were candles used for special occasions like Christmas." Benji ran her thumb along the bottom of the line of candles. Bayberry wax coated her hand.

"Doesn't that burn?" Hayden asked.

She shook her head. "The candles are warm, but they cool off enough to touch after a few seconds out of the wax. Bayberry makes your hands smell good too." She wrinkled her nose. "This is much better than making tallow candles, which are made with animal fat. Those stink."

"Eww," Hayden said.

"Hayden," I said from the doorway.

My son turned and his entire face lit up. "Mom! Where have you been? We've been here forever." He ran across the shed and threw his arms around me like he hadn't seen me in weeks.

I buried my face into his neck and fought back tears. I would take as many of Hayden's hugs as I could get. I worried about the day when he would no longer want to hug me in public.

Eddie laughed. "We've only been here for an hour, H, and you know your mother has been working."

Eddie followed Hayden and me out of the shed.

"Where's Krissie?" I asked.

Eddie frowned. "Ladies room." He checked the time on his iPhone. "That was a while ago. I wonder why she's not back yet."

"I can go check on her," I said. "Do you know which restroom she was headed to?"

"The visitor center. I think that's the closest."

"It is. I'll go get her now."

"Can I come with you?" Hayden tugged on the hem of my polo shirt.

"You stay with me, H." Eddie pried his hand from my shirt. "Why don't you go back inside? I want to talk to Mom for a second."

I frowned. Eddie rarely wanted to talk to me alone.

"Okay," my son said good-naturedly. "Can I dip candles?"

"Under Benji's close supervision," I said. "And be careful and do everything that she says. Remember, she is the professional."

"Yea!" he cried as if it was the best news that he had ever heard and disappeared inside the building.

Eddie squinted into the sun. "I heard about the guy dying on the battlefield today."

I folded my arms. "From who?"

"Everyone here is talking about it. Even your candle dipper mentioned it."

I made a face.

"Are you really sure Barton Farm is best place for Hayden to live? Maybe he would be better living with Krissie and me."

"Is that a threat?"

He scolded. "It's a question, but now that I'm getting married and will have more help at home, I think it's time to revisit our custody agreement."

"More help at home?" I snapped. "Is Hayden too much work to have just on your own? Because it's just him and me ninety percent of the time."

"You know what I mean." He swatted at a mosquito.

"No, Eddie, I don't know what you mean." I lowered my voice. "And as far as custody goes, I'll fight you, don't think I won't. I will fight you with everything I have."

"It seems to me that I'm the one more concerned with our son's safety."

I felt like I had been slapped across the face. Hayden was my number-one priority. He would always be my number-one priority. Eddie knew better than to question that. I ground my teeth. "I'm going to go find your bride." I marched away, seething with every step.

Inside the visitor center, I stepped into the women's restroom. There was a middle-aged woman at the counter washing her hands, and I heard sniffles and whimpers coming from the stalls. The woman at the counter jerked her thumb at the handicapped stall at the end of the room.

After she left, I walked over to the stall and knocked on the door with the back of my knuckles. "Krissie? It's Kelsey. Are you all right?"

"No," was the wail that came in return. The stall door unlocked. "Come in here," she said.

Was she kidding? After the many reasons why I shouldn't go into the stall flashed across my mind, I went through the metal entry anyway. As soon as I cleared the door, Krissie slammed it closed and relocked it. Then, she sat on the toilet, fully clothed, thank heaven.

She buried her face in her hands. Okay, this was weird. I was in a locked handicap restroom stall with the twenty-two-year-old my ex-husband was set to marry and raise my son with.

I leaned on the sink inside the stall and folded my arms. "What's wrong?"

She gasped. "Wesley is dead. I went to his tent to say hello and there were police all over the place. He's dead. He committed suicide."

I dropped my arms. "I'm so sorry. I know he was your friend."

"I—I just saw him yesterday and he was fine. I was just so shocked I didn't know what to do, so I came back here." She blew her nose in a wad of toilet paper. "I didn't want Hayden to see me cry."

"I appreciate that," I said, meaning it.

"The police said Wesley murdered that man. I know I haven't seen him in years, but the Wesley that I knew would not have done that. He wouldn't!" She shook the wad of toilet paper at me for emphasis.

"Did Wesley give you any indication that he planned to kill himself yesterday?"

"No, not at all. He was genuinely excited to see me. We talked about college and where our other friends are now."

"Did he say anything about Maxwell?"

"He mentioned that he was dead and that he was engaged to Portia. That was a shock to me. I thought Portia and Wesley would be together forever." She rubbed her eyes.

"You knew Portia too?"

She nodded. "She went to college with us. She and Wesley lived together most of that time. It was hard to see Wesley and not see Portia too. I didn't know her as well as Wesley, but I always thought she was a sweet girl. Maybe a little shy. I was surprised to hear she was marrying such a powerful man, but then, Maxwell had money."

"Money was important to Portia?"

"Wesley hinted to me once that Portia was very poor. I think she came from a foster family. I could be wrong on that."

"Did Wesley confess to you that he killed Maxwell?"

"No, he did not." She balled the paper in her fist. "He didn't do it."

"I don't think he did it, either," I said. "The police are wrong."

She lifted her head. Tears streaked her face, and her bottom lip quivered. She looked like a little girl. Her expression made me feel incredibly sad and incredibly old.

"Really?"

"I'll find out who really killed Maxwell," I said.

"You will?" Tears hung on her eyelashes. "You'd do that for me?"

"I'm not doing it for you," I said. "It's for Wesley, and for Cynthia, who has a right to know what really happened to her nephew."

Outside the stall, the bathroom door slammed closed, startling us both.

"Was someone listening to us?" Krissie whispered.

I stared at the stall door. "I don't know."

"You won't tell Eddie where you found me, will you? I haven't told him about running into Wesley yesterday. It would just upset him."

I opened the stall door. We were the only ones there.

She followed me out of the stall. "Are you going to tell him?"

I sighed. The situation with Hayden came to mind, but that was something Eddie and I needed to discuss as parents. I wasn't going to get Krissie involved. At least not yet.

"I won't tell him."

She let out a breath. After washing her face and reapplying her makeup, I led Krissie back to Hayden and Eddie at the candle making shed.

"Mom," Hayden said when we arrived. "Look, I made these!" He held up a dip stick holding three tiny candles hanging from the stick by their wicks.

"That's awesome, Hayden!" I said.

Eddie wrapped his arm around Krissie's shoulders. "Everything all right, honey?"

She nodded.

He frowned and gently brushed her hair out of her eyes. I had to look away.

Eddie, Krissie, and Hayden left shortly after that. My cell phone rang as I waved good-bye to their car. It pained me to watch them drive away.

"Hey," Justin said in my ear. "I just heard that Wesley Mayes was the one that offed Maxwell. I guess you're no longer in need of my lawyerly services."

"The police have the wrong guy."

He groaned. "I thought you would be glad that you're no longer a suspect."

"I am, but I know Wesley didn't do it."

"How?" he asked.

"Krissie said he was innocent too."

He choked a laugh. "Wait, do I have the right number? I am talking to Kelsey Renard Cambridge, am I not?"

"Yes," I said through gritted teeth.

"What, did you and Krissie braid each other's hair or something? Since when have you cared anything about her?"

"I'm just saying I'm not the only one who believes he's innocent. I just have to prove that to the police."

"Kel." Justin's voice turned serious. "Don't do anything stupid, okay? Even though my brother and you aren't married anymore, I still care about you."

I always suspected that I fell in love with the wrong Cambridge boy. I slid the phone into the back pocket of my jeans after disconnecting and returned to the cottage to clear my head. Dad was in the living room with arms raised, shouting boos at Frankie and Tiffin. Neither animal appeared overly concerned; they were used to Dad practicing his lines on them.

I waved at Dad and went upstairs. I stepped into Hayden's room and sat on his bed. Action figures and Lego blocks were strewn across the floor. I had asked him to pick them up before he left with this father, but I knew that was just force of habit. Finding them still on the floor was not a surprise.

I knelt on the floor, pulling one of his toy crates across the navy blue carpet. One by one, I tossed the action heroes into the crate.

Dad knocked on the doorframe. "How is my favorite child?" he asked. His eyes drooped downward with concern.

A yellow minion fell into the crate. "I'm your only child."

Frankie walked into the room and grabbed a plastic Spider-Man, dragging it under the bed like a spider taking a fly back to her web. I didn't have the energy to wrestle it away from him. That particular Spider-Man was on his own.

"That's good because I couldn't like another one more than I like you."

I fought back a smile as a sat back on my heels. "Did you hear about Wesley?"

He sat on Hayden's bed. "I did."

"I don't think he did it."

Dad tapped his cheek with his index finger. "Then, find out who did. You're a smart girl, you can do it."

"As my father, shouldn't you encourage me not to get involved?" Two more minions went into the crate.

He waved his hand. "Bah! As your father, it's my job to encourage you to do the right thing. If you don't think Wesley murdered Maxwell, then find out who did." He stood. "Now, I must head to the playhouse. The big show is tonight. You are still coming, aren't you?"

I smiled. "Yes. Both Laura and I will be there."

"Good, and for one night put this murder behind you and enjoy yourself. You'll come to the right conclusion in the end."

"You act like that's easy. The police can't even figure it out."

"I know you can do it, Kelbel," he said and left the room.

I stood, picked up the crate, and slid it into its place on Hayden's bookshelf. "I wish I had your confidence."

TWENTY-SEVEN

MY RADIO CRACKLED. "KELSEY? It's Ashland. Come in?"

I picked up my radio from where I left it on the kitchen table while foraging in the refrigerator for something to eat. "What's up, Ashland?"

"I found him," she said.

I put my can of pop on the table. "Found who?"

"Jamie Houck. You wanted me to find him, didn't you?"

I had completely forgotten about Jamie with Wesley's death.

"Maybe it doesn't matter now that Wesley has confessed to the crime and is dead."

"It matters," I said. "Where is he?"

"Meet me outside of the visitor center and I'll take you to him."

"Be there in five minutes." I left the house with my uneaten sandwich on the counter.

I decided to take Tiffin with me to meet Jamie Houck. He had spent much of the day trapped in the house, and I knew he was itching to get outside and see the camps. I wrapped his leash around my right hand but let him walk untethered beside me. Ashland was already at the visitor center when I got there.

"Where is he?" I repeated my early question.

"Follow me."

I frowned. I would have much rather Ashland just answer my questions, but if my assistant wanted to present me with some big reveal, I wouldn't rob her of that. She headed straight for the Confederate camp, and Tiffin and I followed.

She led me to a tent in the middle of the camp. Three men in Confederate dress drank coffee and laughed. Two of the men I didn't recognize, but the third one, in the middle, was familiar. As we got closer, I realized it was the same Confederate corporal who had accused Wesley of stealing his canteen on the first day of the reenactment.

Ashland marched up to the men with a new self-confidence. "Henry Adams, we would like a private word with you."

Adams's two friends laughed at Ashland's formal announcement.

One of his comrades stood up. "Looks like you're in trouble, Adams."

Adams frowned. "Give us a minute, boys."

Still laughing, the other two men sauntered away. After they were gone, Adams sat on a camp stool at the entrance of his tent. "What can I do for you, ladies?"

Ashland folded her arms and glared down at him. "Your real name is Jamie Houck, and we want to talk to you about Maxwell."

I stared at Ashland. *This* was Jamie Houck? The same guy I saw on the first day of the reenactment in a yelling match with Wesley over a missing canteen?

He scowled but didn't deny her accusation. "What does it matter what my name is outside of the reenactment?"

"It matters," Ashland said, "because your business partner is dead."

Adams—no, Jamie Houck—poured what was left of his coffee into the grass. The dark liquid disappeared among the thick green blades. "Do you think that I'm happy that Maxwell is dead? After this weekend, I have to go back into the office and clean up the mess he's left behind. I'd appreciate if you let me enjoy my last few hours of make-believe before reality sets in."

"When you say mess," I said, speaking for the first time, "you mean the construction site on Kale Road."

His neck jerked up and he glared at me. "Not that it is any of your business, but yes. We were just about to sign a new deal with an anchor store for the mall with the backing of Cynthia Cherry's fortune. Now that Maxwell is gone and that money is out of my grasp, I don't know what will happen." He shuddered. "I'm left with a multimillion-dollar pile of dirt."

"You and Maxwell argued about this," I said.

"It was no secret that we argued over the plans for the new mall, but we both wanted it to happen. It was going to be a lucrative deal for us both."

"And that deal can't go forward without Maxwell?" Ashland asked.

"I just said that." He looked from Ashland to me and back again. "You don't think I had anything to do with Maxwell's death, do you? That Union sergeant killed him and then killed himself. I can't say that I'm at all surprised. The kid was a punk and stole my canteen."

I balled my hands into fists. "His name is Wesley."

Jamie shrugged. "Doesn't matter. That kid cost me a canteen and millions of dollars, so excuse me if I don't feel bad that he's dead."

"Wesley knew Maxwell. He even worked for Maxwell for a time," I said.

"He did?" Jamie's eyebrows shot up. "I didn't know that. It is a small world." He shook the last remnants of coffee grounds from his cup. "If he worked for Maxwell, then I'm even less surprised he killed him. Maxwell was a terror to work with. I wouldn't have gone into business with him at all if I didn't need a money man in my corner."

I didn't like Maxwell, but it was hard to listen to someone else talk about him so disparagingly, especially since I knew Cynthia was at home grieving his loss.

"All Maxwell's death did was cause more headaches for me." With that, Jamie Houck/Henry Adams turned and walked away from us.

As Tiffin, Ashland, and I walked back to the visitor center, my assistant said, "Maybe Wesley did kill Maxwell. He had the best motive to kill Maxwell, and the police believe his confession was real."

"I just can't believe that."

She frowned.

Laura walked up to us. She was now in her street clothes, ready for the theater. "Kelsey, take Tiffin home and get changed or we're going to miss the first act!"

"I'm on my way now." I patted Ashland on the shoulder. "Thanks for your help."

She gave me the smallest of smiles before she turned away.

Laura watched her go. "You should be careful and not praise that girl too much; she already idolizes you. Next thing you know, she's going to be gunning for your job."

I rolled my eyes. "Don't be ridiculous."

"I'm not," Laura said.

———

During *Hamlet*, my father gave the performance of his life. I felt bad for the young man with the title role, as my father outshone him in every scene that they shared. When the play ended and the house lights went up, Laura stretched. "Your father plays a good ghost. Let's hope he comes back someday to haunt the Farm. We would make a fortune in ticket sales and maybe even get on one of those ghost hunter shows on cable TV."

I laughed. "He's going to be wired tonight. I'm so proud of him." I hadn't felt this relaxed in days. I didn't know what it said about me that watching a play about another person going insane over a murder relaxed me.

"Do you want to go backstage and see your dad?"

I shook my head. "I'll see him back home eventually, and I don't want to get in the way of his adoring fans."

Laura laughed.

We followed the throng of playgoers back into the lobby. A huge chandelier hung from the ceiling, and floral carpeting covered the floor. Even though the New Hartford Community Theater was small, it was well funded with an arts endowment. It was one nonprofit in the town that didn't have to ask the Cherry Foundation for money.

"I need a drink," Laura said, making her way to the bar. "Watching people talk so much makes me thirsty."

As we threaded our way across the crowded room, I blinked a couple of times to make sure I wasn't imagining what was before me. Cynthia stood with Portia near the bar. A glass of sherry was in her hand. She wore a rose silk pantsuit and had a black shawl wrapped around her shoulders. I hurried over to her. "Cynthia."

"Kelsey, my dear," she said and reached for my hand. "It's so good to see you here. I loved your father's performance. His talent is wasted here in our little playhouse."

I smiled. "I'll tell him that you said that."

"Please do."

"I'm so happy that you came." I paused. "But I'm a little surprised to see you here. I thought that you wouldn't be up to coming, considering..."

She clutched her shawl close to her shoulders. "Maxwell wouldn't want me to be cooped up in the house all day. The play has been a welcome distraction from my grief." She squeezed Portia's hand. "It's been a welcome distraction for us both."

Portia fidgeted beside her.

"I'm glad to hear it," I said.

Cynthia placed a hand on my arm. "I'm glad that I saw you, Kelsey. I want you to know that I've taken care of everything. You won't have any worries over the Farm after I'm gone."

I covered her hand with my own. "Cynthia, please don't talk about after you're gone."

She released my arm. "At my age, I need to be prepared. I don't want to leave a mess behind me for others to clean up. The Farm will be fine, trust that."

"What do you mean?" Laura, who now had a glass of wine in her hand, asked.

Cynthia shook her head. "We shouldn't spoil the evening by talking about business."

"Did you hear what happened during the reenactment today?" Laura asked.

I stepped on my best friend's toe.

"Ouch," she muttered.

Cynthia nodded. "We did. I'm happy that Maxwell's case has been laid to rest. It won't bring my nephew back."

"I don't—ow!" This time, Laura stepped on my toes. Since she was wearing three-inch heels, it hurt a lot more than when I stepped on her with my flat.

"I'm sorry for the family of that young man," Cynthia added.

I watched Portia as Cynthia spoke. The young woman held onto a lock of her black hair and kept her head bent down. She refused to look at me.

I wanted to ask her about Wesley, but clearly Cynthia didn't understand the connection between Wesley and Portia. She

226

may not have even realized Wesley was the young man who yelled at Maxwell on the first day of the reenactment.

Cynthia slid her arm through Portia's. "I'm starting to feel a little tired. Portia, can you take me home?"

Portia set her own glass on the bar. "Of course."

Laura stepped forward. "Portia, why don't you go pull the car around for Cynthia, so she doesn't have to walk through the dark parking lot?"

Portia hesitated.

"That would be very nice," Cynthia agreed.

"I'll only be a minute," Portia said, and she headed to the playhouse's entrance.

Laura widened her eyes at me and mouthed, "Follow her."

"Excuse me, Cynthia," I said. "I think I'll go to the powder room."

Cynthia simply nodded. She leaned heavily on Laura, fatigue etched on her face.

I caught up with Portia in the parking lot. She was headed for a black Lexus. "Portia!" I called.

When she turned, I saw that her face was tear-streaked. "Leave me alone."

I jogged to catch up with her. "I want to talk to you for a moment."

She stopped and turned. A full moon hanging overhead and a large lamppost in the middle of the parking lot were the only light.

"I don't want to talk to you."

"I just want to make sure that you're all right."

"I'm fine." Her tears belied that.

"I don't think so."

"I don't care what you think. What right do you have to asking me how I am, after I lost two men I loved in a matter of days?"

I chewed on my lip. "I don't have a right."

"At least we agree on something."

"Just answer me one question, and I'll go away."

She gripped her ponytail. "If it means you'll leave, fine."

"Did you hear from Wesley since you saw him at the reenactment or after Maxwell was killed?"

"No." Tears rolled down her pale cheeks. "And that is my biggest regret. Maybe if I'd reached out to him and explained, he wouldn't have done these horrible things."

I blinked. "You think he killed Maxwell and committed suicide?"

She rubbed a tear from her cheek. "I don't know what to believe anymore about anyone, including myself." With that, she turned and sprinted to Cynthia's car.

TWENTY-EIGHT

I asked Laura to drop me off where Maple Grove Lane met the pebbled path that led to the visitor center. "Are you sure you want me to drop you here?" she asked. "I can at least drive you to the visitor center."

I unbuckled my seatbelt. "No thanks. This way I'll have a chance to walk through the camps on the way to the cottage and make sure everything is all right."

She nodded as I got out of the car. "See you tomorrow. It'll be the last day of the reenactment. After tomorrow, we can put all of this behind us."

I waved at the taillights of her car until they disappeared. I didn't think I could put what had happened at the Farm the last few days behind me.

Reenactors waved and smiled at me while I walked past their camps. I steered clear of the Union camp and Chase. I wasn't ready to see him or the chief yet. I couldn't believe that I had been dumb enough to trust him. How many times would I get burned before I learned my lesson?

I walked to the visitor center and unlocked the employee entrance. The building was dark and quiet. My shoes clicked as I walked across the lobby. In my office, I tucked my purse in my desk drawer and grabbed my radio, which I hooked on the belt of my dress. I would collect my purse before I went to the cottage, but first, I wanted to check the camps one last time.

Outside the visitor center, a man walked up to me with a smile. "We haven't had the honor of seeing you in our camps as much as you have been visiting the Union."

With surprise, I realized that it was the same Confederate private who fought with Wesley over his rifle in the middle of the battlefield.

I smiled. "I'm sorry to have been away. The weekend was more work than I expected." I refrained from saying "the reenactment." I sensed this reenactor was a stitch counter and would pretend he didn't know what I was talking about. He wasn't just in character; as far as he was concerned, he was back in 1863 fighting in the War Between the States.

"We appreciate everything that you are doing. It's been a trying weekend with so many causalities. It reminds me of the Battle of Shiloh in that way. The Yankees refuse to understand that we have a right as much as they do to build our own country, one that respects state's rights. The Union never will. Mark my words, if they are victorious, the power in Washington will grow that much stronger and the states will grow that much weaker." He relaxed. "But enough politics for one day. Can I give you a tour around our encampment?" He held up his gas-lit lantern. "I'll lead the way."

"Sure," I said eagerly. I had run in and out the camps numerous times after the last few days but hadn't taken the time to really look at them. Hayden was with his father, and my father wouldn't be home until very late because there was a cast party after the opening performance. I was in no rush to go back to the quiet cottage.

"My name is Matthew Richardson, by the way. The general is really the man in charge and should be the one showing you around. He's already retired to his tent for the night." He pointed to the largest tent in the camp. A table covered with maps and surrounded by three camp chairs sat outside. A sleepy-looking private drinking from a tin cup stood guard. "Our general is a good man," Matthew said. "But he's no General Lee."

"Few men are." I smiled.

He removed his forage cap and held it to his chest. "Truer words were never spoken." He pointed at a tent with a wash tub and an old-fashioned washboard. "Here's where we do the wash and cleaning."

Civil War reenactors were like a traveling circus. They carried everything that they needed with them. The Farm had just provided the land. It was an expensive hobby. The men and women who participated had to be truly dedicated to the pastime. I didn't know if I could show that kind of devotion to it, but I had to respect their abilities.

A Confederate private pulled a sizzling skillet of bacon out of the flames. He used a flimsy cotton towel to protect himself from getting burned as he forked out one of the pieces.

231

Matthew laughed. "Late-night snack."

The private held up the piece of bacon. "Want some?"

I shook my head. "No thanks."

Matthew and I walked through the rest of the Confederate camp. We stood on the edge of it about twenty yards from the Union camp.

"I appreciate the tour," I said.

"Did you want to see the Union camps as well? I'm sure one of the Yankees would love to take a pretty lady like yourself on a tour." He smiled. "I know I enjoyed it."

"No. Like you said before, I have been to the Union camp many times."

He nodded. "Tomorrow will be the last battle and the ball. We'll make due with one man down on both sides."

"One man down?" I asked.

"You know about Wesley Mayes, of course." He held the lantern higher. The yellow light bounced off his pronounced cheekbones.

"I do."

"Very sad turn of events, and we lost a solider on our side too."

"A Confederate soldier died too?" I felt my pulse quicken three dead people? Could it even be possible?

He shook his head. "No one died outside of the battlefield, but on Friday morning one of our privates deserted."

"Deserted?"

He lowered his voice. "He was diabetic and all of his medicine for the weekend had spoiled. He had to leave. I hated to lose him. He was a very good solider, one of my best really. We're hoping that he'll meet us at our next encampment. I'm thinking that we should try to invade the North once again. If they are in the same agony as the South, they would want to end this war in a hurry."

"Was he a type one diabetic?"

He rested his free hand on the hilt of his revolver on his hip. "I think so. He gave himself insulin shots every so often."

"That doesn't guarantee that he was type one, but it does mean he would have insulin with him."

Matthew lowered his voice. "The cooler with his insulin became too warm. The whole supply was ruined, and Private Darling even claimed one of syringes and a couple of vials of his insulin were missing. I can't say I believe it; Private Darling can be flighty. I wouldn't promote him to officer, if you know what I mean."

My father was flighty too. He was an eccentric professor and actor, but one thing he knew was where his syringes were and how much insulin he had. At all times. He had to know it.

"Did you tell the police?" I asked.

He jerked his head back. "Why would I tell the police something like that? Private Darling left early morning on Friday of his own accord."

Friday. The morning that I found Maxwell in the brick pit.

Who would know there was a type 1 diabetic in the encampment? A Union soldier? Wesley Mayes was dead, so I couldn't ask him. The only other soldier with a connection with Maxwell was the Union medic, Chase Wyatt.

What would I do with this information? The last time I thought I had made a breakthrough in the case, Chief Duffy had laughed at me. I wasn't ready to go through that again, but I couldn't keep it to myself either in case the police didn't know about it. Then I spotted Officer Parker walking toward the visitor center, waving a flashlight back and forth on the path in front of him.

"Wait right here," I told Matthew.

He lowered his lantern. "Okay."

"Officer Parker," I called.

The police officer spun around with arms up, poised to block an attack.

I slowed. "What are you doing?"

"You s-scared me. This place gives me the creeps. Grown men walking around playing dress up and acting like it's a hundred years ago. It's too weird. Chief Duffy said I needed to patrol until most of the reenactors went to bed. Most of them are in their tents, so I'm out of here."

"I thought Chief Duffy was convinced that Wesley was the killer. Why would he ask you to patrol the Farm?"

"I don't know, but I can't wait to go home. These people are crazy."

"Before you go, you need hear something."

"What?" His eyes flitted back and forth.

"It's not from me. One of the Confederate private has important information about the case."

He didn't move.

"Come on, Officer Parker, the reenactors won't bite."

He sighed and followed me into the Confederate camp. When I found Matthew again, I told him, "Tell Officer Parker what you just told me about Private Darling."

"Why would the police what to know?" Matthew asked.

"Just tell him," I urged.

He shrugged and repeated the story about Private Darling's ruined insulin.

Officer Parker folded his arms. "So what?"

I scowled. "Insulin was used to subdue Maxwell in order to put him in the brick pit with the bees."

"So now we know where Wesley Mayes got his supply. It doesn't change the fact that he's the killer. The case is closed."

I gritted my teeth. "Will you at least tell the chief?"

He grunted. "Fine. I will, but not until the morning. I have to get home and take a shower after being in this place all day long." He shivered and stomped away.

I said good-bye to Matthew and left the Confederate camp. Across the street in the village, I saw a flashlight moving around the barn. Hadn't Officer Parker checked to make sure there wasn't anyone wandering around the village? With no electric lights, the village was strictly off limits after dark. I sighed. A reenactor probably wandered over there even though it was forbidden.

During the day the chief stationed Officer Parker as a guard over a brick pit so that the scene would be left undisturbed by visitors. At night, he relied on the crime scene tape as a deterrent. I looked back at the encampments. All of my staff had gone home, and the reenactors had either crawled into their tents or were sitting around campfires smoking and drinking more "cider" from brown jugs.

The light was probably Jason, and this was my chance to confront him about his fake home address. If I caught him in the act of sleeping on the Farm, then I would—I hope—finally be able to talk to him about his living situation and why he gave a false address on his job application.

Before crossing the street, I picked up one of the lanterns hanging from a pole at the end of the Confederate camp to light my way. I wished that I had Tiffin with me, but it would take too long to run to the cottage to fetch him and by then Jason might be too hard to find.

I held the lantern straight out in front of me. It was heavy, and I had to lower it a few inches to stop my arm from shaking. I crossed the road at a run. At night, teenagers joyriding through the park flew down Maple Grove Lane. I didn't want to chance meeting any of them head on.

The barn was dark. From the outside, I could hear animals moving about as they settled in for the night. I placed the lantern on the ground next to me, so that I could use both hands to push open the heavy sliding door. It took a couple of hard shoves, but finally it opened enough so I could fit through. I picked up my lantern and slipped inside.

Scarlet, the mare, hung her head over her stall and blinked at me. Miss Muffins buried her face under her paw as if to block the light from my lantern. The two oxen didn't stir, but several of sheep *baa*ed in protest of my disturbing their beauty sleep.

I held the lantern high. "Jason? Jason, it's Kelsey. I need to talk to you."

No response.

I stepped under the ladder to the hay loft. He could be up there, but I wasn't going to chance breaking my neck to climb the ladder in the middle of the night.

"Okay," I said, lowering the lantern. "You win for now, but we do need to talk. I know you're living here. I went to the home address you listed on your job application. There was nothing there. I'm not going to kick you out onto the street, if that's what you're afraid of, but you can't keep hiding here at the Farm. We have to talk about some kind of compromise or arrangement that works for both of us."

I waited and there was still no response. A sheep *baa*ed, sharing her irritation with my speech.

I sighed. "I just want to talk to you, Jason. You know where to find me." I took my lantern and slipped out the barn door.

I walked down the path between the barn and the brickyard. From my vantage point, I could see all the way across the green. Most of it was cloaked in darkness, but just in front of Barton House a light bobbed in the dark. It's up and down motion made it appear like someone was running across the green.

"Hey!" I called. "Jason!"

The light didn't stop and disappeared between Barton House and the next building.

I ran down the path toward the village, stopping at the edge. "Jason?" I called.

Still nothing.

I saw blur of light near the far corner of the Barton House.

"Hey!" I called again. I was shouting so loud, I was surprised a dozen reenactors didn't cross the street to find out what all the commotion was.

I took a step forward and stopped. Maybe I was wrong, and it wasn't Jason. It could have been a reenactor or maybe a camper from one of the campgrounds in the park. Then again, the closest campground was over four miles away. That would be quite a long hike through dense forest in the dark. It was late, and clearly Jason or whoever it was didn't want to talk to me. I kept my eye on the corner of the house the light had disappeared behind. Nothing stirred. Occasionally, a lightning bug lit up the gloom. A half moon hung high in the sky and provided minimal light when it peeked through the clouds.

Whoever it was wasn't my problem. I wasn't going to chase them all over the village. The buildings were locked down. The artifacts were secure. It was time to go to bed and hope tomorrow was better.

I heard a rattle behind me like a large stone being kicked and bounced off another stone.

I turned and lifted my lantern high but saw nothing. Absolutely nothing. It may have been Jason, and he didn't want to be seen. I'd deal with him after the reenactment. That's how I thought of things: before and after the reenactment, before and after Maxwell was killed.

And then something smacked me in the back of my head.

The lantern fell from my hand and shattered on the path. I swayed, grabbing the air for something to hold onto. There was nothing there. Another blow came, and I fell to my knees. Hayden's smile came into my mind's eye, and then everything went dark.

TWENTY-NINE

I SMELLED DIRT. I tasted it too. I rolled over onto my side, and my head felt like it was split in two. Tentatively, I reached behind me and touched the back of my head. There was a lump there about the size of a tangerine. I didn't want to raise my head. I was too afraid I would throw up, so I lay in the dirt with my cheek on my hand. I would get up in a minute.

I woke up a second time. I didn't know how long I had been asleep. I raised my head an inch off of the floor. It still hurt, but I didn't feel the nausea that plagued me the first time I had awoken. Slowly, I pushed myself up into a sitting position. I waited for the dizziness to pass before I opened my eyes.

Across from me I saw a line of moonlight. I crawled in that direction. Something light and furry scurried across my hand. "Ahh!" I squealed and waved my hand in the air even though the creature was long gone. No longer caring about my head, I doubled my pace to the line of light. It was a hatch in the low ceiling above me. The ceiling was so close I could touch it from a kneeling position.

I pushed up on the hatch. It didn't budge. Panic crept into my chest. I knew where I was. I was inside the Barton House root cellar. We had used it last year as part of our Underground Railroad program. The only way out was through the hatch, which opened in the corner of the home's living room. There was no lock on the hatch and usually we have a heavy steamer trunk over it, so that the visitors didn't notice it. Sweat trickled down my back. I'd bet the trunk was on it now.

I took a deep breath and pushed with all my might; the hatch rose less than an eighth of an inch. I crumbled back to the dirt floor. I allowed myself to lie there a moment, just a moment. *Think, Kelsey, think.* There must be a way out of here. Hastily I ran my hand over myself. I still wore the summer dress I had put on to go to my father's play, but my radio and cell phone were both missing. I shivered. Whoever put me in the cellar wanted to make sure I wouldn't get out any time soon.

Think.

Worst-case scenario, I would have to stay inside the root cellar until the next morning when my staff opened the building. I'd scream and yell, and they would let me out. That was only hours away. My mouth felt dry. Hours. How many was unknown. Could I stay in the cellar for hours and not go crazy?

Maybe my cell phone *was* in the cellar with me. I could look for it and that would pass some of the time until morning. I swept my hand back and forth over the dirty floor. If I ran into the furry creature again, which I prayed was a mouse or chipmunk and not a rat, I would lose it. Maybe searching for my phone wasn't a great idea.

Above I heard footsteps. I froze. Was it a rescuer or the person who put me down here, coming back to finish the job?

Maybe I wouldn't have the chance to wait until morning to be rescued.

Above I heard a loud scrape, like a piece of furniture was pushed away from the hatch. No longer caring about what small animals might be hiding in the corners of the root cellar, I ran my hands along the dirt floor, search for anything that I might be able to use as a weapon. My left hand bumped into a piece of wood. I ran my hand over it and squinted at it. It felt like a piece of handle to a rake or broom. It was the best I had. My fingers curled around it.

More scraping came from above. Now I wondered if furniture was being moved away from the hatch or onto the hatch. The hatch opened.

The sudden brightness that spilled into the cellar hurt my eyes. I shielded them with the hand not holding the stick.

A face appeared in the opening. "Kelsey?"

Despite my squint, I made out the features of Chase's face.

"Chase!" I crawled forward. He jerked his head out the hole when he saw me crawling toward him. I stopped. Was he leaving me? A second later both his hands were reaching into the cellar for me. I grabbed his forearms and let him take me out of the pit. He pulled me out and I lay there on his chest for a moment, willing my heart rate to slow down.

He brushed a hair out of my face, which was when I realized that I was still lying on top of him. I rolled off of him onto the hardwood floor of the Barton living room. The movement caused the world spin. I held the back of my head.

Chase sat up and watched me. "Are you hurt?"

"I'll be all right," I murmured, but I didn't remove my hand from the back of my head.

"What happened?" he asked as he scrambled to his feet. He wore sweats and a T-shirt. Apparently, he didn't sleep in reenactor clothes. I shivered to think what I must look like.

"I don't know exactly. I noticed that someone with a flashlight or some kind of light was moving through the village. I was calling out to the person to answer me, but they didn't. Instead someone knocked me on the back of my head. Twice. I remember clearly they hit me a second time. I guess my head is pretty hard to have to take two hits before I fell."

"I'm not surprised at all." He stepped forward. "Let me see."

"Oh no, I'll be fine." I kept my hand on the back of my head.

He smiled. "I'm a paramedic, remember?" He helped me to my feet.

"Right. Sorry," I murmured.

Still holding me as if he thought I might topple over without his steady grip, he grabbed a ladder-back chair leaning against the wall. He moved it in front me. "Sit and I will check your head."

I stared at the chair. It was an original to the house. The Bartons brought it with them from their suburban middle class home in Connecticut when they came to the Western Reserve in 1808.

"I can't sit on that. It's an artifact."

"Sit," he said leaving no room for argument. "An old chair is not more important than your skull."

"I'm not so sure of that," I said, but I sat because dizziness overpowered my concern for the chair.

Delicately, I felt his fingers tickle through my hair and probe the bump. The room was dim. There was just a large battery-powered lantern sitting on an end table. I was thankful for that. Any light seemed to irritate my pounding head.

"What's your name?"

I scowled. "Kelsey Desdemona Renard Cambridge."

"Desdemona?"

"My dad has always had a thing for Shakespeare. He wanted that to be my first name. My mother wouldn't let him."

"Smart woman. I don't remember Desdemona having a happy ending."

I shivered, telling myself it was from the pain but fearing it was from something else.

"Why did you keep your ex-husband's last name?"

I swatted at his hands. "If you are asking me questions to make sure that I don't keel over, you should pick a better one. *That* is none of your business."

Chase stepped around to face me. "You have a pretty large contusion back here, but the skin isn't broken so that's a great sign. In any case, you might have a concussion." He held the lantern in my face.

I winced and held up my hand to block the light.

"Your pupils aren't dilated, that's a good sign, but you're sensitive to light."

"I've just been in a root cellar with no light for who knows how long—of course I'm sensitive to light."

"You had better go to the ER and get checked out. A concussion is nothing to mess around with."

"I can't go to the hospital. I need to be here for the reenactment."

"You were almost not here for the reenactment permanently," he said. "Don't you understand that whoever did this to you could have killed you? This was a warning, and we both know what the warning is about."

"If Wesley is the killer like you and Chief Duffy believe, then this has nothing to do with Maxwell's death."

"Don't lump me in with the chief. I never thought Wesley killed Maxwell, and this just confirms it for me." He lifted the hair from the back of my neck and I shivered.

"Then why did you act like you agreed with your uncle when I told you both about the bees?"

"I didn't act like I agreed with my uncle. You stormed off and didn't give me enough time to explain." He sighed. "Whoever did this doesn't want you involved in Maxwell Cherry's case. He must think you're close to solving it."

I leaned forward to escape his touch. "Well, he's going to be disappointed. I'm nowhere near solving the case."

"You're close enough to make this person nervous."

A shiver ran down my back when he said this, and despite the terrible headache, I popped out of the chair. I ran to the far wall and place my hand on it for support.

"Hey, what's wrong?" His eyes were wide.

"How do I know it wasn't you? Maybe you knocked me on the head and pretended to come to my rescue."

He sighed. "It wasn't me, I promise."

"You promise?" I snapped, holding my head with my right hand. "I'm just supposed to take you word for it. As far as I know, you killed Maxwell and are trying to stop me from finding the truth." If Chase was the killer, I needed to get out of there. But how? My head hurt so much, I didn't know if I could open the door.

"I didn't kill Maxwell," he said slowly, giving each word extra emphasis.

"Prove it," I said.

"I have an alibi, an airtight one."

My mouth fell open.

"I was sleeping at the firehouse the night of the murder. Six other guys can and have vouched for me. The police know this. I finally had to tell them. Candy wouldn't get off my case."

"Why didn't you mention your alibi from the start?" I folded my arms and leaned on the wall.

He ran a hand through his hair. "Because I didn't want my uncle to find out that I didn't sleep here. You don't know how important these reenactments are to him. If he had it his way, he and I would do this every weekend. I give him two weekends a year for this, and by leaving just because I wanted to sleep in a comfortable bed, I was letting him down."

I frowned. "So he didn't know that you left."

He shook his head. "After he went to his tent for the night, I snuck off to the firehouse."

"When was that?" I asked. I still wasn't sure I believed him.

"Ten. Hours before Maxwell was attacked."

I licked my lips. "How did you know I was here? Did you know about the root cellar?"

He walked around the chair and perched on the antique steamer trunk. I bit my tongue to keep from telling him that the trunk was a Barton family artifact too and shouldn't be sat on.

"Will you at least sit down before I answer that question? You look like you are about to fall over."

I did feel a tad wobbly. Against my better judgment, I shuffled back to the chair and sat.

"I saw you come back and tour the Confederate camp," he said. It looked like he blushed when he said this, but I couldn't know for sure in the dim lighting. "After you left the camps, I walked to your cottage because I wanted to talk to you about Wesley and explain that I didn't agree with my uncle that he was the killer. I got to your cottage, and Tiffin barked and barked, but no one answered the door, so then I headed to the Rebel camp to see if anyone had seen where you had gone." He placed his elbows onto his knees. "A Confederate private told me he thought he saw you take one of their lanterns and cross the road into the village. When I got to the village, I found the shattered lantern near the brickyard and knew something terrible must have happened. I was running back to the road when Jason stopped me and told me he knew where you were. He brought me here."

I shivered and wiped cobwebs off of my arms. "Jason?" Jason would be the last person I'd expect to save the day. "Please thank him for me."

"You can thank him yourself," Chase said. "He's right there."

I slowly turned my head, so that I couldn't jar my neck. Jason stood in the corner behind the door like Boo Radley. Seeing him there made me jump, which just made my head hurt more.

Chase frowned. "You do realize you behaved exactly like the person with the flashlight wanted you to."

"You think I was lured out here to be thrown into the Bartons' cellar?"

"I can't think of any other reason that you were knocked on the backside of your head." Chase raked his hand through his hair. "It's pretty stupid to follow someone in the middle of the night. What were you thinking?"

I winced. He was right. I had been really stupid, and I could have paid dearly for it. Hayden could have paid dearly for it. I felt tears in my eyes. I was tired, that was all. I was really tired.

Chase squatted down in front of me, taking both of my hands in his. "Don't cry, okay? We'll get to you the ER. They'll check you out. I don't think they'll keep you overnight as long as you have someone to sit with you to make sure you don't fall back asleep for a few hours."

"I'm not going to the ER," I said. The tears evaporated.

He squeezed my hands harder. "You have to. Between the two of us, I'm the professional when it comes to head injuries, and I say that you have to go."

I scowled at him. I wasn't going. "My dad will sit with me. Poor Dad! He must be terrified over where I've been. What time is it?"

"It's just before midnight."

"Oh, good," I said. I hadn't been in the cellar as long as I feared. "Dad might not be home yet. I don't want him to worry."

Jason pushed off of the wall as if he was set on leaving.

"Jason, wait," I said. "Thank you for what you did."

"You're welcome. I'm glad you're okay." His voice was scratchy from underuse.

Then, because I didn't know if I would get another chance, I said, "Jason, we have to talk about you living in the barn."

He wrapped his arms around his own waist. "I'm sorry. I know it's wrong. I don't have anywhere else to go. You're going to make me leave, aren't you?"

I shook my head. "No. We'll have to talk about it. We will have to find you a better sleeping arrangement. You can't sleep in a barn for the rest of your life."

"I don't mind it." His voice was low.

"You sleep there in the winter?" Chase gaped at him.

"The hay and animals kept me warm enough," Jason said as if it wasn't a big deal.

I shook my head. I couldn't fathom sleeping in the barn on a cold Ohio night. Jason could have easily succumbed to hypothermia.

"Or if it got really cold, I'd sleep in the visitor center."

"You don't have a key," I said. "How did you get in there?"

Jason turned bright red. "I can get in."

I stood on shaky legs. Chase jumped off of the trunk and steadied me. "I'm all right." I hobbled toward Jason. "Thank you, Jason. You may have saved my life."

He nodded. His face was an even deeper shade of red. "Can I go back to the barn now?"

"Sure, but we are going to need to talk about your living arrangements. You can't avoid the conversation forever. I'm pretty persistent."

Chase snorted when I said that. Jason nodded and left through the house's front door. I wrinkled my brow, wondering how my attacker had gotten into Barton House despite its padlock. I guessed if Jason could break into the visitor center, the newest structure, there wasn't any building in the Farm that was truly secure. I wavered on my feet; standing took more out of than I expected. I gritted my teeth. I wasn't going to the hospital. The room was beginning to spin again.

Chase lowered me back onto the chair and touched my back. "Sit until the dizziness passes."

I did what I was told and took some deep breaths. As much as I hated the idea that Hayden was with Krissie, I didn't know what I would have done if I'd known he waiting for me at the cottage. I didn't want him to see me like this.

"We have to talk to my uncle and tell him what happened."

"No," I said, raising my head too quickly. I moaned. Big mistake.

"What do you mean *no*?" Chase stared down at me with folded arms.

"There's been a murder, a fatal accident, and now an attempted murder." I ticked each event off on my fingers. "The chief knows about the first two. I'm afraid if he knows about the third, he'll close the reenactment down completely and we'll never know the truth. He's not going to look for it. He already thinks the case is closed."

"Won't this prove to him that it's not?"

"I don't know. Will it?" I asked. "He's your uncle."

Chase frowned, which I took as my answer. "Is the truth worth being knocked out and left for dead?" he asked.

"I wasn't left for dead. If whoever did this wanted to, they could have killed me while I was unconscious." The idea made my head swim. I bent over my knees again but kept talking. "Like you said, this was a warning."

He grunted. "That didn't work."

"Nope." I struggled to my feet again. "I have to save the Farm." I wobbled.

"Hold still." Chase said, and he put one arm behind my legs and another behind my back.

"What are you doing?" I demanded as he scooped me off of the chair like I was a doll.

"I'm taking you back across the street. You can barely stand up straight. There's no way you can walk over yourself and it'll take too long to run to the visitor center for a wheelchair."

I kicked my legs. "This is so embarrassing. I can't let you carry me back into the reenactment in front of the all the soldiers."

"First of all, it's after midnight, so most of the soldiers are asleep and the rest are drunk. Second of all, you don't have a choice and are far too weak to fight me on it."

I ground my teeth. My anger at Chase helped clear my head like nothing else could.

THIRTY

CHASE CARRIED ME ACROSS the street and after a while, I stopped fighting him. I was just making the trip take longer.

He chuckled when I stopped kicking. "See. It's not so bad, is it?"

I let my full weight fall against his chest. It wasn't so bad, but I wasn't going to tell him that.

"I'm going to take you straight to the hospital."

I kicked him hard with my heel.

"Ouch!" he cried. "I'm really getting tired of that."

"I'm not going to the hospital."

"Okay, if you are going to be so stubborn, I'll take you back to your cottage, but I'm going to stay with you."

"Stay with me?" I asked. "In my home?"

I felt his shoulders rise in a shrug. "That's my offer. Take it or leave it. But if you don't agreed to my terms, I will take you to the hospital even if I have to call your dad and Laura to back me up."

"You wouldn't," I said.

"How do you know?" He winked down at me.

I glared at him. "Fine, but we have to stop at the visitor center for my purse. My house keys are in there."

"Okay," he agreed with a smile.

When we reached the visitor center, Chase set me on a bench outside. I gave him my employee keys from my skirt pocket. "It's in the second drawer of my desk. My office is always unlocked." I might want to rethink leaving my office unlocked from now on since I knew Jason could get into the visitor center anytime he wanted.

"Got it." Chase disappeared around the side of the building to the employee entrance.

The camps were quiet. That was good. Maybe no one saw Chase carry me across the street. As far as I was concerned, no one needed to know about it.

Chase had left his battery-powered lantern with me. I held it up and the light reflected off of something shiny in a huge potted plant by the visitor center's main doors.

Stifling a groan, I stood up and hobbled over to the potted plant. My mouth fell open when I saw what was sitting in the dirt. My cell phone and my radio.

Chase came around of the visitor center with my purse over his shoulder. He carried it like he wore a purse every day.

I held up the radio and cell phone. "Look what I found."

"So?" Chase asked.

I frowned. "I had them when I crossed the street. Whoever hit me over the head must have taken them and put them here for me to find." I shivered.

"So they didn't want you dead, they just wanted to hurt you really bad. And they didn't want you to lose your phone permanently."

Somehow that didn't make me feel better.

Chase bent down as if he were going to pick me up again.

I stepped away and smoothed my dress, which was beyond saving after my time in the root cellar. "I can walk there myself."

"You'll fall over."

"No, I won't." I stumbled.

He whistled. "I don't know if I have ever met a woman as stubborn as you before."

I raised my chin. "I take that as a compliment."

He wrapped my left arm around his waist. "You should. Because I like it."

I frowned.

The trip to the cottage took much longer than it would have had I let Chase carry me, but I wasn't going to give him the satisfaction of asking him to pick me up.

The cottage was dark. Dad wasn't back yet from his party. Knowing my father, the festivities could go into the wee hours of the morning. As soon as we stepped through the white picket fence that surrounded the yard, Tiffin began barking his head off.

Still holding onto me, Chase asked, "Should I be worried about your dog?"

I laughed. "No. Tiffin isn't much of a guard dog. He's never met a person he didn't like."

I unlocked the door. When I turned on the overhead light, I saw both Tiffin and Frankie waiting for me. Tiffin shook his tailless rump and hopped in place, barely able to contain his joy about seeing me. I felt bad for cooping the poor guy up so long in the house. Usually, he has a pretty free range on the Farm after hours, but with the reenactors here, I felt it better to keep him in the house at night.

Frankie sat beside him and narrowed his one good eye. He kneaded his claws into the rug.

"Okay," Chase said as he stepped into the house. "Forget the dog. Should I be worried about the cat?"

"Yes. That's Frankie. And you should always worry about Frankie."

"Duly noted."

I found myself smiling. "Frankie is Hayden's cat, and Hayden is the only one he loves. He tolerates the rest of us for my son's sake, but don't cross him." I realized that Chase still had his arm wrapped around me. I slipped out of his grasp and walked over the couch.

Chase sidestepped Frankie and came into the living room too.

I looked down at my skirt. The dress was mud streaked. I hoped all that was on it was mud. I knew I should go upstairs and change, but not at the moment.

"Hey." Chase shook me. "Don't close your eyes. You can't fall asleep."

"I'm just resting my eyes." I murmured. My eyes remained closed.

"Yeah, right." He shook my shoulder a little more forcefully. "Wake up."

I opened one eye and suspected that I looked a lot like Frankie. "There's something I don't understand. What about the stolen canteen and musket that Wesley supposedly took from the Confederate camp? How is that connected to the murder?"

"It's not. It was a prank. One of the Confederate privates hid the canteen and other items in Wesley's tent just to cause trouble. After Wesley died, the guy went to my uncle and made a full confession. I think he did it half because he felt bad that Wesley died and half because he was afraid that his fingerprints were all over Wesley's tent."

Another dead end. My head lulled to the side. I was so tired.

"Hey, you need to wake up." Chase shook my shoulder.

I squinted at him. "I'm going to ask the police about your alibi. You know that, don't you?"

He smiled. "I wouldn't expect anything less."

I frowned at that. Maybe Chase was telling the truth about sleeping at the firehouse since he wasn't concerned about me confirming it. "I'll stay awake if you tell me how you know Maxwell."

He sat beside me couch. "Let's not get into that."

"You want me to stay awake, don't you?" I opened my eyes.

"Fine. But I'm going to need coffee to tell this story and if I'm going to be able to stay awake to make sure you don't go to sleep. Care if I make some?"

I shook my head. Ouch. "No," I said. I needed to remember that moving my head was a bad idea.

The main floor of the cottage was just one big room, so I could see him from my post on the sofa. "There's coffee in the freezer. Sugar should be on the counter and creamer is in the refrigerator door."

He smiled around the freezer door. "Don't worry. I got this. I know my way around a kitchen."

He started the coffee. I calmed as I heard the soothing sound of water bubbling in the machine. He leaned on the kitchen counter.

"So, how do you know Maxwell?" I asked.

He opened cupboards, and when he found the right one, removed two mugs. He held them up. "Batman mugs?"

I frowned. "I have a son."

He grinned. "I like it. You're full of surprises, Ms. Cambridge."

"You're avoiding my question."

"Yep." He turned and filled the mugs with coffee, then added cream and sugar to both. He carried the mugs over to me on the couch and handed me the one with Robin on it.

"How did you know I like cream and sugar in my coffee?"

He laughed. "So suspicious. I could just tell you were a cream and sugar girl."

I frowned into my coffee, which was just how I liked it. I found that annoying.

He chuckled. "And when you told me where everything was, you told the location of the cream and sugar, from which I concluded, rightly, that you liked both in your coffee."

"Oh." I sipped from the mug. It was perfect. "Now, answer my question."

He sat on the opposite end of the couch and turned toward me. "I knew Maxwell because he swindled me on a business deal."

"I thought you were an EMT." I set the mug on the coffee table and pulled a blanket off the back of the couch and wrapped it around my shoulders, dirty dress be damned.

"I am, but I inherited a nice nest egg from my parents. Both of them died in their sixties and I got all the money they had socked away for their retirement. My father was thrifty and worried about having enough when he retired." He stared into coffee. "He worked hard and never got to enjoy it."

"I'm sorry about your parents."

He wouldn't meet my eyes. "Thank you. They were good, honest people. My father would be disappointed with me and what I've done with everything they had saved."

"What was that?" I asked. I was no longer feeling the least bit tired.

He frowned. "I knew Maxwell from charity fundraisers at the firehouse for the paramedics, and he told me once that if I ever came into money, he would help me invest it, which would triple my return. When I got the nest egg from my parents, I called him. That was four years ago."

Four years ago, I thought. That's when Maxwell and Jamie Houck bought the eyesore property on Kale Road. I cupped my mug in my hands. "You invested your money in the mall that wasn't on Kale Road."

He nodded. "It was stupid and something my father would have never dreamed of doing. Dad never took risks with anything."

"How much did you lose?"

"All of it," he said matter-of-factly.

I winced. "Can you get any of it back?"

He shook his head. "I hired a lawyer and tried to sue Maxwell, but he was too powerful. His lawyer crushed mine. I guess there was this tiny clause in the investment contract that I didn't read or fully understand that said if things with Kale Road went south, Maxwell and his partners weren't responsible."

I sat up straighter. "So you have a good motive for murder."

He shrugged as if I'd said something about the weather. "Sure, I did, but that was four years ago. If I was going to kill Maxwell, I would have done it four years ago when I was furious about it. Now, I've accepted it. I don't like it, but I've learned from it."

"So do you know Jamie Houck? He's reenacting her under a different name."

"No. I never met Jamie, only Maxwell. I can't say I really want to talk to him about any of this, though."

"Thank you for telling me," I murmured.

He smiled. "You're easy to talk to, even if you are prickly at times."

I narrowed my eyes. "Prickly?"

The front door opened and my father waltzed in. He was still wearing his ghost costume and clearly running high on a great performance. He pulled up short when he saw me on the couch. "Kelbel, you didn't have to wait up for me." He spotted Chase. "Oh, you're not alone. You have a man in the house."

Chase shot out his seat like someone had jabbed a pin into his backside. When he did, my father seemed to notice Chase's sweatpants and T-shirt. That somehow made it worse.

"Dad, this is Chase Wyatt. He's one of the reenactors."

"Oh!" my father said, sounding and looking like a ghost.

"Sir, this isn't what it looks like."

"What does it look like?" my father asked.

Good question.

"I had an accident in the village after Laura brought me home from the play. Chase was sitting with me to make sure I didn't fall asleep."

"Why wouldn't you want to fall asleep?"

Chase quickly explained about finding me in the root cellar and about my injuries. I was grateful when he didn't mention Jason.

"Oh, my," Dad said. He stepped forward and extended his hand to Chase. He shook it and then yanked Chase into a hug. "Thank you for saving my daughter."

Chase appeared taken aback for the first time since I had met him. "You're welcome."

Dad released him. "How much longer does she need to stay up?"

"It's probably safe for her to go to sleep now."

"How is she?" Dad asked Chase.

"She'll be fine. I don't really think she was in any real danger of a concussion. She was able to tell me her name and what happened. She wasn't disoriented at all."

I gritted my teeth as I listened to this.

Chase continued, "It's been almost four hours since she was hit on the head."

"What was she hit with?"

Tiffin whimpered and licked the hand that hung loosely at my side.

Chase opened his mouth to answer.

"Hey, I can answer for myself," I snapped. "I might not be able to stand up straight, but my mouth isn't broken."

Dad grinned. "Oh good, they didn't knock the spunk out of you. I would hate for you to lose your spunk." He lowered his voice. "She got that from her mother. My Pamela could sass anyone."

"She still has more than her share. I'm not sure what I think about it being heredity."

I narrowed my eyes at Chase, but considering my woozy condition, I think it just looked like my eyes were rolling back into my head. "I was hit on the back of the head with a brick."

"How do you know it was a brick?" Chase asked.

"It felt like a brick." I stood. "And if Chase says I can go to sleep, I'm ready for bed."

"Let's get you to your room before you keel over," Dad said.

Dad and Chase helped me up the stairs. Again, I was thankful that Hayden wasn't there to see me. I prayed that Eddie didn't find out about this. It would just be more ammunition for him and Krissie, the teenaged bride, to take Hayden away from me.

Dad flicked on the overhead light in my room. I covered my eyes. He turned it off and switched on my bedside lamp. "Better?"

Much to my horror, I whimpered, "yes." I shuffled to my bed and sat down. Ahh, that was better. A little rest and I would be able to finish out the reenactment tomorrow. I didn't know if I would be able to find out who killed Maxwell. Suddenly, I felt dizzy again. This entire situation was unreal.

"I'll go get you a glass of water." Dad left the room.

Chase picked up the Spider-Man stuffed toy that sat in the middle of my bed. "Cute."

"It's my son's." Tears rushed to my eyes. I looked away.

"Hey, he's safe." He brushed my hair out of my face.

"I know." I wasn't going to tell Chase my fears that Hayden was safer with his father. I never thought I would think that, but being knocked over the head and thrown into a root cellar gave me a new perspective on my job.

"Sit back," Chase said.

"What?"

"Sit back, so I can take off your shoes."

"I can take off my own shoes," I said stubbornly. I leaned over, and the world tilted on its axis.

Chase knelt. "Sure you can. Sit back." Chase removed my shoes.

I made a motion like I was going to stop him, but he was right, I was a mess. But I would be better with a little sleep.

"Sit back," he ordered.

"You shouldn't have to do this."

He looked up at me from a kneeling position. "Can't you let someone else take care of you for once?"

"I'm not very good at that," I admitted. I blinked. "I'm a mom."

"Moms need to be taken care of too."

"I guess," I said groggily.

"Do you want to change into pajamas?"

"No!" I yelped, covering my chest. No matter how bad of a killer headache I had, I wasn't going to let Chase help me change my clothes.

The corners of his mouth quirked up. "I wasn't going to help you with that."

I blushed and hated myself for this. "No, this is fine. I'll just sleep in my clothes. This dress is very comfortable." *I'll throw the whole mess into the wash tomorrow.*

He swung my legs onto the bed and settled me back against the pillows. "All right. Get some sleep."

As soon as I was prone on my comfortable bed, my eyelids drooped closed. Sleep. That was all I needed, and then I could face whatever tomorrow brought. It couldn't be worse than today, which included a slain reenactor and a near-death experience. No, tomorrow would be a breeze. I smiled to myself. "Good. Sleep is good." My eyelids fluttered opened for a moment. There was something important I thought I had to say. "I'm still mad at you, you know."

He looked down at me. "Oh?"

"I'm still mad at you for not sharing the information that you had about the bees. That wasn't very nice, Chase. What if I had done that to you?"

He smiled. "I wouldn't like it."

"Right." My eyes closed.

I may have imagined it, but it felt like someone kissed my forehead before I drifted off to sleep.

THIRTY-ONE

THE BUGLER PLAYED THE reveille in the morning, and I could understand why someone may be tempted to murder another human being. If the bugler had in my bedroom at that very moment, he wouldn't have stood a chance.

Tiffin went to the window and barked in the direction of the encampments.

"Tiff," I muttered into my pillow. "That does not help."

Frankie then jumped onto my pillow and started to meow about his breakfast. He knew I was awake since I had spoken to Tiffin.

I felt disgusting from sleeping in my dirty dress, the same clothes that I had worn when I crawled around the Barton Farm root cellar. My comforter would need to be washed. My tongue felt too big for my mouth, and my teeth were fuzzy. I didn't dare look into a mirror until I showered and brushed my teeth, and even then my reflection might cause a horror movie–worthy scream.

The problem with the cottage was that the bathroom with the shower was on the first floor. There was only a tiny half bath on the second level, where Hayden's and my bedrooms were. Cynthia had it added before we moved into the cottage. She would have paid the expense for a full bath or at least a shower, but there wasn't enough room without giving up one of the two bedrooms, and that would never work. Dad slept in the small bedroom off the kitchen during summers. In actuality, I suspected that it was meant to be a pantry and not a bedroom.

Shower. That's what I needed: a shower. Toothbrush. I'd keep my thoughts to a singular mission until I was coherent enough to move it up to complete sentences.

Then I remembered Chase having been in my room, removing my shoes, kissing me on the forehead goodnight … or not. The last part may have been a dream.

I couldn't stand wearing the dress a second longer, so I removed it and pulled on my robe. As I walked down the stairs I was happy the world was no long spinning when I turned my head. Excellent progress. On the first floor, I placed a tentative hand to the back of skull. The bump was still there, but it felt smaller. Then again, I might just be telling myself that to feel better. It might have no longer seemed like the world was turning, but I had a splitting headache. On the way to the bathroom, I would stop in the kitchen for aspirin. I kept all the medicine on the highest shelf in there because it was the one place Hayden couldn't get into.

Dad was sitting at the kitchen counter drinking a cup of tea, but he wasn't the person I was staring at. Chase lay sprawled on my couch on his stomach. He had his face buried in my throw pillows.

"What is *he* doing here?" I hissed.

"Chase?" Dad raised a bushy eyebrow.

"Is there another man sleeping in my house?" I downed four aspirin with a swig of water from the tap.

"I let the guy crash here. He's been sleeping on the ground for the last three nights." Dad finished his cup of tea. "And he did save your life, so I think we owe him a good night's rest."

"Why didn't you tell me?" I asked.

Dad's brow furrowed. "You were dead to the world."

"Well, wake him up and tell him to go back to his tent."

Dad hopped off the barstool. "Why don't you wake him up? He'd like that." Dad folded the morning newspaper under his arm and head out the front door to read it in his lawn chair.

Why don't I wake him up?

Chase's T-shirt was pushed halfway up his back. I tried not to stare at his bare skin and failed. I picked up the other throw pillow, which had fallen on the floor.

I tickled his nose with the fringe.

He waved it away. "Reload your muskets, men," he murmured into the pillow.

Was he reliving a reenactment in his sleep? I dropped the pillow and bumped his leg with my knee. "Chase, wake up."

"I'm not going to make it. Leave me, boys," he said dreamily.

I inched toward his head. "Chase. Chase, wake up. You are having a bad dream."

"It's an angel come to collect me from the battlefield," he murmured with a hint of smile on his face.

Faker.

I punched him in the side.

"Ow!" He sat up and rubbed the spot where I hit him.

"Oh, I didn't hit you that hard."

He opened one eye. "I like the robe."

I stepped back and wrapped my arms around my chest. "Don't you have a war to fight?" I stomped to bathroom.

"The war doesn't start until I get there," he called after me.

That I believed.

By the time I got out of the shower, Chase was gone. I told myself I was relieved not disappointed.

Dressed and feeling more human, I braided my hair. Before going back downstairs and despite the early hour, I had to make a phone call. I called the New Hartford police department and asked to speak with Detective Brandon. I told the operator it was about Maxwell Cherry's murder, and I was patched right through to the detective's cell phone.

"Brandon," the detective barked.

"Detective Brandon, this is Kelsey Cambridge."

"What do you want, Ms. Cambridge?"

Apparently the police detective didn't have time for pleasantries. "Is it true that Chase Wyatt has an alibi for the night of Maxwell's murder?" I decided to ask the detective and not Chase's police chief uncle about his alibi because I suspected that she wouldn't lie to cover for him.

There was a paused, and then she said, "Yes. We have six eyewitnesses who put him at the firehouse at the time of the murder."

"He's not the killer," I whispered.

"No. Disappointing, isn't it?" she said. "I told you he was trouble. I suggest that you run as far away from him as possible."

I was still mulling over my conversation with the detective when I went downstairs again. Dad was back in the kitchen. "I made you breakfast," he said. "Monster pancakes." He presented me with a plate of pancakes. He had drawn a monster's face on the top pancake out of fruit and chocolate syrup.

"Dad, you make these for Hayden. I'm not a child."

"You're still my child. I can make these for you if I want to. It's a father's right."

I smiled. "Thanks." I picked up one of the pancakes and ate it dry. Before I knew it, the plate was empty. I had been hungry.

"I knew you would be hungry. Did you eat dinner last night?" Dad asked.

I thought about it. "I don't remember." It was difficult to remember to feed myself when Hayden wasn't around. I sighed. I wouldn't see my son that day at all. Even before Eddie announced his engagement to Krissie, he and I had agreed that Hayden would stay with Eddie on Sunday because I would be busy with the last day of the reenactment all day, and the Blue and Gray Ball all night. I sipped from the glass of milk that my father had paired with the monster pancakes. The ball. I hoped everything would go off without a hitch. I had planned to go over all the details last night after the play, but under the circumstances, that hadn't happened.

"I need to check on the plans for the ball." I took a gulp of milk.

"Take it easy, Kelbel. You had quite a scare last night."

"I'll be fine. I might not be up to going into dark confined spaces for a while, but other than that, I'm great." I shivered and wondered if I would be able to go into the Barton House root cellar ever again.

He pursed his lips.

"How bad do I look?" My voice sounded hoarse.

"Like you got kicked by one of the oxen." He grinned.

I laughed but stopped abruptly because it made my head hurt.

"I'm worried about you. I don't want you taking these kinds of chances anymore."

I searched in my cupboard for the largest mug that I could find. When I didn't find one that would work, I selected a deep soup bowl and filled it with coffee. After a sip of the scorching liquid, I was refreshed enough to return to the conversation. "Dad, I have to save the Farm." I grimaced. I sounded like one of Hayden's action hero cartoons. "And," I added, "I need to find out who killed Maxwell for Cynthia. She's done so much for Hayden and me. This is how I can repay her."

"You're stubborn. I know." He shook his head. "You're as bad as your mother."

"I'm glad."

"I love that about you." His eyes turned downward. "I loved that about her too. But you can't put yourself in harm's way. Think about Hayden."

"I always think about Hayden."

Dad pursed his lips.

"I won't take any more stupid risks." I set the soup bowl on the counter and hugged him. "I promise."

"I've enjoyed the reenactment, but all things considered, I'm glad this is the last day of it."

"Me too," I admitted. I walked to the front door and removed Tiffin's leash from the peg on the wall. "I'm going to check on the grounds."

Dad sighed. "Be careful."

"I will," I promised.

Tiffin ran ahead of me on the pebbled path, and then he ran back and ahead again. The poor dog had been cooped up in the house way too long. I headed straight for the visitor center. Chase, wearing his Union medic uniform, sat on the bench outside the visitor center, holding two steaming blue tin cups of coffee. I stopped in front of him. "What are you doing here?"

He grinned. "Waiting for you."

"Why?" I asked as Tiffin ran circles around us and the bench.

"Primarily, to keep a close eye on you, and secondly, to expose you to some decent coffee unlike that sludge that you subjected me to last night." He wrinkled his nose.

"Are you insulting my coffee?" I asked.

"You bet I am." He handed me the mug.

I accepted it. I never turned down a good cup of coffee. "This is good," I admitted.

"The best Colombia has to offer. I order it direct."

I arched an eyebrow. "Would a Union medic during the Civil War have access to great Colombian coffee?"

He winked. "We'll just keep it our little secret."

"Another secret."

"Sure. You made me promise I wouldn't tell my uncle about you getting knocked over the head last night, didn't you?"

I sipped from the cup. "Oh, right." I paused. "I spoke with Detective Brandon this morning. You will be happy to know that she confirmed your alibi for me."

"Ah, I'm guessing she hated doing it." He sipped from his mug. "Did she say anything else?"

"She told me to run away from you," I said.

He furrowed his brow. "And will you follow her advice?"

"I haven't decided yet." I held up the cup. "Thanks for the coffee." I continued down the pebbled path toward the village.

A second later, I realized Chase was following me.

I turned. "What are you doing?"

"I'm coming with you."

"You don't need to. The sun is up. No one is going to come out of the woods and knock me on the head in the light of day." I quickened my pace.

He walked ahead of me and started to walk backward so that he could face me. This was getting to be a habit. His forage cap was low over his eyes and his cartridge bag thumped against his hips with each step. "I wouldn't count on that. No one is in the village at this time of day. Besides, Tiffin wants me to come."

Tiffin barked in agreement.

I frowned. "Did the two of you talk about this last night when I was sleeping?"

"Yep," Chase said.

Tiffin danced in place.

"Fine," I mumbled and kept walking.

Tiffin and Chase fell in beside me.

"Where are you going exactly?" Chase asked when we reached the road.

"Back to the scene of the crime."

Chase and Tiffin followed me to the brickyard. "Where did you find the broken lantern?" I asked.

Chase scanned the ground. "It was right about here, but it looks like it's been cleaned up."

"Jason?" I asked.

Chase frowned. "Maybe." He squatted on the path.

I squatted next to him and ran my index finger along the pebbles, looking for any evidence of the lantern. A glass shard plunged into my fingertip. "Ahh!" I cried waving my hand.

Chase caught my wrist. "Hold still."

I relaxed. He removed the tiny shard from my index finger. It was hard to believe something that tiny could hurt so much.

"When was the last time you had a tetanus shot?"

I winced. "Last year."

"That's good news or I would threaten to take you to the hospital again." He opened his ammunition bag and removed an antiseptic towelette, antibiotic cream, and a Band-Aid. "I suspected that I would need these today, especially if I was hanging out with you." He opened the towelette. "The cut is not deep, but we still need to patch you up." He quickly cleaned and bandaged my finger.

Standing up, I noticed a spot of blood on my Farm polo shirt.

He stood and put his first-aid supplies away. "That's going to stain."

"I have a five-year-old, I can get any stain out. Let's look at Barton House." I turned so that he wouldn't see my face. I told myself the tingling in my hand was the loss of blood not from his touch.

I started toward Barton House and unlocked the padlock with my key. In the living room, the ladder-back chair was still in the middle of the room where I had sat on it and the hatch was open. "Good thing we came back," I said. "We forgot to shut the hatch to the root cellar."

Tiffin lay on the threshold of the open door. He knew that he wasn't allowed inside any of the historic buildings.

"We should take a look down there to make sure there aren't any clues to who may have hit you."

"Good idea." I went to the supply closet in the next room, the Bartons' dining room. It was where we kept supplies for the whole village, so I knew there would be an industrial-sized flashlight there. The flashlight was exactly where I expected it to be, hanging from a nail just inside the door.

Returning to the living room, I hesitated over the opening in the floor.

Chase took the flashlight from my hand. "Let me."

I frowned. I didn't want to appear weak, but I really didn't want to climb back down into the hole. Before I could protest, Chase lowered himself through the hatch. He was only gone for a couple of minutes. The root cellar was tiny and wouldn't take long to survey with a strong flashlight.

Chase reappeared. "There's nothing down there." He climbed out of the hole without my help.

"I don't know if I'm relieved or disappointed."

"Makes sense to be a little bit of both," he said as he lowered the hatch over the hole. "And I guess I wasn't being completely honest."

I froze. "Why not?" I asked.

"The cellar wasn't completely empty."

"What did you find?"

"A pair of red eyes." He moved the heavy trunk over the closed hatch. The root cellar was again hidden from visitors. "Could have been a raccoon, but you might want the place checked for rats. That would be my best guess. By the look of its eyes, it was Chihuahua-sized."

I shivered.

THIRTY-TWO

"No, no, no," I said moving across the green, waving my trusty notebook.

Two large men holding up a pole to erect the food tent for ball froze. The pole tilted at a diagonal.

I waved at them. "The food tent goes ten yards back."

The men sighed and lowered the pole and carried it to the place I pointed out. When the food tent was finished, all the tents would be erect. While those men worked on raising the small tent, another team of men laid the wooden floor for the dancing in the middle of the large tent. Others set up round tables that could seat eight and high tops that could comfortably accommodate six people standing. I hoped there would be enough tables and food for everyone. I ordered extra of everything, and so far only a handful had canceled their RSVPs. This would be the single biggest event I had ever pulled off.

It was midmorning and despite the misplaced pole, the Blue and Gray Ball was coming together more smoothly than I expected.

Except for my audience. Chase sat a few yards away on a park bench next to the church watching all the proceedings. He had followed me around all morning. At first I thought it was cute, but the cuteness was waning.

I marched over to him. "Chase, you need to leave."

"What?" he asked looking up.

"You need to leave. You are going to miss your battle."

"Bah," he said, waving his hands. "I'm keeping an eye on you."

"You don't have to. There are forty people here setting up for the ball. My assistant Ashland is here."

"Ashland won't be any good if someone tried to knock you over the head with a tent pole."

I pulled him to his feet. "Go. The morning battle starts in fifteen minutes. Get over there. You're making me nervous."

He grinned. "I make you nervous?"

"Go."

He sighed. "All right. I suppose my regiment needs me." He winked and finally sauntered off.

After Chase left, Laura walked up to me with her period sunhat dangling from her hand. "What was Medic Hotness doing on that bench all morning?"

"Watching me. He was worried someone was going to knock me over the head again or some other ridiculousness." I had told Laura about last night when she arrived at the Farm. As my best friend, she was required to hear about my near-death experiences.

Laura put a hand to her chest. "He's your knight in blue wool blend."

"Can we leave the dramatics to my father?" I asked. "He's the professional."

She laughed. "Whether you like it or not, I think Chase's chasing you is adorable."

"Chasing me?"

She laughed. "You've spent too much of your time wasted on Eddie to know the signs."

I frowned. Was she right? It felt strange to be pursued by a man, and I realized that I never had been. Eddie and I fell in love like you fall in love with familiarity and comfort, but it certainly didn't involve a chase. Our love could have been better described as a stumble.

"I need to get back to work."

She grinned. "Got you thinking, didn't I?" She headed back to Barton House, swinging her hat as she went. She called over her shoulder, "Don't forget. I'll be at the cottage at five sharp to get you ready for the ball." She twirled. "You'll be a fine lady."

I winced. As much as I loved history, I didn't like being part of it. Thank goodness Hayden wasn't there to see me stick out my tongue. He would never let me forget it.

I went back to supervising the food tent. As I went around the village green, checking on the flower arrangements and number of chairs, I felt Ashland staring at me the whole time. Every time I turned around, she was there. I was used to Ashland shadowing me and following me from place to place, but this was to the extreme. I showed the party company where I wanted the candelabras to be in the dance tent and spun around. I hit Ashland in the face with my braid.

"Oh," she cried and rubbed her nose.

"Are you all right?"

"I'm fine," she said quickly. Her notebook was at the ready so that she could jot down notes on directions I might have.

I folded my arms. "You're not fine. You've been acting strangely all morning. Ashland, what's wrong?"

"Wrong? Nothing's wrong," my assistant said.

"You've been staring at me all morning and following me."

She looked at the ground. "You keep touching the back of your head. Are you okay?"

I dropped my hand from the back of my head, not realizing I'd even put it there. Maybe she was right and I had been touching my head all day. I was paranoid about the size of the lump. Thank goodness for my thick brown hair, a gift from my mother, or I would have had a complex about it. I sighed. "I had an accident last night."

"An accident?"

I explained to her about the brick attack and the Bartons' root cellar.

Her hand flew to her mouth. "You could've been killed."

I shook my head. "Whoever hit me just wanted to scare me."

Her bottom lip stuck out. "Why didn't you tell me?"

I smoothed the white linen tablecloth over the table. "I didn't want you to worry."

The radio on my hip crackled. "Kelsey. Kelsey come in? It's Judy."

I removed the radio from my belt. "What is it, Judy?"

"We need you on this side of road." It was hard to hear her over the noise in the background.

"Why? What's going on?"

"There seems to be an incident going on with the reenactors."

"What kind of incident?" I asked. The last time I got a call like this, there was a dead body in the middle of the battlefield.

"I don't know," she said. "Just get over here quick."

"On my way." I clipped my radio back on my belt. Couldn't we get through one mock battle without an altercation? "I need to go to the battlefield," I said to no one in particular. I started for the road. I looked over my shoulder to find Ashland following me. "Ashland, stay here and supervise the setup."

She kept following me. "But what if you need my help?"

"I do need your help. Here at the tents."

She frowned but turned back to the tents, and I broke into a run.

The oxen stared at me as I raced past their yard. Jason stood with them and watched too, open mouthed.

I hit the pebbled path on the other side of Maple Grove Lane at a sprint. A large group gathered at the edge of the battlefield closest to the camps. I pushed my way through the crowd.

Some teenagers were yelling, "Fight, fight, fight!"

Oh boy. This wasn't good. This wasn't good at all.

I peeked around the arm of a barrel-chested man and saw the back of Chase and just the side of another man in a Confederate uniform.

I slid around the man. Sometimes it paid to be small. Now I was just two rows back from the arguments. I could now see Jamie Houck with his hands on his hips.

Chase balled his fists at his side. "My parents worked hard for that money."

"We're talking about millions of dollars lost." Jamie glared at Chase. "Your pitiful little investment isn't even worth my time!"

Chase decked the man in the jaw, and Jamie flew backward into the split-rail fence. He slid down a fence post and lay on his side.

THIRTY-THREE

"DAD," A PRE-TEEN BOY said. "This is awesome. You didn't tell me that there would be real fights at these museum things. I totally would've come before!"

I didn't wait to hear his father's reply. "Excuse me, excuse me," I said as I forced my way through the crowd. "Excuse me. Director of Barton Farm coming through."

Finally, I broke through the cluster of people.

Chase stared at Jamie with his mouth open, as if he couldn't believe what he had just done.

Jamie rubbed his chin. "I'm going to sue you. After I'm done with you, you won't have a penny left."

Chase's uncle, in his full Confederate uniform, stepped forward. "Now Sergeant Adams, you wouldn't want to do that and put at risk your place in my regiment, would you? You did swindle my *nephew* after all, so I'd say that was just cause to lay you flat on your back. But what do I know? I'm only the general of this Confederate Army and the police chief of New Hartford. I can't imagine what I think accounts for much."

Jamie Houck/Henry Adams kept a hold on his jaw as if he thought it would become detached from his face. "H-he's your nephew?"

"Sure is. My beloved late sister was his mother. I'm disappointed to hear that you have no concern for my sister and brother-in-law's hard-earned money." The police chief leaned forward and extended his hand to Jamie.

After a moment's hesitation, Jamie took his general's hand. "Thank you, sir," he said.

"I'm sorry," Chase said. "I shouldn't have let my temper get the best of me like that."

"Oh, it's all right," Jamie said as if he hadn't threatened to sue Chase two minutes ago. "I can understand why you were upset."

"You see," the police chief said. "That wasn't so hard to make up, now was it?"

Both younger men shook their heads.

The crowd, seeing that there wouldn't be any more punches thrown, started to disperse.

"Let's resume the battle, shall we?" Chief Duffy asked.

"Wait," I said.

Chase turned and frowned when he saw me standing there.

"Adams," I said, calling Jamie by his reenactor name. "Where were you when Maxwell was killed?"

"Oh, Ms. Cambridge," the New Hartford police chief said. "I thought we put all that murder business to rest."

"It's a simple question," I said.

281

"It is," the chief agreed. "But it is also one I can answer. Adams was with me. We had a late council of war that night. It went into the wee hours of the morning. Sergeant Adams had nothing to do with Maxwell's death. I can vouch for that."

Jamie nodded. "That's right."

My shoulders drooped. An alibi doesn't get any more airtight than one that comes directly from the chief of police. I wouldn't give up that easily. "Chief Duffy, what about the insulin used to subdue Maxwell?" I asked, pulling him aside.

He sighed. "What about it?"

"Detective Brandon took a needle and insulin sample from my father."

He nodded.

"Did Officer Parker tell you about Private Darling's ruined insulin? I discovered it last night and asked him to tell you."

"He did, but I already knew about Private Darling leaving the reenactment because of that. He's in my regiment, after all. Of course I had his insulin tested as well as your father's. Interestingly enough, they both use Humulin R and the same prescription of needle, both of which are consistent with what was used on Maxwell. Toxicology will have to confirm that, which takes time. It turns out your father and Darling even go to the same diabetes specialist in Akron." He smiled.

I bit the inside of my lip as I digested this information.

"Now," Chief Duffy said. "I know if might seem like it, but I don't sit around and twiddle my thumbs when it comes to murder. Since your father claims not to be missing any medicine or syringes, I suspect our killer stole Private Darling's insulin. Darling said—because I did track him down and ask him what happened—that three doses of his insulin were missing. The killer tripled the dose he gave Maxwell." He paused as if to let that sink in. "All of the regular reenactors, including Wesley, knew about Darling's condition. We took it upon ourselves to keep an eye on him during the battles."

So my discovery of Private Darling's insulin proved nothing. In fact, it made the case against Wesley that much worse. Could I be wrong? Had Wesley killed Maxwell? I rejected the idea.

The chief patted my arm and said in a low voice only I could hear. "It will all become clear. You'll see."

I stared at him, and he winked at me.

"Now, to battle," Chief Duffy said. Still with a hand on his face, Jamie followed his general to the Confederate encampment.

When they had gone, I grabbed Chase by the arm and pulled him away from the split-rail fence.

"Hey," he protested. "I thought you wanted me to participate in today's battle."

"That was before you decided to deck someone. Come with me." I pulled him toward the visitor center.

Chase was three times my size. I couldn't pull him anywhere that he didn't want to go, so he came willingly.

We entered the visitor center through the main entrance. Judy was on the other side of the door. She had a hand on her cheek. "What is the world coming to? It just seems like one thing after another for this reenactment!"

Truer words had never been spoken.

I led Chase to my office. When we got inside, I pointed to the empty chair that the chief sat in just two days before to question me about Maxwell's murder. Had that only been two days ago?

It seemed like months—or years. So much had happened in such a short amount of time. It also seemed like that the North and South encampments had always been here. It would feel strange when they packed up to leave the next day, but it would also be a relief. There were many things that were going to change for the reenactment next year—and there *would* be a next year. Despite murder and brick attacks, the Farm had made more in the last three days than we had made in the entire previous season. Next year, I would be more careful who I invited to take part in the reenactment.

Chase had a light scratch over his right eyebrow that I just noticed. It gave him a roguish look.

"Did Jamie hit you?"

Chase shook his head. "I got this during the battle. I got a little too close to a Rebel's bayonet. Reenacting is a full-contact hobby."

"What was going on out there?" I leaned on the side of my desk.

"I don't know. I saw him in the field and just sort of snapped. I didn't know Adams was Jamie Houck until my uncle told me right before the battle. I figured I'd ask him if he knew that Maxwell's business partner was at the Farm, and he told me Jamie's alias. Talking to you last night about how I wasted all my parents' money brought up all those hard feelings, feelings I thought I was over." He placed his head in his hands. "When there was a break in the action, I went over to Jamie just to talk. I thought—I don't know what I thought—maybe I hoped that he had a way to get my investment back." His hands balled into fists. "But he turned out to be as pompous and egotistical as Maxwell. I never intended to hit him. I was going to walk away, but then he said something that made me react..."

"I heard," I said. "I can't have people hitting each other on the Farm, and you're really lucky your uncle stepped in there. I have little doubt that Jamie would have sued you if your uncle hadn't asserted his authority."

His face fell into hands again. "I know."

I pushed off of the desk. "I need to get back to the village. You can hang in here as long as you want to calm down."

He looked up. "I could come with you."

"Bad idea. I have too much to do and you are a distraction."

He smiled at this.

I fled my office before he could make a smart remark. After checking in with Judy at the ticket counter, I went outside. The sound of cannon fire ripped through the air. The Rebels charged the Yankees on the field.

As I walked back to the village green to check on the tents, I stopped. Portia stood under an oak tree near the path, combing her ponytail with her fingers over and over again. I hurried over to her. "Portia, what are you doing here?"

"I—I don't—I just felt like I need to come here, close to where..." She couldn't finish her thought.

"Can I get you something to eat or drink? You are really pale."

"No. I haven't eaten in a few days. I don't think my appetite will ever come back after what I've done."

"What do you mean?" My pulse quickened. Was she about to confess to Maxwell's murder?

"I left the man I loved for money and now he's dead because of it."

"You mean Wesley."

She nodded and dabbed at her eyes with the ends of her hair. "I didn't love Maxwell," she whispered as if we were in confession and I was the priest. "I never loved him, but I thought I could be happy with him because of what he could provide me."

I chewed on the inside of my cheek.

She looked up at me with her big eyes as if she could read my mind. "That doesn't mean I killed him."

I folded my arms. "I didn't say that."

She tugged on her hair. "You thought it."

I didn't deny that. "Where did you and Cynthia go after the play last night?"

"We went back to the estate and had a late dinner. Cynthia ate, and I watched her eat. Nothing appealed to me. Then we went to our separate rooms."

"What time was that?"

She thought for a moment. "We finished dinner around nine. Cynthia likes to take her time when she eats. I don't mind. I have nothing else to do and nowhere else to go."

That meant they were still eating dinner when someone hit me on the back of my head. It would be easy to check her story out with Cynthia.

"Why do you ask? Did something happen?"

I shook my head. "It's not important." The lie slipped easily off of my tongue.

"I should let you go. I know that you have a lot to do for tonight's ball. Cynthia's looking forward to it."

A crack of cannon fire interrupted our conversation. Portia and I both looked over at the battlefield. This time the Union made an assault on the Confederate Army. The Rebel line fell back behind their makeshift trenches."

Portia shook her head. "I don't understand why anyone would want to pretend killing people like that. Don't you think it's horrible?"

I watched as a Confederate fell in a spectacular death scene. "War is horrible," I said. "That's why museums and historic sites like this one are important. They are here to remind us of our past, both good and bad. It's the only way to learn from it and avoid the same mistakes. Most of the time, history repeating itself is a very bad thing."

She frowned. I hadn't convinced her.

"If you'd like, you can come with me to village. We're in the middle of setting up for the ball. I could use some extra hands," I said, knowing that Chase had offered his help and I had turned him down. The difference was that Portia didn't make me nervous; Chase did, and I kicked myself for letting him know that.

"It would be nice to feel useful. Are you sure I won't be in the way?"

"You won't be in the way. Let's go."

She followed me down the pebbled path, and the sound of the guns and cannon fire faded but didn't completely fall away.

Portia was quiet while we walked. She said finally, "I wasn't the only girl to fall under the spell of the comfort Maxwell could provide. I was the lucky one—or unlucky one—that he chose in the end."

I stopped so abruptly that I skidded on the pebbles. "What do you mean, other girls?"

She squinted into the sun. "Maxwell always had a string of young women hanging around. It wasn't until we were officially engaged that he told them all to leave."

"Anyone I know?" I asked.

She shook her head. "I don't know. I never saw any of the others. I knew of them, but Maxwell was very careful to keep us separated. Whoever they were, they must have hated me."

And Maxwell, I thought. Did any of them hate him enough to kill him?

THIRTY-FOUR

ASHLAND MET US NEAR the dance tent. "Kelsey, I think everything is ready. All that's left to do is for the caterer to arrive and set up the food." She checked her watch. "It's noon now, and they'll be here at three to have everything ready by six. The band will arrive at four."

I gave a sigh of relief that at least one thing this weekend had gone as planned. I walked into the dance tent. Until the Farm closed to the general public; we would leave the sides of the tent rolled down. When the Farm closed at five, the waitstaff would open both tents.

The inside of the tent was exactly as I envisioned it should be. A big dance floor lay in the middle. It would be large enough to accommodate the parlor room dances that were popular during the Civil War. The far end of the tent was where the six-piece string band would be, playing favorite pieces from the era. A glass chandelier hung from the center of the tent, which would provide electric light—I was all for being historically accurate, but not in the case of a fire hazard. Chairs and benches circled the perimeter, so that those unable or who didn't want to dance would have places to sit. I grinned. "It's perfect."

Portia cleared her throat. "If everything is done, then you won't need my help."

"We do," I assured her. I removed my notebook from my back pocket. "How is your handwriting?"

"Okay."

"Can you write in cursive?"

She frowned. "Yes."

"Perfect. I had to ask. They don't teach cursive in schools any longer. Hayden will learn keyboarding instead." I unfolded a list that was tucked into the pages of my notebook. "This is a list of all the ladies who RSVPed. I would like you to write their names on the front of these dance cards."

Portia took the list from me. "There are three hundred names on this list."

"Actually it's three hundred and six, but if you and Ashland work together, you should have it completed in no time." I sighed. "I had planned to do it myself earlier in the reenactment, but as both of you know, this weekend did not go as planned." I removed a large box from under the table closest to where the band would be. "The printing company delivered the dance cards today." I set the box on top of the table.

I removed one of the cards from the box. It was printed on white linen stationary. On the front there was the logo for the Farm and the insignia for the Blue and Gray Ball. It was all done in blue and gray lettering. Inside the cards were the names of all the dances that we would have in order. There was the waltz, the Virginia reel, the polka, the quadrille, and many others. We would host twenty-four dances throughout the evening. The more common ones like the waltz would repeat four or five times.

I found the box of felt-tipped pens I'd grabbed from the visitor center earlier that afternoon. "Next year, we should be more historically accurate and use inkwell and quills. It's too late for that now." Setting the small box on the table next to the larger one, I said, "After you're done, place the cards in alphabetical order by last name on the table at the entrance of the tent. I'll have a seasonal worker standing there during the ball to make sure everyone finds their cards."

Portia sat down at the table and took a pen and a large stack of dance cards from the box. "This sounds like it will be fun."

I hoped she'd still think that when she got to dance card number 153.

Ashland frowned. "She can do this by herself. I'm sure there are better things that I need to be doing."

I arched an eyebrow at her. "It will go more quickly if you do it together."

Ashland pursed her lips.

"After it's done, we should be all set and you can go change for the ball. Thanks girls. I'm going to the visitor center to make sure everything is in order there for tonight." I headed for the tent's exit.

Unsurprisingly, Ashland followed me. She frowned. "What is she doing here?"

"She wanted something to do and she's helping out. I thought you would be glad about it. Those are a lot of dance cards. Without her help, you'd be writing them all yourself."

"She shouldn't even be here. She's not a Farm employee." Ashland frowned at her notebook.

"No, but today she is a Farm volunteer. Ashland, do you have a problem with Portia?"

"No," she stepped back, bumping into the side of the tent. "Why would you ask that?"

"I don't know," I shrugged. "Because you're all uptight that she's helping you with the dance cards?"

"I don't have a problem with her. I don't have any problem at all."

"Great." I pointed to the tent. "Because those dance cards aren't going to write themselves."

She turned and reentered the tent.

I removed my cell phone from my pocket and scrolled through the numbers until I found the one for Detective Brandon.

"Brandon," her sharp voice came through the phone's speaker.

"Detective Brandon. This is Kelsey Cambridge."

"What do you want, Ms. Cambridge?"

Okay, I thought. *Still not one for small talk.*

"I wondered if you got any results back yet on Wesley Mayes's toxicology report."

"We have preliminary findings." She said nothing more.

I gritted my teeth. "Can you share those results with me?"

"I have no reason to. You're not next of kin."

"I know that, but I think it would be helpful to know what caused his death. If it was poison as the police chief suspected, I need to know if that poison was found on Barton Farm grounds. If it was, I need to remove it as soon as possible."

"Oh," she said a little less sharply—just a little less. "I suppose in that case it would be all right if I told you. It's not a secret."

"So?"

"He ingested lily of the valley. Highly toxic. He must have eaten if right before he marched on the battlefield. The medical examiner said that he had never seen anyone consume such a large amount of it. It was clearly evident in his stomach. It will go to the lab for confirmation, but the medical examiner is very confident that the test results will support his theory. Official results will take several weeks. I'd appreciate it if you kept this information to yourself."

I suddenly felt sick. I knew lily of the valley was deadly poisonous, and we had plants growing in the medicinal garden under lock and key. In the nineteenth century, families like the Bartons would have used it as medicine for everything from heart failure to pink eye. "He's sure that's what it was?"

"Yes," the annoyance was back in her voice. "The medical examiner is a very thorough investigator. You do know that you have a large number of poisonous plants at Barton Farm."

"They're part of our medicinal garden. Visitors can't go in there without staff, and the gate is always locked when there's not an employee around. The gardener keeps a close eye on those plants. We wanted to show what would really be in an

Ohio garden during the nineteenth century, and some of those plants are poisonous."

She sniffed. "History at what cost? I'm en route to collect some samples from your gardens." She hung up.

I shivered.

Across the green, I saw Shepley weeding in his garden. He seemed to be content, or as content as was possible for Shepley.

The medicinal garden was just outside the main garden. The gate was indeed closed and locked.

Shepley tossed a handful of weeds into his bushel basket. He didn't wear gloves while he worked. Shepley thought gloves were for wimps. "What do you want?"

I folded my arms. "Has anyone one been inside the medicinal garden during the reenactment?"

He eyed me and straightened up as much as he could with his ruined back. "It's been open off and on throughout the weekend, but I've always been there."

"Have you taken any plants from it?"

Bent at the waist, he hobbled to a garden bench a few feet away and sat. "I take plants out of it from time to time, but I haven't removed anything recently."

"Has anyone else?"

"How could they without my permission? No one does anything in my garden without my permission."

I frowned. How could he be sure? He didn't live here. He didn't spend all his time here.

"But if you think someone has been in the garden, we can check." He stood.

I followed him to the corner of the enormous garden at a painfully slow pace. When he reached the medicinal garden gate, he fumbled to get the key into the lock. I resisted grabbing the keys away from him and doing it myself when I realized that Shepley's hands shook. His fingers were covered in dirt. The nails were jagged and cracked from digging in the dry summer soil. He wasn't a young man any longer and hadn't been for as long as I had known him. I frowned. How much longer could he keep up the backbreaking work of caring for the gardens? He would have to tell me when it was time. I would never suggest that he wasn't up to it. That would just make him hold on that much longer.

The fence around the garden was six-foot-high iron work made by a local blacksmith who sometimes visited the Farm as a special event. It wasn't impossible to climb, but the nasty looking spikes at the top of each fence post were a pretty good deterrent. At least I thought they were until I realized someone must have gotten into the garden to harvest enough lily of the valley to kill Wesley. It could have even been Wesley himself.

The gate swung inward with a creak.

Shepley moved down the woodchip-covered walkway. "All seems well." He glanced over his hunched shoulder. "Why the sudden interest?" Before I could answer, he said, "What's this?"

"What?" I caught up with him.

Shepley crouched next to a garden bed. His knees cracked as he moved. I winced at the sound.

"It looks like someone yanked a third of my lily of the valley out of the ground. It was done blooming of course, but the plant withers and dies back on its own accord. That feeds the bulbs

295

for healthy plants next spring." He spat. "Scoundrels. First my bees are violated and now my garden." He jerked upright, and his knees cracked again. "You can't let this happen! These people shouldn't be on the Farm!" He shook his fist.

I took two steps back from him and held up my hands. "Shepley, you need to calm down."

"Calm down? It's not your life's work someone is playing with or killing people with," he growled.

"What do you mean?"

"I heard the symptoms that the soldier who died in the middle of the field exhibited. The tourists love to talk about the grotesque. What's more grotesque than death? I'm just a simple gardener to them. I'm scenery and they don't notice me." He pointed at the ground where the lily of the valley should have been. "Lily of the valley is toxic. Eat a few leaves, and you're dead."

"Who can get into the medicinal garden?" I asked.

"You and I have the only keys," he said.

He slipped his hand into the hip pocket of his overalls and produced a key ring. "Here's mine. Where's yours?"

I knew where my keys were. They were in the key box in my office. My office, which is always unlocked and had been unlocked during the entire reenactment.

I left Shepley muttering to himself in his prixed medicinal garden and headed to the visitor center. More and more I was convinced that whoever killed Maxwell and maybe Wesley was connected to the Farm. That person knew where everything was. The reenactors hadn't had the time to get to know the Farm so well. I frowned. My only Farm suspect left was Shepley, but he had seemed genuinely upset when he thought his garden had been touched. I couldn't know for sure, but I didn't think he was acting.

I waved to Judy and the rest of the gift shop staff as I crossed the lobby. I was relieved to see Chase was no longer in my office. I had too many thoughts about murder rolling around in my head to be bothered with how I felt about him.

I went straight to the key cabinet on the wall beside my bookshelf, the same bookshelf that Detective Brandon had leaned on. I opened the cabinet. The key to the medicinal garden was there right where I expected it to be. I took it off its hook and slipped it into the pocket of my jeans.

THIRTY-FIVE

"Hello, hello, hello!" Laura crowed as she entered my house at five sharp with a garment bag.

I had just beaten her to my house after overseeing the caterers set up for the food for the ball. It would be a spectacular event if I could shake the melancholy feeling I'd had ever since Detective Brandon told me Wesley had been poisoned by lily of the valley.

I placed a hand on the side of my head, and Frankie jumped off my lap.

"Oh, sorry," my best friend said. "Do you still have a headache?"

"Just a little one." I didn't tell her, but my headache was more from guilt about Wesley's death than from being walloped over the back of the head the night before.

"Maybe you shouldn't go to the ball tonight."

I jumped off of the couch. "Are you crazy? This is what I've worked for all year. I'm going."

She beamed. "Okay. Then we have to make you look the part." She dropped the garment bag on the couch. "I have your dress. I can hardly wait for you to see it."

"Okay," I whimpered.

She unzipped the garment page. "Ta-da!"

The dress was a satin royal blue with lace at the collar and bodice. "It's very pretty."

"Pretty?" She sniffed. "It's gorgeous. You'll be the belle of the ball, as you should be." She rubbed her hands together. "Let's do your hair first." She set out her makeover arsenal on the kitchen table. Makeup, hairspray, brushes, combs, tweezers—I didn't want to know what those were for—and pulled out a dining chair.

"Can't I just wear a braid? They braided their hair back then."

She shook her finger at me. "Little girls did, not ladies. And we're going to make you a lady. Sit."

Resigned to my fate, I sat on the chair.

She ran the brush through my hair. "The reenactment has gone beautifully today. You'd be so proud, Kelsey, not a dead body on the place."

"That's something to strive for. But I think you're being a little too generous. Chase did get into a fistfight with another reenactor."

She shivered. "I'm sorry I missed it. How are you feeling? I've watched you fly all over the grounds today, which you probably shouldn't have been doing with your head injury."

"My head injury is a bump, and Ashland helped out a lot with the ball."

"There was a lot of chatter in the camps today about Chase carrying you through the encampment late last night. Some thought they were watching a scene out of *Gone with the Wind*."

I groaned. I felt my cheeks grow hot. I must have looked so pathetic cradled in Chase's arms like a damsel in distress, which I most certainly was not. "He wouldn't let me walk," I said in my own defense.

She teased my hair. "I'm not knocking it. If a fine man like that wanted to carry me around, he's welcome to. Of course, I don't weigh a hundred pounds like you do, so I don't know if he could pick me up."

"Please, I don't weigh anywhere close to a hundred pounds, and he could pick you up no problem," I said. I hated it when Laura commented on her weight. She was beautiful just the way she was.

"Maybe he would sling me over his shoulder, pirate style," she chuckled.

"Ow," I cried.

"Sorry, I must have gotten a little carried away with my teasing. Your dramatic rescue is all anyone has talked about today."

"I bet. That's so embarrassing."

She selected a round brush from the table. "A normal woman would be thrilled with having a handsome man rescue her."

"I'm not accustomed to being rescued and can't say that I like it." I winced as she tugged on my hair. What was she doing back there?

"You should be glad that Chase came along. Who knew how long you might have been down there, or if whoever put you there was on his way back to finish the job?"

I shivered. I knew I was lucky, but I had someone to thank more than Chase: Jason. I hoped he wouldn't leave now that he knew I knew he was living on the Farm. That's not what I wanted. "Have you seen Jason today?"

"No, but I hardly see him on a normal day, and this is not a normal day."

"Far from it," I agreed.

"Why do you think you were hit on the head?"

"Whoever killed Maxwell must think I'm too close to discovering who he or she is. The truth is, they're wrong. I couldn't be further from knowing who the killer is."

"I think you should pay attention to the warning. The reenactors will be leaving tomorrow. Let it be."

"I can't," I said.

She sighed. "I can see from the look on your face that you're determined to ignore me."

"Maybe we can run through the suspects?"

She sighed again. "Fine."

"There is Jamie the business partner."

"What's his problem?"

"He and Maxwell were the main investors in that failed construction project. They lost a huge amount of money in the mall on Kale Road, but the police chief gave him an unbreakable alibi. He's out."

She waved her brush in the air. "Besides, if Maxwell was going to be given power over millions of dollars from Cynthia, why would Jamie knock him off? Now he has no money and a lot of useless land."

"Good point. There's Shepley."

"Shepley?"

"He is in charge of the beautification project for New Hartford. Cynthia was planning to support it, but Maxwell promised not to."

She grimaced. "I'm glad I wasn't there when Shepley was told. Did his head start to spin?"

"And it was his bees that were used for the murder. Plus, I learned today that Wesley died from eating lily of the valley." At her silence, I added. "Lily of the valley is a toxic plant, and Shepley has a crop of it in his medicinal garden."

"That garden is built like a high-security prison."

I nodded.

"Wouldn't that be kind of dumb for him to use his own bees and his own flowers? And I can't see Shepley plotting such a methodical murder. I mean, it's never any secret what the guy is thinking or feeling. He screams in your face on a regular basis, and you're his boss. I would think it would be much more likely if he grabbed one of the soldiers' rifles and shot Maxwell in the heart in front of the entire Farm."

I had to agree that Laura had given a pretty good assessment of Shepley's character. "There's the fiancée, Portia."

"If she was marrying him for his money, she won't get any now. If I were her, I would have waited a few years after the wedding and then poisoned him."

"Should I be concerned that you've thought out the best way to kill people?"

She grinned. "Not at all."

"She's also Wesley's ex-girlfriend. She dumped Wesley so she could marry Maxwell for money."

"See, there you go. She'd have no reason to kill her sugar daddy until he put a wedding band on her finger." She selected another brush. I was beginning to wonder how many brushes were necessary in a normal woman's daily routine. I was more of a wash and braid girl. Laura waved the paddle brush back and forth over my head as she spoke. "Wesley is the young man the police believe is behind it."

"Right."

"The confession letter that the chief found sounded pretty convincing."

"Did you see it?"

"Heard about it. You know how everyone talks around here."

"I'm not convinced…" I trailed off. "Then there's Chase."

She yanked on my hair. "The Union hero? No way."

"Ow!" I cried. "Be careful. I did just get knocked on the back of the head with a brick."

"I'm sorry." She pulled the brush through much more slowly this time. "If you didn't braid your hair so tightly, you wouldn't have these kinks." She clicked her tongue. "How can you even think it was Chase after he saved you?"

"Saving has nothing to do with it. He has an alibi," I said. I told her about Chase's sleeping at the firehouse the night of Maxwell's murder.

"I knew he couldn't have done it." She pushed four bobby pins into my head. "Wanna know what I think?"

"Not really," I said as another bobby pin jabbed into my scalp.

"Too bad. You're going to hear it anyway." She removed the last bobby pin from her mouth. "I think you're afraid of him."

"What?" I jerked forward in my seat.

She pulled me back me by the shoulder. "Don't move, you'll ruin my masterpiece. And I'm right; you're afraid of Chase."

"That the most ridiculous thing I've ever heard."

"You're afraid of him because you're attracted to him and don't know what to do about it. You've been in love with Eddie since you were fourteen years old. It must be odd to have romantic feelings for someone else."

I stared at my hands clenched together on my lap. How was Laura able to nail me so well? It wasn't until she said this that I knew it was true. I had only ever loved Eddie. I'd never looked at another man in that way, even since the divorce. Hayden, the Farm, and even my father were distractions from finding someone else. Little did I know I would stumble over someone playing dead on my pastureland. But even if Laura was right, that didn't mean I had to admit it to her.

"I *might* find him attractive."

She laughed. "If that's as far as you are willing to confess, I will take it." She patted my hair. "My masterpiece is done. Now get upstairs into your dress."

In my bedroom, I stepped in the hoop skirt and slipped on the corset. Laura stood behind me. "This is going to hurt."

I held up my hand to stop her. "Don't pull too tight."

"I just pull tight enough to get the dress on you. It's tiny. There wasn't a whole lot of selection in the costume closets. Most of the women's clothing was everyday dresses and aprons." She pulled on the corset strings. "Suck it in."

I took a deep breath as she pulled the string. I felt like my ribs were about to crack. "Okay, okay! That's tight enough."

"Are you sure? With another tug, I can take your waist down another inch."

"No. This is fine. Breathing is really important to me."

She tied the strings. "Okay, it's my turn. Pull as tight as you can. I'm willing to sacrifice breathing."

I rolled my eyes and stepped behind her. I yanked on her corset strings with all I had.

"Ow!" she cried.

I froze. "Am I hurting you?"

"Nope," she winced. "That was just right. Tie it off."

I did as I was told and she admired herself in the mirror. "I have to say I'm looking pretty good. I would wear this every day if it didn't threaten to break one of my ribs or cause internal bleeding."

I lifted her heavy dress over her head and helped her into it. I did the buttons up her back. "You're beautiful."

"I'm not bad, but I can't wait to see you in your dress." She picked the blue gown off of the bed and slipped it over my head. With practiced fingers she fastened the dozens of cloth buttons up the back.

Side by side we stared in the mirror. "Don't we look like a couple of fine ladies?" she asked. "I feel like Robert E. Lee or someone equally grand should escort us to the ball."

I arched an eyebrow. "Not Grant?"

"That guy was a drunk."

I twirled in front of the mirror, a move I wouldn't have done in front of any person other than Laura. I had to admit, I didn't look half bad, but Laura—with her peaches and cream skin and sparkling green eyes—was gorgeous. Her dress was off the shoulder, like mine. The cut made me look smaller, but it enhanced all Laura's curves. She would have a full dance card tonight.

"Well, we'll have to be satisfied with my father as an escort." I glanced at the clock on my bedside table. "He should be home soon from his matinee performance of *Hamlet*."

"Works for me." She examined my dress. "I did a wonderful job making you up. This might be some of my best work. You look like Scarlett O'Hara come to life."

I snorted. "Right."

"No really, Kelsey, you are beautiful. Chase Wyatt doesn't stand a chance."

I peered into the full-length mirror. Laura was wrong. It was I who didn't stand a chance.

"Hello, hello," my father called from the bottom of the stairs. "I'm home and changed from my fifteen-century attire to my nineteenth-century. Are you ladies ready for the ball?"

Dad waited for us at the bottom of the stairs. He wore his Union dress uniform—all of it for the occasion of the ball. He grinned. "My. Aren't I lucky man to escort you two beauties to the ball?"

"Thank you, Mr. Renard." Laura looped her arm through his.

Tiffin placed his head on his pillow. He didn't like the idea of being left at home during the ball, but I couldn't have him barking at everyone or trying to herd the guests during dances.

THIRTY-SIX

It was a perfect early summer night. I smiled. The weather was another thing that went right this weekend. Maybe it wasn't a complete disaster. Grandmother Renard would be proud of me for counting my blessings.

Ladies and gentlemen poured out of the visitor center in their best 1863 garb. Some of the women carried ruffled parasols and shaded their faces from the setting sun. Others dripped with jewels that I prayed weren't real. I wouldn't comment on the historic inaccuracy of the jewels. Women of the time didn't have so much finery. If they had it, they certainly would not have worn it in public and attracted attention. Instead many wealthy ladies buried their jewelry in their gardens and prayed it would still be there when the war was over.

Union and Confederate privates stood shoulder to shoulder outside of their respective camps. Those that had dress uniforms changed into them, but not all did. Just like during the

Civil War, some men couldn't afford more than one uniform. I caught myself searching the Union side for Chase.

One of my seasonals, a teenager dressed as a New York newsie, directed traffic.

My father nodded and smiled at anyone who passed him. I hid a smile as he fully embraced his Civil War–era persona. The only thing I wished was that Hayden was there. It would be a great experience for my son to see history really come alive. Of course, living on the Farm he saw that more than any other child his age, but this was a special event. Maybe next year he would be able to attend.

We crossed the road into the village. As I had directed, the sides of the tent had been rolled up, and the period band was in the corner of the tent playing chamber music until the ball really began.

Ladies and gentlemen walked arm in arm around the green like they were on a promenade in Washington DC. Most of my staff was there in period dress, including Benji, who was stunning in a canary yellow gingham dress. It was the first time I had seen her out of her dusty brickmaking clothes. Jason, unsurprisingly, was MIA.

I let go of Dad's arm. "I'm going to check on the caterers." I headed to the food tent. My stomach rumbled with the welcoming smells. The dishes stayed warm in chafing dishes along two long tables. I couldn't remember if I ate much during the day, but I was sure hungry now. A woman in a white chef's hat stood behind one table slicing an enormous roast. Beside the roast were an uncut turkey and a ham. In addition to traditional banquet food like the meats, salad, steamed vegetables, and potatoes, I also asked the caterers to make special dishes that were popular during the Civil War, like soda biscuits, sweet potato wafers, and Kentucky snap peas. Because food was so scarce during the war, especially in the South, I suspect that our period food tasted a lot better than what the men had eaten on the front.

Drinks consisted of lemonade, sweet tea, coffee, and hot tea, and there was a cash bar for anyone who wanted something stronger. Mason jars served as the cups.

I smiled at the caterer. "Everything looks perfect. I'll announce the opening of the ball in the big tent soon, so get ready. They'll flock your way right after that."

She smiled. "We'll be ready."

I returned to the big tent. In addition to the chandeliers overhead, electric lanterns hung from iron posts outside the tent and around the grounds. The waiters—also in costume—passed appetizers on trays among the guests.

The chief in his dress uniform walked into the tent holding the hand of a dowager-looking woman in a velvet evening gown. To my surprise Detective Brandon was behind them, and she wore an emerald green ball gown as well. She was breathtaking. I found myself gasping. Suddenly I wasn't feeling quite as confident in my own gown as I had just a few minutes ago.

The chief smiled broadly at me. "Quite an event you have here, Kelsey. Wonderful job."

"Thank you," I said.

He placed his hand on the hilt of his period revolver. "I'm glad that this business with the murder has been all cleared up before today. Nothing should ruin the ball. May I present my wife, Mrs. Edith Duffy."

I got the feeling that the chief wanted me to curtsey. "Nice to meet you."

The woman examined me. "Yes, my nephew Chase has mentioned you. I can see why. You're a lovely girl. It would be nice if he took an interest in a lady for once."

I found myself blushing. Truth be told, I wasn't much of a lady. I spent most of my days in jeans. Behind Edith, Detective Brandon stiffened. It was very subtle, but I noticed it.

"You have a nice spread for the ball tonight," Mrs. Duffy continued. "The roast looks delicious. And I'm surprised at the turnout. This is the first reenactment event the chief has been able to drag me to. I'm afraid I'm not much for history," she said apologetically.

I smiled. "I hope you enjoy your evening."

Behind her I saw Cynthia accepting a glass of punch from a server. "Oh, I see Cynthia. If you excuse me, I'd like to say hello to her."

"Of course," Edith said. "We already gave her our condolences."

I nodded and wove through the dance tent to the punch bowl. "Cynthia?"

She turned and smiled. It wasn't her typical bright smile; that would take some time to return.

I squeezed her hand. "Cynthia, I'm so happy to see you here, but you didn't have come."

"I didn't want to miss your big moment, my dear. I'm finding going out and seeing people helps. I was refreshed after the play last night."

I covered her hand with mine. "Then I'm glad you came. This event is as much your doing as my own. You know I can never thank you enough for everything you've done for the Farm and for Hayden and me."

She smiled. "Please stop thanking me. You know the pleasure is all mine. You look so lovely tonight, Kelsey. I know you'll worry about all the little details of the ball, but I want you to let someone else worry about concerns for a change. This is your moment. Enjoy it."

Ashland stood beside the band and waved to me frantically.

I laughed. "I think that's my cue to open the ball."

Cynthia smiled. "Go on, dear."

I crossed the tent and took the microphone from Ashland. "Ashland, you look beautiful."

My assistant wore a floral ball gown that was off the shoulders, showing off her delicate clavicle bones. Even though the rest of her was covered, I had never seen her in something so revealing. I was surprised by the firm muscles in her shoulders.

Her face, neck, and chest turned bright red. "Thank you."

"Good evening," I said into the mic.

When the crowd continued to talk, I spoke a little more loudly. "Good evening!"

The ball goers quieted down.

"For those who don't know, I'm Kelsey Cambridge, the director of Barton Farm. I would like to thank you for coming to our first annual Blue and Gray Ball."

The crowd applauded. I waited for the noise to die down before I continued. "I would like to thank everyone who made the ball and the reenactment this weekend possible. First, I thank

Cynthia Cherry and the Cherry Foundation. We could not have done this without their continued support. In particular, Cynthia, I give you my personal thanks for everything that you've done for Barton Farm, my family, and for me. Your selfless giving is a true inspiration to everyone in New Hartford and at Barton Farm." I fought back tears. Cynthia beamed at me from the crowd. I cleared my throat. "I would also like to thank all the reenactors who camped out on the grounds over the last four days. Thank you for sharing your hobby with our visitors. I think many of them have new appreciation for American history, especially the Civil War. I also have to thank the wonderful staff here at Barton Farm, especially my assistant Ashland George, who took on so much planning for this weekend."

Beside me Ashland squirmed at the praise.

"On the table near the front here, there are dance cards for all the ladies. Ladies, find your dance cards. I'm sure they will fill up in no time with so many handsome privates and officers from both sides here with us tonight."

I hesitated in my speech. "However, this weekend hasn't gone flawlessly. I would be remiss if I didn't mention the sad events of the weekend. Maxwell Cherry and Wesley Mayes are both gone. I hope you will join me in keeping their families and friends in your thoughts and prayers. Both men were taken before their time.

"It's my opinion the Wesley Mayes was wrongly accused of Maxwell's murder. He was a depressed young man, and someone, maybe even someone here, took advantage of that. I, for one, will keep looking for the person who is truly behind

312

Maxwell's death until Wesley's name is clear. I think we should honor his and Maxwell's memories in our festivities tonight."

An eerie quiet settled over the partygoers as I spoke.

"The buffet and dance floor are now open. Enjoy your evening. The first dance is a waltz." I handed Ashland the mic.

The band began the first waltz and men and woman slowly inched to the dance floor.

"Kelsey, what were you thinking by saying that?" Ashland stared at me with wide eyes.

"I wanted to make sure that the person who hit me on the back of the head knows he or she doesn't scare me."

"But—"

"I've witnessed a lot stupid stunts in my life," a voice said behind me. "But that one takes the cake."

I recognized the voice.

Slowly I turned around. It was Chase. He was so handsome in his dress uniform. Had he been with the Union soldiers marching on Atlanta with Sherman, the Southern ladies in his path would have fainted dead away. As the director of Barton Farm, swooning was not an option.

"Hi," I squeaked.

"I agree with Ashland: that was a pretty dumb stunt you just pulled. Why don't you just wear a sign that says 'Kill me next'?"

I frowned. "I was making a point."

He grunted. "Your point was clearly made. My uncle's eyeballs just about popped out of his head during your little speech." He nodded to Ashland. "You'll excuse us."

She chewed on her lip.

I touched Ashland's arm. "Don't worry about me. I know what I'm doing."

Her brow wrinkled. "I know you do."

He led me to the middle of the tent. Couples spun on the dance floor with their partners, and there was already a long line leading to buffet table in the dining tent.

Chase removed a card from the inside pocket of his dress coat and handed it to me. "I took the liberty of finding your dance card for you."

I took the card from his hands and opened it. "Why is your name on here twenty times?" *Chase Wyatt* was next to every dance except for the polkas.

"I also took the liberty of filling out your card."

I peered up at him. "And the polka?"

He grinned. "I don't polka. We can eat then."

"Do you expect me to stay with you all night?" I tried very hard not to smile.

His grin widened. "I thought that was a given." He bowed. "May I have this dance, Ms. Cambridge?"

I slipped the dance card ribbon over my wrist. "I suppose, since your name is on my card." I placed my hand into his. He gripped it firmly and confidently led me to the center of the tent.

The crystal chandelier sparkled above us. Men in their blue and gray dress uniforms bowed to their ladies, and the ladies curtseyed in return. The music started again, and the men spun their partners. Flowered, gingham, satin, and silk ball gown skirts in every shade imaginable fanned out over the dance floor and collided with each other in a swirl of color. I was so mesmerized by the scene that I forgot I was twirling around the dance floor with my very own soldier.

"You look beautiful," he whispered, and he turned me around the floor.

I looked up at him. "Are you trying to sweet talk me?"

"Is it working?"

"No," I lied. "Where did you learn to waltz?"

He smiled. "My uncle required it. Any Union officer worth his salt can waltz. I can cha-cha too. Of course that would require a different outfit, but I think it's important that you know all I have to offer."

I looked up at him. "And why is that?"

He smiled and didn't answer. We passed Laura and a Confederate lieutenant on the dance floor. She grinned and wiggled her eyebrows at me.

I looked away. "You seemed to have gone to great lengths to indulge your uncle's hobby."

Chase's face clouded over. "It's the least I could do after everything he's done for me." He changed the subject and we chatted through two more dances until polka music started. "That's our cue for dinner," Chase said.

We walked off of the dance floor. Detective Brandon stood just outside the tent glaring at us. A Union soldier was talking to her, but she was ignoring him. Her eyes were fixed on Chase.

In the dining tent, one of the servers brought me a note on a silver tray as Chase and I sat at a table.

"Thank you," I said, accepting the note.

"What is it?" Chase asked.

I unfolded it. "It's from Ashland. There's some kind of emergency at Barton House." I refolded the paper. "I knew the evening was going too well—no party goes off without a hitch. I'd better take care of this."

Chase started to get up. "I can come with you."

"Don't be silly. Enjoy the ball. I'm on the clock. This is my job."

He frowned.

"Dance with Laura," I said "She'll be thrilled. The two of you can plot against me."

He grinned. "That's tempting."

I stood up. "I'll be back in no time."

Chase's grin faded, but he let me go.

THIRTY-SEVEN

THE NOTE FROM ASHLAND asked me to meet her inside Barton House, which was only a few yards from the tent. I wondered what had gone so terribly wrong that we couldn't speak about it in front of the guests. Surely nothing as awful as a murder.

A couple sat on the house's front porch eating their dinner. I smiled at them and was surprised to find the padlock on the house. I had figured Ashland would be waiting inside. I unlocked the door and stepped inside. With no electricity, the home was cold and dark. The front door opened into the living room, and I was happy to see that the trunk was still over the root cellar's hatch. It was dusk now, and the only light in the room was ambient light from setting sun, which just made the shadows grow long and monstrous. I decided to leave the door open. I could hear the muffled sounds of laughter and music from the dance.

"Ashland?" I called.

There was no answer. I frowned and walked through the home. Nothing appeared out of the ordinary or disturbed. I peered through the kitchen window over the sink and saw Ashland in the back yard. She had her arms wrapped around her body, and she was crying.

I went out of the house through the back door. "Ashland, what's wrong?"

She looked up. "You came."

The trees in the woods cast dark shadows over the lawn. Even in the dimness, I could see tears glistening on her cheeks. "Of course, I came. What's this emergency you have? Does it have something to do with the reenactment or the ball?"

"No," she cried harder. "Yes."

That wasn't confusing or anything.

Something about her tragic expression, like a lost puppy, connected the scattered thoughts in my head. She'd had that same look on her face when Maxwell, Portia, and Cynthia were at the reenactment—like someone had just kicked her. I had thought at the time that it was just her moody nature, but I'd been wrong. All this time I had a gut feeling that the killer was connected to the Farm and not the reenactment. All this time I had been right. Click, click, click. The clues lined up in my head like grooves in a zipper. Who else would know everything about the Farm like I did? Ashland. Who else spent their time emulating me? Ashland. Who tried to set me up for murder? Ashland.

"Ashland, why did you kill Maxwell?" I whispered.

"He threw me aside for that dumb girl because she's better arm candy than I am at events like this one." She glared at me. "She even told me while we worked on those dance cards that

318

she didn't love him. She was in love with that worthless reenactor."

"You loved Maxwell?" I wrinkled my nose. I couldn't help it. I couldn't understand how anyone could fall in love with such a jerk.

"He wasn't always so harsh," she said.

"How did you even know each other?"

"When you would send me to Cynthia's estate to make reports and deliveries, we struck up a friendship. And then it became more. I know he loved me and not her." She balled her fists on either side of her hoop skirt. "I tried to make him see, but he just wouldn't."

I always asked Ashland to go to Cynthia's estate because I'd hated running into Maxwell every time I went. When she went, she'd be gone for several hours, but I had assumed that she spent her time drinking tea with the Farm's benefactress, not flirting with the foundation's heir.

My fingers turned ice cold as I realized I hadn't seen Portia at the ball with Cynthia. "Ashland, where's Portia?"

"It doesn't matter. She doesn't matter."

"It matters a lot," I corrected. "You didn't hurt her, did you?"

"She gave me no choice. She wouldn't shut up about how much she hated Maxwell and loved Wesley. She couldn't talk about the man I loved like that!"

"The man you killed," I corrected.

She glared at me. "I didn't want to. It broke my heart when I had to kill him, but when he met me here in the village that night, it was clear he wasn't coming back to me. It was my last resort. I had no choice." She started to cry again. "He was knocked out when I rolled him into the pit. He never felt the stings."

"And Wesley?"

"I just showed him a way to escape his misery."

"You gave him the lily of the valley."

She glared at me. "*He* made the choice to eat it. I didn't shove it down his throat."

"What are you going to do now?" I asked.

"I don't know," she whispered. "It's gotten so complicated. I thought I'd feel better if I knew Maxwell couldn't be with anyone else, but it's not working."

"You can run," I said. "Just tell me where Portia is and you can run away and start over."

She stared at me as she considered this. "Will you help me get away?"

"Tell me where Portia is, and I'll help you," I lied.

"That agreement doesn't work for me." Detective Brandon appeared around the side of the Barton House with her gun drawn. I guess she had hidden it in her massive ball gown. "You're under arrest."

Ashland stared at her.

"Ashland," I said. "Tell me where Portia is. The police will go easier on you if you tell us where we can find Portia."

"Don't make promises we can't keep," Brandon barked.

I glared at her.

"It doesn't matter now," Ashland said and turned and ran. She was crying and ran blindly, failing her arms and legs.

"Stop!" Detective Brandon ordered. "Or I will shoot!"

"You can't shoot her in the back!" I yelled.

Jason popped out of the woods and made a move to catch Ashland. She screamed and made a sharp turn, running directly into the first beehive and knocking it to the ground. She fell on top of it and the bees buzzed and swarmed. Jason melted back into the safety of the woods.

I didn't wait to see how Ashland fared with the bees. It seemed a fitting punishment given what she'd done to Maxwell. I ran into Barton House and headed straight for the living room. I yanked the steamer trunk off of the root cellar's door. "Portia," I cried as I lifted the latch.

There was no answer. Could I be wrong? Did Ashland stash her someplace else? Was she already dead? Swallowing my fear about the giant rats, I bunched up my lovely skirt and climbed into the hole. It was a tight fight with the hoop skirt. "Portia?" I heard crying from the back corner of the root cellar. "Portia, it's Kelsey. I'm here to get you out."

She came at me at a fast crawl, wailing. "She threw me in here. I thought she was going to kill me. She killed Maxwell."

I wrapped my arms around her. "I know. Shh. You're safe now." Her entire body shook as I scanned the dark for mutant rats. "Let's get out of here."

Hands appeared in the root cellar's door, and then a face appeared. Chase's face appeared, a bit wild eyed and smirking. "How many times am I going to have to yank you of here?"

I handed a whimpering Portia to him. He pulled her out of the hole, and then I climbed out without his help. "Is there no limit to your chivalry?" I asked as I cleared the hole.

Chase set me on my feet. "When it comes to you?" He shook his head. "Nope."

EPILOGUE

EVEN THOUGH IT HAD been months since Chase had found me in Barton House's root cellar for a second time, I thought of the events of the Blue and Gray Ball often. Most of the time, I wonder what I could have done for Ashland to help her make other choices—choices that didn't lead to murder.

Hayden wiggled in my lap as we sat in the waiting room of the Cherry Foundation's main office in downtown New Hartford. It had only been a month since Cynthia's funeral, and since then all I had done was worry about the future of the Farm when I wasn't kicking myself over Ashland. What would our fate be? Cynthia's will would be the deciding factor for all of it.

Outside an early November snow covered the parking lot. Flakes continued to fall from the sky. It would be a long and cold winter. Not a good time to move if I was evicted from the cottage.

My thoughts spiraled out of control, bouncing between Ashland and the Farm. What would the Farm do if we couldn't keep funding from the Cherry Foundation? I would have to close it and lay off all of my employees. Who would care for all those historic buildings? What about Barton House? Despite the giant rats in its root cellar, I hated the thought of all the history going away. Maybe there was another living history museum that would take the buildings, or at least one or two. I hated the thought of breaking them up again, but it was better than letting them rot.

I shifted on the hard wooden chair. I'd have thought the Cherry Foundation would have more comfortable chairs in their waiting room.

"Mom, when can we go home? We've been here forever."

We had only been there twenty minutes, but Hayden was right. It did kind of seem like forever.

The door to the inner office opened and an elderly man named Mr. Culpepper emerged. He was Cynthia's primary lawyer. He scowled. "You brought your son."

Mr. Culpepper wasn't a fan of kids. I could tell. "I didn't have anyone to watch him. My father is teaching today."

His scowl deepened. "He can't listen to what I am going to share with you."

I frowned in return. "You should have told me that before you beckoned me to your office," I said.

The receptionist peeked out her office door. "He can stay with me. Hayden, do you like to color? I have some crayons."

"Coloring is okay," Hayden agreed, and he walked into her office.

I smiled at her. "Thanks."

"I have three kids. I always have emergency crayons and paper," she whispered.

Mr. Culpepper held the door for me into his office and gestured that I should sit on a leather couch. He sat across from me in an armchair. "Ms. Cambridge, thank you for coming in today. I suppose you are wondering why I called you in here."

"I imagine that it has something to do with Barton Farm and Cynthia."

He nodded and removed his glasses. "As you know, the Cherry Foundation has been more than generous with Barton Farm over the years. It truly was Ms. Cherry's pet project."

I folded my hands on my lap. I was wearing jeans. Maybe I should have chosen something more fitting for this occasion, but Mr. Culpepper had called late that morning asking to meet me in the office, so it hadn't given me much time to consider my wardrobe. "She cared a lot of about history, especially local history."

"Yes. Unfortunately, now that she is gone, circumstances have changed too because of the untimely passing of Maxwell, her heir. You must know the Cherry Foundation cannot support Barton Farm in the same way it has been doing for these many years."

This was it. This was the moment where I would find out the Farm had to close. I felt tears gather in the back of my eyes, but I would not cry. I didn't cry when I was thrown into the root cellar or when Ashland, who was now awaiting trial after somehow surviving hundreds of stings from Shepley's bees, betrayed me and the Farm. I wasn't going to start now.

"Barton Farm has been named benefactor of a sizable trust from Cynthia."

I blinked. "What?"

He nodded. "You are the trustee with no strings attached. Ms. Cherry is putting the whole authority to make decisions about the Farm on you."

This is what Cynthia meant when she said to me at Dad's play that the Farm would be fine. She had already made her decision then. My elation was quickly followed with the feeling of a great weight being lowered onto my shoulders. "How long will the trust sustain the Farm?"

"That is up to you and how you choose to spend the money." He leaned back in his chair. "If the money doesn't last, that will be on you."

His bluntness made me shiver, and the weight on my shoulders grew heavier, threatening to push me through the couch cushion and into the floorboards. "So I'm in charge free and clear. No strings attached?"

"You have all the power to distribute the funds, but there is one stipulation of the trust," he said.

I knew it sounded too easy. Money was never this easy.

"What's that?" I asked, anticipation growing in my gut.

"You will be required to live on the property for fifteen years and hold the directorship for all of that time. After which, if you chose, you may leave and select a new director."

"Fifteen *years*?" I had no intention of leaving Barton Farm now, but how did I know that wouldn't change for fifteen years?

"That's the stipulation of the trust. Will you comply?"

"What happens if I don't?" I asked.

"The trust is null and void. Ms. Cherry was very clear on that."

I swallowed. If I didn't agree, the Farm would close. I gripped my hands so tightly my knuckles turned white. "I'll do it."

He nodded. "I know Ms. Cherry would be pleased with your decision."

I knew that too.